Fly by Night

Laurinda Wallace

Fly by Night

Cover Design by Annie Moril

Author Photo by Reign Photography

ALL RIGHTS RESERVED

This is a work of fiction. Any references to real events, businesses, organizations, and locales are intended only to give the fiction a sense of reality and authenticity. Any resemblance to actual persons, living or dead is coincidental.

DEDICATION

For my Dad, with love.

ACKNOWLEDGMENTS

As always, many thanks to my awesome beta readers, and to my editor, Rose.

PROLOGUE

The splintered, half-rotted platform complained under the weight of its occupant. The deer stand had the perfect vantage spot. A trial run from the stand to the edge of the field and back again proved that it *was* perfect. Timing would be everything for this meeting. Then again, timing was everything—always.

A hand pushed the jagged leaves of the maple aside to reveal a better view of the field, which now lay in semi-darkness, the air heavy with the smell of hay ready for cutting. Exhaling slowly, the figure leaned back against the shaggy bark.

Fumbling in the pocket of the denim jacket, strong, latex-gloved fingers extracted two red-and-brass shotgun shells in a plastic bag and, reaching overhead to a cup-like crotch of branches, deposited the small package into the natural deep container.

Blue-and-white lights burst through the darkness and swept the field. A gasp of fear was quickly swallowed. A thin humming sound broke the silence.

The flashing stopped and the lights became steadier, slowly pulsating while hovering over the shadowy woods on the other side of the wide field. A cigar-shaped object glimmered under the blue-and-white lights. The faint, high-pitched hum competed with the steady chorus of peepers in the swamp that lay to the west of the deer stand. A flash of white light etched the black sky. And then all was quiet.

After a cursory check of the area around the base of the tree, the figure hastily descended from the treetop perch on short lengths of two-by-fours nailed into the tree trunk.

Slinking through the murky woods, the figure looked back only once to make sure no one was following. Shuddering, the silhouette then jogged down the narrow lane and disappeared into the darkness. The peepers resumed their serenade as if nothing had happened.

CHAPTER 1

"Mornin', Chief. Take a look at the paper."

Jim Taylor dropped the front page of the newspaper on his business partner's desk. Gracie Andersen glanced up from the computer monitor and swung around to look at the headlines. A big black Lab stood and shook herself, rattling the tags on her red collar. She ambled from her corner bed to greet Jim.

"Hey, Haley," Jim said, rubbing the dog's head and then scratching her wagging butt.

"I saw that story. Things are getting pretty exciting for little ol' Deer Creek," Gracie replied.

"A little too exciting, maybe. The paper's been full of the wind farm controversy for two months and today we've got little green men up in Greerson's Meadow."

Gracie laughed and pushed back her chair from the desk. "Don't forget the lawsuit between D. B. and the environmental group. What's their name? Renew Earth, I think. That's even been on the TV news."

"You're right. Forgot about that. It's been a bonus news week for the media." Jim poured himself a mug of coffee and dumped a generous slug of half-and-half from the carton next to the coffeemaker. "I'd like to get a good look at those mysterious lights. I'm betting it's a hoax or some military exercise."

"Maybe it's true. You need to keep an open mind."

"Sure. Just like you do," he teased. "Well, I'd better get back to cleaning runs." He took a gulp from the mug before heading for the doorway.

"Kibble delivery comes at 9:30 today. Don't keep Harry waiting," Gracie called after his disappearing back.

"Got it!"

He began whistling a boisterous rendition of "Jimmy Crack Corn." An enthusiastic chorus of yips, barks, and howls joined in as backup. Gracie shook her head and turned back to the computer screen.

The invoices for the week were now paid and there was a comfortable balance in the account—finally. It had been a tough start, but the kennel was officially in the black. She clicked the print button and waited for the small laser printer to slide out the report. The front door to reception jangled.

"Good morning, Gracie," a young feminine voice sang out.

Haley eagerly trotted to the reception area to greet Trudy, their newest kennel assistant. She was young, pretty, and energetic. Trudy Wilcox had been a teller at the Deer Creek Bank, and when Gracie had advertised the job opening, she'd been the first to respond. She felt that standing behind a counter and counting money just wasn't exciting enough. So far, Trudy was good with the dogs and customers.

The bell jangled again, signaling the arrival of Marian Majewski, the part-time groomer. Marian had been drawn out of retirement to work at Milky Way almost from day one. Gracie didn't know what she'd do without the woman who kept the grooming portion of the business thriving. She grabbed the grooming and the occupancy schedules from her desk.

"Here's the paperwork for today, ladies." She handed them each a schedule.

"All right. Looks like I'll be busy all day," Marian said and tied on the black groomer's apron.

"I think it's getting busier every week, Gracie," Trudy remarked as she glanced over the pick-up and drop-off schedule.

"That's good, and July is already starting to fill up." Gracie crossed her fingers on both hands and grinned.

"I'm not surprised. Our reputation is building the business. Midge gave us some good advertising yesterday when I stopped in for lunch," Marian replied, exiting for the grooming room.

"Midge is our biggest fan. She always promotes us," Gracie added.

Midge owned Midge's Restaurant in Deer Creek and had been Gracie's very first customer. A successful two-night stay for her nervous Chihuahua, Taco, was Milky Way's inauspicious opening. Gracie had refused to leave the poor dog alone in the huge empty kennel, so she'd just taken him in the house to hang out with Haley. After Haley had recovered from her initial shock to discover Taco was actually a canine, they had a rip-roaring good time, chewing bones and chasing squeaky toys.

"I'd better go help Jim," Trudy said, looking at her watch.

"He's down in 'C,' I think," Gracie informed her, turning back to the office.

Marian rattled around in the grooming room, getting ready for her first customer.

"Did you hear about that UFO sighting on the radio today?" Marian stepped into Gracie's office, holding a large pump bottle of shampoo.

"I read about it in the paper. Jim thinks it's a hoax."

"Not from what I've heard," Marian countered. She leaned against the doorframe. "Quite a few people have seen those lights up at Greerson's Meadow. Reputable people."

"Since when?" Gracie poured herself a cup of coffee.

"Since a month ago, at least. Tobias McQuinn says he's got pictures from the other night."

"Toby's not exactly what I'd call a reliable witness."

Gracie would have a hard time giving him any validity as a witness in general. Tobias McQuinn was the local hermit, having lived up in the woods near Greerson's Meadow in an Airstream trailer for years. He worked sporadically, picking up calf-feeding jobs and handyman projects. Mostly he cut firewood to sell. Every once in a while he'd claim he'd been abducted by aliens as a child.

"He's a little strange, but he seems to know a lot about UFO stuff," Marian sniffed. "Did you hear that D.B. Jackson is trying to buy that property from him too? D. B. wants to lease it to the windmill company that's putting up wind farms all over the place."

Gracie almost choked on her coffee. "You've got to be kidding. Why would D. B. want to stick those awful white giant windmills up there? The view and that pond ..."

She was sputtering now. A ton of fond childhood memories centered around the Meadow. Her favorite was the night excursions in the summertime with her parents and brother to watch fireflies make it a fairyland with their twinkling lights. The road would be flanked with vehicles and families leaning out car windows to watch the show. Several times a year, biology departments from local universities conducted studies on the wildlife and plants. It was a natural gem, tucked away on a back road that saw little traffic and hardly any maintenance.

"Don't worry. Tobias won't sell to him," Marian said confidently. "He's a little eccentric, and not stupid. I think that environmental group is trying to stop it too. D. B. usually gets his own way, but I'd be surprised if he does this time."

Before Gracie could respond, the bell on the door jingled, and Marian went to greet the customer.

*****

Haley stood panting at the rear entrance ready to go back to the house, while Gracie finished the final bed check on their canine guests and set the alarm. It had been a long day, and she could hardly wait to stand under a hot shower.

"Okay, girl. Let's go." Gracie pushed open the door, and Haley made a beeline for the kitchen steps.

The sun lingered in a gold-and-pink streaked sky. Gracie took a deep lungful of lilac-scented air and admired the scene. The old ranch-style house had been under renovation and now had a second floor with dormers and a wrap-around porch. The contractor had finished the outside construction and the upstairs addition. With another bedroom, bathroom, and large office, the house had doubled in size. It had seemed silly to add on for just one person, but somehow it seemed more like home to her. The rambling farmhouse she'd lived in for almost 16 years with her late husband was sometimes like a distant memory. It was hard to believe she'd lived at Milky Way without Michael for more than two years.

The gardens in the backyard were overgrown, but the lawn looked like a golf course. Her dad kept it mowed and the yew hedge near the driveway trimmed. She'd have to get the flower gardens in shape soon. There just wasn't enough time to do everything. Gracie sighed. Her mother yearned to get her hands on the gardens and was itching to be asked. A lot of free advice came with the help. Asked or not, her mother would probably show up if she couldn't find time in the next couple of weeks. The flowers struggled to be seen through the jungle-like mess. Somehow it had all gotten out of control during the house renovation and the building of the new training barn next to the kennel. She needed to check on when the fence guy planned to put up a new fence around the backyard too. He'd already postponed installation twice. With the new training facility finished, Gracie wanted a little more privacy from the bustle of the kennel. Cheryl, their most senior kennel assistant, was working hard to get kennel clubs and 4-Hers to use Milky Way's latest venture.

Haley barked and pawed at the kitchen door.

"All right. I'm coming," she told the dog. "You're probably hungry, aren't you?"

A school-bus-yellow compact car swung into the driveway before she was through the door. Haley offered a "somebody's here" bark. Gracie shooed her inside and walked down the steps to the new flagstone path.

A lanky man with longish dark hair and a well-trimmed dark brown beard strode toward her across the crunchy driveway gravel. He had a clipboard tucked under his left arm.

He was dressed in a light blue button-down shirt and gray dress pants.

"Hello. Mrs. Andersen?" He smiled and pushed his sunglasses up on his head.

"That's me. Were you dropping off a dog tonight?"

"No, no. I'm Ben Richter. I live over on Stillwater Road. I'm hoping you'll sign a petition to stop those wind farms from ruining our views and damaging the environment here."

The massive white turbines that spiked the green rolling hills of dairy country seemed to be everywhere in rural Western New York. Gracie quickly sized up the man, whose tone and slightly haughty manner made her immediately go on the defensive. So this was D. B. Jackson's current foe. The picture in the paper hadn't captured the overconfident attitude that radiated from the man.

"You must live near the Jackson farm then," she said, watching for his reaction.

"Unfortunately, yes. Mr. Jackson and myself ... we don't really see eye to eye. However, someone has to keep large businesses accountable." The man shifted uneasily in what looked to be expensive alligator leather shoes.

"Let me take a look at the petition," she said, reaching for the proffered clipboard. "Is it connected to any particular group?"

"It's a concerned citizens' petition," he answered. "We're trying to raise awareness about the dangers of these horrible windmills and their effects on our health and, of course, our wildlife."

Gracie scanned the signatures. Ben and Autumn Richter were at the top. Tobias McQuinn was the third signature, and then there were a half-dozen names she didn't recognize. The wording seemed innocuous enough, but she wasn't getting a warm fuzzy. A logo at the bottom of the page confirmed her hesitation. A globe with an outer circle of stars filled the right corner. It was the Renew Earth logo she'd seen in the article about the lawsuit. Besides that, the guy's attitude was a little high and mighty.

"You know, I really need to talk to my business partner about this. I understand your concerns and I share some of them, but I'm not comfortable signing right now." She handed the clipboard back to the man whose smile had quickly turned to a scowl. Ben Richter stroked his beard and then recovered his smile.

"Sure. I understand. How long have you had the kennel?"

"Just a couple of years."

"We'll have to look into your services next time we're out of town."

"I'd love to give you a tour sometime. What kind of dogs do you have?" Dogs were an infinitely friendlier subject than wind farms and the environment.

"We've got just one right now—Aristotle. He's a shar-pei."

The way the man said "shar-pei" was reminiscent of her cousin Isabelle's imperious tone, making her bristle.

"We see quite a few of those," she fibbed and enjoyed the look of disappointment on his face. Milky Way had hosted only one of these wrinkly canines, and they *could* see a lot more of them. "He'd be welcome anytime. Can I get you a brochure?"

Haley was whining at the screen door, begging to come out.

"No, thanks. I'll have my wife give you a call if we need your services. Big dog you have there." He waved his hand that held the clipboard toward Haley who pressed her muzzle against the screen.

"That's Haley. She loves everybody, but she can be a little rambunctious."

"Looks like it. Thanks for your time. I'll stop back again."

"Sure. Nice to meet you."

From her kitchen window, she watched the small car loop around the driveway and head down Simmons Road.

Just as she stuck a fork into the plate of salad that was supper, her cell phone rang. The caller ID indicated it was Jim. He wanted her to join him to check out the mysterious lights at Greerson's Meadow.

"Not tonight, Jimmy. I'm really beat. Let me know if you see E.T.," she joked.

"Your loss," he bantered back. "If I don't show up in the morning, you'll know I was abducted."

"All righty. Have fun!"

She didn't see a hint of any colorful lights in the sky later, when Haley made her final potty run for the night. Shivering in the chilly night air, she called for the dog. Maybe Jim was having more luck.

CHAPTER 2

"It was quite a show last night," Jim announced triumphantly, pouring a cup of coffee.

It was already lunchtime and the first chance for a conversation between the partners.

"Really? So you saw flying saucers?" She arched an eyebrow at her tall, dark, and handsome partner.

His almost black hair was cut short and his icy blue eyes were fringed with long lashes. His eyes always drew comments from those of the female persuasion. A confirmed bachelor, Jim lived in a log cabin he'd built 10 years ago with some help from his two brothers and her late husband, Michael. It was just a couple of miles from his parents' house and about the same distance from the kennel. However, the log cabin was not primitive living. He'd had some help decorating over the years from various girlfriends and Gracie. The Jacuzzi on the two-tier deck overlooking the lush Genesee Valley was the crowning accessory for Gracie. She'd always been envious of his view and the hot tub. Of course, Jim thought it was the combination of the hot tub and huge flat screen TV that made his house perfect. He was the host of choice for football parties. If only the Buffalo Bills could actually have a winning season again.

He smirked. "Not quite the show I expected," he said, reeling her back into the conversation.

"What do you mean by that?" she asked.

Gracie was collecting leashes to get the next group to a play session. She grabbed a chocolate chip cookie from the plate by the coffeemaker and bit off a chunk of soft cookie. Marian's grooming skills were only exceeded by her baking prowess. She'd brought a plate of huge cookies still warm from the oven as a treat for everyone.

"There was quite a group of people. More than I thought would show up. D. B. made an appearance and people were arguing with him about putting up any more windmills. Then Toby jumped into it. He told D. B. to take a hike; the property still belonged to him. D. B. got mad and went home. It was a pretty tense scene. Now there's some big rally planned to promote green power, but this Renew Earth organization is hot to oppose it. I'm not sure their position makes sense. Anyway, a couple of people were passing out flyers about how windmills cause cancer and make your cows give less milk. Didn't see any—"

"That reminds me," Gracie cut in. "A Ben Richter stopped by with a petition to stop the windmills. I didn't sign it because I saw the Renew Earth logo on it. I'm not sure we want to be associated with that group."

"I don't think so after last night. I'm not sure what they're up to, but between windmills and cow manure, they have a real ax to grind with D. B." Jim finished off a cookie and took another one for the road.

"So when's this rally ... uh ... protest?" Gracie followed his lead and took another cookie herself.

"Friday night at seven o'clock sharp. The town council has some politician showing up and said the windmill company will make an appearance. Renew Earth's gonna have their chance to speak too. Could get pretty interesting, if last night is any indicator."

"It does sound like a fascinating evening. How about we check it out?"

"Sure thing. I'm in. The bonus is that Toby is making noises about designating the Meadow a preserve of some sort. I'd like to see him do it. The Meadow's too pretty a place to be wrecked by windmills or anything else."

"I like that idea too. It's a place that should be protected." She bent to check that her shoelaces were tied. Straightening up, she said, "Gotta run, Jim. It's exercise time for some beagles."

*****

By Friday morning, Gracie and Jim decided they needed another kennel assistant or, more realistically, two. She'd spent the better part of Thursday going over their income and expenses to see if adding two more part-time employees was even viable.

Jim had his hands full with maintenance. The kennel, which was mostly renovated, still had a small section that really needed some work. Jim was updating the plumbing and electric. When those projects were finished, he needed to install a new air conditioning system. Summers weren't long in Wyoming County, but they were plenty humid. A reliable air conditioning system was a necessity. Well past its retirement date, the current setup worked only sporadically. When it did, it burped and gurgled ominously.

Gracie leaned back in her chair and adjusted her drooping mass of red hair in the hair clip. She must be a real mess. She'd have to be ready to go to her parents' in a couple of hours.

Friday nights had been reestablished with her parents after Michael's death. Her dad got a stack of crispy fish fry dinners from Midge's, and the Clark family ate dinner together. Most of the time, it was her parents, Haley, and herself. Her brother Tom and his daughter Emma usually joined them, but not tonight. Tom's ex-wife, Jan, had requested their presence at one of her family's gatherings. Surprisingly, Tom had agreed. Gracie could only hope that Tom's relationship with Kelly, her best friend and the kennel's on-call veterinarian, would survive. Jim would join the remaining Clarks tonight.

Gracie sighed and dumped the scattered papers on her desk in the wire basket. It was time to clean up here and hit the shower. Haley was close on her heels as they did a final check on their guests, and Trudy straightened the reception area. There were 35 boarders for the weekend. Haley, the goodwill ambassador, greeted each one with a perpetually waving tail.

"Looks like everybody is all set. Thanks for your hard work today, Trudy. See you in the morning."

"All right. I'll be back bright and early." Trudy grabbed her bag from the bottom desk drawer and patted Haley before she left.

Dinner was a fast affair. Everyone was anxious to get somewhere else, so there wasn't much conversation. Gracie's parents, Bob and Theresa Clark, were going to a movie and didn't want to miss commandeering good seats. Theresa even allowed them to eat out of their Styrofoam containers, which was usually a big no-no.

"So, this protest is about the windmills?" Bob asked Jim as he finished the last bite of perfectly deep-fried haddock.

"Partially," Jim managed, wiping his mouth with a paper napkin. "There are a lot of negative feelings about D. B. right now too. He's doing a great job of ticking off Toby and just about everybody else. No one wants to see those windmills ruin that property. But I think a congressman is coming tonight who is actually in favor of the wind farms. There's a lot of government money for green energy out there."

"I hope it doesn't get ugly. Are you sure you and Gracie should go?" Theresa asked.

She was already clearing the table. Gracie knew her mother hated to be late for anything. She took her mother's cue and began to collect napkins and silverware.

"The sheriff's department will be there because of the congressman. It's just some people blowing off a little steam," Jim assured Theresa.

"It's Wyoming County, Mom, not exactly a hotbed of political unrest." Gracie teased her mother. "We promise to come home early and not get in any trouble."

Her comment was rewarded with the "look," which hadn't changed since she was in kindergarten.

"All right, you two. Get out of here. We have our own plans. Come on, Bob. Are you ready? I don't want to sit way down front for this movie."

"I'm ready, dear. Let me get my keys."

"We're outta here, Mom. See you later." Gracie kissed her father's cheek and hugged her mother, who was wiping down the counters.

"Your dad and I will be over tomorrow. He's mowing, and I'm going to get started on that mess in your backyard that's supposed to be a flowerbed."

"Great. Thanks. The fence guy's coming tomorrow too."

Gracie could only hope the fence guy and her mother would take a shine to each other.

*****

Jemison Road was lined with vehicles for at least a half-mile. Pickups, cars, motorcycles, and even a tractor were parked along the dirt road. Everybody was apparently getting involved with the Greerson's Meadow issue. Three sheriff's cars were strategically placed and a deputy was directing traffic. Jim drove slowly, searching for a place to park. Four other vehicles crawled ahead of them, looking for a spot too.

"I guess we'll have to walk back from the old Everett place," Jim complained, shaking his head. "I can't believe this crowd."

Gracie nodded in agreement. There had to be at least a hundred people already gathered in the large alfalfa field. More people with signs piled out of cars. It promised to be a stimulating evening.

"Isn't there a lane that goes down into Toby's woods? People might have missed that." Gracie scanned ahead, not seeing a break in the line of vehicles. Toby's woods were only a few hundred yards farther; it beat walking a quarter of a mile from the abandoned Everett farm.

"Good idea. Looks like these folks will just park in the field. It's pretty wet out there in some spots. I don't want to chance getting stuck."

The narrow farm lane that wound back into the thick woods hadn't been snagged by anyone. It was easy to miss, camouflaged by massive sugar maples. Jim backed in for an easy exit. Tire tracks showed in the soft ground and then disappeared over a rise in the narrow road. About a cord of firewood stood stacked at the crest of the hill. Toby must be cutting wood to sell for the next season already. The smell of fresh sawdust hung in the evening air.

When they reached the Meadow, a representative from the wind turbine company loudly extolled the benefits of renewable energy sources. Unenthusiastic applause went around the crowd. Congressman Streeker then gave an impassioned speech about the local economy and the importance of green energy. The chintzy sound system snapped and squealed, giving the congressman's aide fits. She whispered incessantly to the sound person, who shrugged and kept adjusting the small soundboard without much success. There were a few cheers from the bunch nearest the platform, but a lot more booing from the west side of the crowd. Gracie shaded her eyes to check out the dissenters, who had the setting sun at their backs. She recognized Ben Richter and several people from town, but there were a lot of unfamiliar faces, who, in Gracie's quick assessment, had to be ringers. Some applause broke out as the congressman and a couple of aides stepped down from the makeshift plywood platform. D. B. pumped the politician's hand and then made a little jump to reach the small podium.

D. B. Jackson seemed to fill the platform. Imposing at well over six feet, he had broad shoulders, a square jaw, and ham-like hands that smoothed his shirt. He took off a white cowboy hat and wiped his gleaming forehead with a handkerchief. His salt-and-pepper hair was slicked tight to his head. Replacing the hat, he grabbed the microphone. Gracie and Jim edged closer through the crowd toward the platform to get a better view.

"Well, folks, you heard our good Congressman Streeker. Renewable energy is just what I want to promote here in the Deer Creek area. Our economy can use the help, and as a dairy farmer, I can say these windmills haven't done a bit of damage to my herd or to other herds in the county. The Jackson Hilltop Farm over in Strykersville has been sharing space with these windmills, and milk production is up. Sure, they're big, but they're doing a lot of good. In a few years, everybody'll see how they're benefiting the local economy and providing cheap, clean energy for us." He mopped his head with his red handkerchief again and smiled broadly at the crowd. The microphone squealed when he drew it back to his face.

Before he could continue, a man shouted from the group of protesters.

"What about all that greenhouse gas you're making up there on your farm? When are you going to stop polluting the ground water?"

A woman, waving a sign that said "Free the Cows," called to D. B. "You're just a big hypocrite!"

Gracie kept her eyes on Ben Richter, who looked like the Cheshire cat. His arms were folded across his chest. She nudged Jim.

"That's the guy who stopped at the house."

"I've seen him around town. Hey, watch out!"

Jim suddenly ducked, pulling her to the ground as a small rock came flying overhead. It thumped harmlessly on the soft ground behind them. A shower of small rocks scattered across the platform as a surge of people ran toward D. B. The majority, meanwhile, hightailed it for their cars.

D. B. jumped off the platform. A group of men in suits hustled him into a black SUV. Two state trooper cars had pulled up, lights flashing and sirens blaring.

"What's happening?" Gracie shouted over the noise of the crowd and sirens.

She and Jim crouched in the hedgerow that separated the field from the woods.

"Beats me. Let's get out of here!"

Jim grabbed her hand, and they ran back up the road to his pickup. They sat in the truck for a moment, catching their breath as cars and trucks sped past the shaded lane.

They could hear someone on a bullhorn, bellowing instructions to regain order.

"What in the Sam Hill just happened?" Jim demanded. His face was pale under his tan.

"Somebody started a brawl, I think," Gracie gasped. Her heart was still pounding. "It must have been the Renew Earth group, don't you think?"

"I'd better go back up there and see if the cops need help. You stay here."

"No way. I want to know what's going on."

She was already getting out of the truck. Jim shrugged and rolled his eyes.

"You head right back here if there's any more trouble, okay?" His voice had a no-nonsense tone. She nodded.

She rewound her hair, which had completely tumbled out of the hair clip, and fastened it more securely. Brushing the dirt off her blue shirt and frowning at the grass stains on her jeans, she trotted after Jim.

The crowd had thinned to a handful by the time they got back to the field. Toby was talking to one of the deputies, waving his hands toward the sky. D. B. had a trickle of blood running down his face from a gash over his right eye. A protester must have found his or her target. Stragglers were standing by their vehicles along the road.

Gracie saw Dan Evans, the owner of the local hardware, talking to Ed Findley, a dairy farmer who lived just down the road from the kennel. Dan was Deer Creek's fire chief, so he had to know something. Jim went to check out the scene around the platform. Gracie walked across the road to Dan's blue Ford pickup.

"Hey, Gracie. Quite the commotion tonight," Dan said grimly.

"No kidding. Who started it?" She watched Jim who was talking to Toby and one of the state troopers.

"Not sure. Probably those tree huggers, but I thought they were supposed to be non-violent types."

Ed chimed in, "Toby might have thrown that rock at D. B. He was spoiling for a fight with him tonight."

"Did you see him?"

"No. There must have been a bunch of people who came with gravel in their pockets and started pitching it everywhere. It was hard to see what was really going on. People were all over the place."

"A rock almost hit us. It wasn't any gravel," Gracie replied, swatting at a mosquito that had settled on her arm for a snack.

"There were a few rocks. It was lucky nobody got seriously hurt," Dan grumbled. "I'm not so sure Toby threw the rock. A lot of stuff happened fast."

"So, D. B. is okay?"

"He's says he's fine," Dan answered. "His head is as hard as rock anyway. I tried to check him out, but you know D. B. He doesn't need anybody's help."

"Well, at least it's not serious."

Gracie saw Jim slap Tobias on the back and begin walking toward them. The state trooper handed Tobias a paper, which he stuffed in his pants pocket.

"Geez Louise, I didn't think those Renew Earth people would go postal on us. They sure didn't win any popularity contests tonight." Ed stuck a thumb in his jeans belt loop and put a foot up on the bumper of his truck. "Guess I'd better get home. It'll be breakfast time again before you know it."

Dan grunted in agreement. He seemed unimpressed with the whole affair.

"You're right, Ed. Looks like the excitement is over for now. I've got an early morning myself." Dan turned and reached for door handle of his truck.

"See ya, Dan ... Ed," Gracie called.

She joined Jim. They walked slowly back up the rutted dirt road to the truck.

"So, did Toby hit D. B. with a rock?" She could hardly wait for Jim to answer.

"He says he didn't, but he got a ticket for disorderly conduct. From what he says, D. B. threatened to call the loan he has on the Meadow today if he doesn't sign the paperwork to sell. It's not going to be pretty. Both of them are plenty mad."

"A loan? Tobias borrowed money from D. B.?"

"I guess. Wasn't very smart. Greerson's Meadow could be a thing of the past if D.B *does* call it."

Jim started up the truck and pulled back onto the road. There were a few vehicles left at the Meadow, including D. B.'s big pickup, which sat near the platform.

The sound guy was hauling his battered equipment to a gray van parked on the shoulder. Gracie smiled feebly at the harried man as they drove past. She was sure the conversation around Midge's counter tomorrow morning over coffee and sweet rolls would be steaming hot. Too bad she wouldn't be able to join the restaurant gang for breakfast.

CHAPTER 3

The gobble of turkeys broke through the songs of the robins and warblers that threaded the woods. There were three hens and one hefty tom moving up the ravine from the creek. The tom kept a lookout, while his harem continued pecking through the layers of wet leaves. Sunlight filtered through the trees, but the morning air was still chilly. A light breeze escorted some rainclouds from the west. The shotgun blast ruffled the watchful tom's tail feathers and sent the big birds scattering in different directions as they attempted to lift off. Their heavy bodies strained to make it through the trees. Another blast brought the rotund tom somersaulting to the ground below.

*****

Gracie rolled over, groaning and slapping at the clock to stifle the annoying alarm.

Haley stood over her face, panting. The long pink tongue hit her cheek. The dog's tags jingled cheerfully. Too cheerfully and too early.

"All right. I'm up. I'm up," Gracie growled as she crawled out of bed. Her mouth felt like cotton.

She tugged at her hair with a large round brush. As usual, the curls went everywhere and her attempts at straightening them were futile. She pulled the hair back into a tight ponytail.

The kennel was open just mornings on Saturdays, but customers would show up by 7:30. She'd have to hurry; it was almost seven. Foundation was a lost cause. It was a freckles thing. She brushed on some eye shadow and mascara to look presentable.

She'd always hated her hair and the freckles that went with it. She was thinking of chopping her hair short, but Michael had loved her long auburn hair. She couldn't quite bring herself to do the deed. Not yet. Her eyes were her best feature, large and brown flecked with green. Looking in the mirror one more time, Gracie determined that she was as good as she was getting today.

Haley began barking as Gracie pulled a tank top over her head and jammed into a pair of jeans. Someone was pounding on the kitchen door. Haley was now alternating between barking and whining.

"Coming. I'm coming!"

Gracie tripped on a braided rug coming into the kitchen and caught herself on the granite-topped island. Haley was jumping at the door. Jim's worried face gazed at them through the café curtains.

"What's going on? Is something wrong in the kennel?" she asked as she let him in.

Maybe it was a sick dog or worse.

"Listen," Jim began urgently, closing the door behind him. "I have to go see Toby. Something bad has happened up there."

She knew by his guarded eyes that he didn't want to tell her exactly what the bad thing was.

"Is Toby okay? Tell me," she demanded.

"He's all right, but D. B. isn't. He's dead. Toby found him up in Greerson's Meadow this morning."

CHAPTER 4

The road was lined with law enforcement vehicles. Red lights flashed from the tops of the SUVs. Deputies were cordoning off the field, pounding in stakes and winding yellow crime scene tape around them. The Deer Creek ambulance squad stood down below, watching the county coroner's ancient black station wagon pull up. Ralph Remington, the coroner, dragged his aging body out of the driver's seat.

The doctor was ready to retire. His wife, however, had decided he should keep working just to stay out of her hair. The short-and-wide white-haired man wore khaki Bermuda shorts, a Madras plaid short-sleeved shirt, white socks, and black golf shoes. He'd gotten the call just as he was teeing off at Silver Lake Country Club. His first game of the year, and it was over before he'd even had a chance to hook a ball into the water.

He walked over to the ambulance crew.

"Don't go anywhere, boys. I'll need some help getting the body in my van. I'm in no shape to be hauling anything around, except myself. And that's questionable some days."

"Sure thing, Doc," Dan Evans answered. "We'll get the gurney out of your car, if you want."

"Have at it, but don't come up there until I say so. You don't want to muck up the crime scene."

A deputy lifted the tape as the coroner bent to duck under it. The ground squished underfoot, and the alfalfa was still heavy with dew. By the looks of the sky, it was going to rain before too long. They'd better get the show on the road. Two state troopers and a group of sheriff's department personnel stood around the sprawled body of D. B. Jackson. A dark bloodstain soaked the front of his blue shirt. His sightless eyes stared at the cloudy sky. A Jackson Farms black, club-cab pickup sat next to the cluster of people.

"Good morning, Dr. Remington."

The voice was cool and very formal. It belonged to a slender woman with fine features, dark brown hair highlighted with strands of gray, and piercing brown eyes. Her right hand rested lightly on the grip of the Glock on her hip.

"Morning, Investigator Hotchkiss. Give me some room here, people!" The old man glared at two deputies who stood in front of the body.

"He's all yours," the investigator said.

The group shuffled back to let the doctor through. The old man knelt down in the grass. His knees were killing him, and he'd probably get blood on his white socks. No doubt he'd hear about that later.

"He's dead all right. Looks like a shotgun to me. Of course, you've probably figured that out already. Help me up." The coroner sat back on his haunches with effort and groaned. A deputy grabbed his arm and pulled him up. "Let me know when you're done, and I can get him outta here. Don't take all day either. It's gonna rain."

He half-limped back to wait with the ambulance crew while the investigator directed her people to process the scene.

*****

Jim squeezed his pickup between a trooper's car and an unmarked police vehicle. He could see Toby standing by a patrol car on the opposite side of the road, smoking. He nervously flicked ashes from the end of the unfiltered cigarette. He took another drag.

Toby was medium height and rangy. It was hard to pin an age on him, but Jim's best guess was somewhere in his 50s or early 60s. His receding hairline extended his forehead and ended in a fringe of stringy gray hair that fell to his shoulders. He was some cousin or other on his mother's side of the family, who'd always been the butt of everyone's jokes. Toby was an easy target. His favorite topics were UFOs, Nostradamus, and a lot of other sci-fi stuff.

Jim felt a couple of drops of rain and looked up. The wind had picked up; trees were swaying in the stiffened breeze. The sky was overcast. Tobias furtively crossed the road to meet him, taking another deep drag on the cigarette.

"Somebody blew his chest wide open. They're gonna blame me. I just know it." Toby's voice trembled. He threw the cigarette on the dirt road and ground it out. He tapped on a pack he took from his shirt pocket, pulled out another, and lit it.

Jim clapped him on the back. "You don't know that. How'd you find him?"

"I was huntin' turkey this mornin', pretty early. Shot a nice fat gobbler and he kinda tumbled into the field." He paused and smiled. "It was a perfect shot. Anyway, I went out there to find him and saw D. B.'s truck up there." He jabbed his thumb toward the black truck. "I went over to tell him he was trespassin'. But, when I got to the truck, he was just laying there with a god-awful hole in his chest."

Tobias shuddered and sucked down another lungful of nicotine.

"Did you hear anybody shooting while you were hunting?"

Tobias flicked ash from the end of the cigarette between his fingers.

"No. Nothin."

Jim watched the group of gray uniforms break up and head down toward the road. The ambulance crew and crusty Doc Remington walked toward them. Tobias ground out his cigarette. He recognized Investigator Hotchkiss right away. Thanks to Gracie, their encounters were getting to be a regular occurrence, which wasn't a good thing. She motioned for Toby. For a second, Jim thought the man might bolt.

"Hang on, buddy," he said grabbing the man's arm. "I'll stick around if they want to ask any more questions."

Toby nodded and exhaled slowly. His eyes narrowed, looking back up toward the black pickup. Jim could just see the top of a dark tarp flanked by Dan Evans and one of the Harwood brothers in the waving ocean of green.

"I guess he finally got what he deserved," Toby muttered under his breath.

CHAPTER 5

Gracie set out a couple of plates, since Jim decided to stay and eat. He'd shown up to help finish the kennel work around noon and then had gone to the Wyoming County Sheriff's Department to lend some moral support to Toby. She knew from experience that Investigator Hotchkiss was a tough cookie, and from all appearances, the policewoman had an excellent reason to hold the odd man.

Gracie had spent the day balancing kennel work with monitoring the fence installation and her mother. The rain had moved out before noon, so work on the flowerbeds and enclosing the backyard had progressed quite nicely. She loved the look of the new English-garden style fence, which was stained a rich walnut color. It made everything look finished in the rear of the house. Zack, the fence guy, promised to be back on Wednesday to install the gates to complete the project. The weeds were gone, and the outline of a real flower garden was emerging under her mother's hard work.

Jim's truck pulled into the driveway just as Gracie slid the chicken-and-rice casserole from the oven. Haley barked energetically, pressing her face against the screen door. Jim had a familiar foam container in his hands as he bounded up the steps and opened the door.

"Hey, Chief. Brought some lemon meringue pie for dessert."

"Good. No time for baking today. It was wild here."

"And other places, too." He grimaced. "The police are questioning Dean, D. B.'s farm manager, about the murder. I talked to him in the county parking lot. Nobody's exempt from the investigation."

"I guess they're covering all the bases. Did he say how Kim is doing?"

Kim was D. B.'s widow. Gracie knew the crushing shock of being told your husband was dead. She couldn't imagine finding out he'd been murdered. Her stomach felt queasy. She forced herself to focus on putting the rest of the meal on the table.

"Not so good. Reverend Minders was over there with his wife helping her with the calls. Sara's a real mess and not much help. Duane's just a kid, but he's going to school in Alfred, so he's not far. I think Amanda lives down in Philly now."

"She'll need help making those calls. It's not easy."

Jim looked at her a little anxiously, but she put on her brave smile. He dug into the hot casserole, while Gracie piled salad on her plate. She handed Jim the basket of rolls and shoved the butter dish toward him. Jim grabbed two rolls.

"Toby was right," he said, buttering the first one. "He doesn't have much of an alibi, and a lot of people have seen the spats he'd been having with D. B. over the Meadow."

"They're sure it's not an accident? Maybe D. B. was hunting up there and fell. It could've gone off, don't you think?" She drizzled ranch dressing over her salad.

"Toby didn't see a gun on the ground when he found him. After talking with my parents today, he's probably going to need an attorney. He hasn't been arrested." He paused, looking up from his plate. "Yet."

"Doesn't he have a couple of brothers?" She pulled a roll apart to butter it.

"My mom is trying to track them down. They don't live around here anymore. One is up in Rochester, and I'm not sure where the other one is. Their parents are gone. Toby hasn't had much to do with his family for a long time. I don't think they want anything to do with him either. One brother's a high school teacher. That's the one in Rochester." He drank some water from the tumbler in front of him. "Mom knows where all these people are. I don't keep track of that stuff." He went back to shoveling food down like he was starving.

Gracie stopped eating and watched Jim wipe the plate clean with his roll and then stuff it into his mouth.

"Haven't you eaten today?"

"Actually, no." He was already spooning more chicken and rice on his plate.

The house phone rang, and she pushed back her chair to check the caller ID. It was her mother.

Theresa was calling on official business for the Fellowship Committee at church. They needed casseroles and salads to take up to the Jackson family. There would be a lot of family coming in over the next few days. Gracie agreed to make a three-bean salad and deliver it on Sunday. She wasn't looking forward to the delivery, but maybe she could help Kim Jackson in this small way.

*****

The Jackson farm overlooked the Genesee River Valley and had beautiful views toward Letchworth State Park, which straddled the banks of the Genesee. Holsteins were grazing in the pastures on both sides of the road when Gracie pulled into the long paved circular driveway that led to the big Victorian house with intricate gingerbread dripping from every inch. Painted in blue, mauve, gray, and cream, its three stories loomed above a grove of blue spruces that provided privacy from the road. The huge front porch (more a veranda than a porch really) had been host to many dairy meetings and cookouts. The house had always intimidated Gracie. The setting was intensely formal, and the barns were more than a polite distance from it. A perfectly trimmed hedgerow edged the driveway to the house. The driveways to the barns led past the house and down a small hill. Only the pervasive bovine fragrance gave the farm away. Gracie smiled to herself. No matter how good you look, cows keep it all real.

Half a dozen cars were parked in the driveway. Conspicuously missing was D. B.'s big black truck. She recognized the white Buick as belonging to Reverend Minders. A trickle of sweat ran down her back, and she felt like running. A lot of memories were wrapped up in the delivery of covered dishes and the awful hushed atmosphere of the bereaved. She was the recipient not so long ago. A fleeting temptation to just knock and leave the salad on the doorstep passed.

A woman with short gray hair answered the door. She smiled and asked Gracie to step into the foyer. Hardwood floors gleamed. Tasteful landscape oils in heavy gilt frames lined the short hallway. A vase of fresh burgundy and white irises filled a crystal vase topping an antique oval accent table. She could hear low conversations in the living room off to the right.

"Hi. I'm Gracie Andersen. I'm just dropping off a salad for Kim and the family."

"Thank you so much. I'm Judy, Kim's sister. Let me take that to the kitchen for you."

"It's pretty heavy," Gracie warned her. "I know my way to the kitchen. It's no trouble."

"Just follow me then. We've got a kitchen crew helping us put together Sunday dinner. The church here is just like family." Judy's voice trembled a bit. "My husband and I live in Virginia, so we don't get together with Kim and … uh … the rest of the family often. I just can't believe this has happened. Who would want to kill D. B.? Kim is just devastated." Her eyes filled with tears that threatened to brim over.

Gracie set the dish next to a tossed salad and a dish of baked beans. Three church ladies were busy peeling potatoes, organizing casserole dishes, and seasoning a sirloin tip roast that was ready for the oven. The kitchen was warm with the smells of good home cooking.

"Why, hello, Gracie," Marilyn Warner said, peering over her reading glasses. She'd been reading cooking instructions for one of the dishes.

"Hi, everyone," Gracie said, greeting the holy trinity of church suppers—Marilyn, Margaret, and Suzie. They'd been in charge of funeral dinners and church potluck suppers for years.

"Looks like you've got everything under control here," she added lightly.

Turning back toward the doorway, she made a beeline for the front door.

"Gracie, please don't rush off," Judy pleaded, hurrying after her. "I'm sure Kim would want to see you."

Gracie's heart sank. Her hand was on the doorknob to leave and with good reason. Comforting someone else who'd just lost her husband so violently was out of her league. Even though the pain of losing Michael and their unborn son was dissipating, she wasn't really up for this task. She swallowed hard and nodded. She'd have to face the music.

"I don't want to bother her," she croaked. She felt the heat of her face flushing with embarrassment.

"Just go on in. I told her you were here."

The plump woman smiled and bustled back to the kitchen. Gracie straightened her back and forced herself to walk through the archway to where Kim was talking with Reverend Minders. Dean, the farm manager, and his wife, Carla, stood at the sunny front windows, talking quietly. The Jackson children—Amanda, Sara, and Duane, all adults—had their backs to the doorway, but Kim immediately stood to greet Gracie. Kim was short and plump like her sister. Her hair was a honey brown with carefully placed highlights. She wore black slacks with a lilac short-sleeved blouse that effectively hid her thickening waist. Her face was almost transparently pale, her eyes red and swollen. A tissue was gripped tightly in her hand.

"Gracie, I ... I ...," she stumbled over her words.

Before she knew it, Gracie had wrapped her arms around Kim Jackson, and they both cried together.

An hour later, Gracie finally excused herself from the Jackson living room. She felt mentally and emotionally drained when she slid behind the wheel of her SUV. She and

Kim had been casual friends for years, but never close. Their similar situations had created an instant bond today.

Kim wasn't involved with farm business like Gracie had been. Kim focused on her family, bridge club, and charity work. Gracie, on the other hand, had handled most of the business end of the farm. Michael and Jim had been happiest dealing with cows, crops, and tractors, not the checkbook. Their small boutique dairy herd hadn't been nearly as large an operation as Jackson Farms though. It gave her a headache to think about all that was required to keep it running smoothly. Obviously D. B.'s right hand man, Dean Jenkins, was perfectly capable of helping Kim sort things out. He'd been managing the Deer Creek farm for years. She wasn't sure who the managers were for the other two Jackson farms. She didn't envy Kim. The woman had a lot on her plate.

Leaning back against the headrest, Gracie rubbed her forehead and sighed. D. B. had been a pushy son of a gun, but why anyone would blow him away was unfathomable. However, as she'd learned the hard way in the last two years, people weren't always who they seemed.

CHAPTER 6

The funeral had been a packed-out affair, which was expected. Everyone knew the Jacksons. Even the weather had cooperated, and the day was sunny and properly May-like. Gracie and Jim slipped out the side door of the Fellowship Hall to head back to Milky Way after the service. She'd felt hollow and shaky seeing the casket at the front of the church, the rich wood draped with a spray of red roses. She'd gripped the back of the pew so hard when they stood for the benediction that her hands ached. Just as she was climbing into Jim's pickup, a male voice called out from the shade of the maples that surrounded the church parking lot.

"Hey, Jim. Got a minute?"

She turned around toward the sound of the voice. Jim, who was already behind the wheel, leaned over to get a better look.

"Hey, Toby. What's going on?" Jim answered.

He got out of the truck, leaving it idling. Gracie decided to stay in the pickup. Toby had always given her the whim-whams, and Jim could take care of this conversation. On second thought, it might prove interesting. The window went down soundlessly when she hit the switch.

The man's long hair was pulled back into a makeshift ponytail. His thin, craggy face was unshaven, and he looked like he hadn't slept for at least a couple of days. Deep lines creased his forehead and around his mouth.

"You know they're gonna get me next. I just want somebody to know. I can't stop 'em this time."

"What are you talkin' about? Who's going to get you?" Jim asked.

"Them. They've done it before. They got D. B. and made it look like an earthling did it." The man's eyes were wide and a little wild. His voice trembled when he said "them" which made Gracie shiver.

"It *was* an earthling who shot D. B., Toby. You know that, don't you?"

Jim stood up and reached out to give the man a friendly pat on the back. Toby recoiled and looked at Jim suspiciously. He rubbed the scruffy growth on his face.

"I told D. B. to stay away from that land. It's mine and he's not gonna take it away. I told him somethin' could happen if I caught him up there."

Gracie gasped, and Jim shot her a warning look.

"Now, hold on," Jim continued as if he'd just heard what the man was having for supper. "You told D. B. that?"

"I sure did." Toby folded his arms across his chest, looking defiant. "He was a liar and slimy as all git out. That land is mine. I gotta protect it for them. They like the Meadow. Now they've come back for me. I've gotta get ready to go again."

He started pacing. His hands jammed into his jeans pockets. Jim glanced back at Gracie with worry in his eyes and a furrowed brow.

"Slow down there. Did you tell the police any of this?"

Toby stopped his pacing and looked blankly at Jim.

"It's none of their business what D. B. and me were talkin' about. I didn't shoot him. I was huntin' turkeys that mornin', not D. B."

"Right. Did you tell the police about 'them' and that they were coming for you?"

"Huh? I don't remember what I told the cops."

"I remember you told me you'd shot a big turkey."

Jim relaxed, leaning against the truck bed. Gracie watched the agitation in Toby's eyes change suddenly to pride.

"I got me a big tom. He was a beauty. Missed him the first time. Pretty crafty old boy, but the second time I knocked him right outta a big oak. I'm gonna put him in the fryer and have a feast. You can come over for some, if you want."

"Sounds good, Tobias." Jim said in a soothing tone.

"We really need to get back to the kennel, Jim. I'm sure Toby has things to do." Gracie tried to sound nonchalant, but she knew her tone was a little more edgy than she wanted.

"Well, Toby. The boss is right. We've gotta get back to work." Jim opened the door of the truck. Tobias inched toward Jim.

"Listen, Jim. You bring Gracie over and your folks too for supper tomorrow night. I'll be fryin' that turkey tonight. Tell your momma to make some of her good potato salad."

"I'll see. We're all pretty busy right now. I'll give you a call."

A shadow crossed the man's thin face. "I disconnected the phone today. I don't want anybody gettin' into my house that way. They have sneaky ways, you know."

Gracie's lips were clamped tight as Jim slid in behind the steering wheel. It took everything she had not to immediately launch into a speech on the questionable mental stability of Tobias McQuinn. He avoided her gaze and turned back to his cousin, who stood fidgeting, waiting for another word from Jim.

"I'll stop by later. You need a ride home or anything?" Jim obliged him.

"Nope. I paid my respects to D. B. I'm goin' home to cut wood. Got my truck here." He jabbed a thumb over his right shoulder toward an old rusty red Chevy pickup, which was held together with baling twine, wire, and duct tape.

"Good enough then. I'll see you later."

Jim put the truck into gear and drove slowly out of the church parking lot, looking intently at the street, still avoiding Gracie's eyes.

When she glanced out of the rear window, she saw a beat-up green compact car behind them.

CHAPTER 7

Before Gracie could express her deep feelings on the subject of dining with Toby and other matters, Jim's cell phone rang. With relief spreading across his face, Jim answered the call. Gracie sat, drumming her fingers on the console, waiting for him to finish. A few "uh-huhs" and a non-committal grunt ended the call.

"My mother," he said, tucking the phone back into the holder on his belt. "The sheriff's department is at the house asking questions about Toby. They're saying something about a mental health exam, and they have a search warrant for his trailer."

"Are you surprised?" Gracie asked.

"No," he said slowly. "Not after *that* conversation. I can't believe he'd really shoot D. B. though. I don't know what's gotten into him today."

"I *can* believe it. He may have thought D. B. was a turkey or something. He's really not right. He needs some help."

"He has some issues, but I don't think he'd really hurt anybody. He's all talk. Always has been. I'll head over to his place after I drop you off. He's going to really lose it when he sees a cop car on his property."

Gracie decided that silence was the highest virtue at her disposal, at least at the moment, and only told her business partner to be careful as he drove off. It wouldn't do any good to tell him anything else.

As soon as the big truck left the circular driveway, the dilapidated, small green car that had followed them out of the church parking lot came sputtering into the kennel's parking area. A plume of oily smoke trailed behind it. Gracie shaded her eyes against the bright sun to get a better look at the vehicle. She hadn't seen anything like it since high school. Something was familiar about it. The car looked like the one driven by a geeky guy who'd had an annoying crush on her in her senior year of high school. She racked her brain for the name, watching the car as it pulled in next to a customer's red Toyota. The guy's name had been Roscoe. She and Michael had been on again and off again that year, and Roscoe had seen his big chance to make a move on her. Michael had found it hilarious, but Gracie not so much.

A man of medium build climbed out of the car, which popped and clicked ominously before shuddering into silence. His brown hair stuck out in all directions. His checked short-sleeve shirt looked like he'd slept in it. He wore black-rimmed glasses and carried a tablet of some sort. He even had a pocket protector.

Recognition washed over her, and Gracie's stomach fell to her feet as if she were on a roller coaster. An uncomfortable blast from the past—Roscoe Myer.

*****

The pickup bounced over the rutted and winding driveway through the woods toward Toby's Airstream trailer. Jim leaned forward, straining to see through the leafy canopy. Two deputy sheriff's cars were parked by the silver trailer. He couldn't see Toby's truck anywhere. Jim unfastened the top button on his shirt and pulled off a dark blue tie. He threw it down on the seat and breathed easier.

The door to the trailer was wide open, and lights were on inside. He pulled in by the shed next to a stack of firewood. A short, stocky deputy, whose stomach strained against the buttons of his gray uniform, carried a shotgun, barrel pointed to the ground, down the steps. He stopped when he saw Jim walking toward him.

"Uh, Deputy," Jim called to him. "Thought it might be best if I was around for your meeting with Toby. Is he here?"

"And you are?" the deputy demanded.

"Taylor. Jim Taylor. Toby is a sort of cousin of mine, and when I heard you guys were up here, uh, I just wanted to make sure he's all right."

"Well, Mr. Taylor, your cousin doesn't seem to be around right now. It looks like he could be in some serious trouble. Do you know where he might be?"

Another deputy, who was taller and much more fit-looking than his partner, filled the doorway. He looked uneasily at Jim and then at the other deputy.

"What's going on here? Are you Tobias McQuinn?"

"No. I'm his cousin, Jim Taylor. Like I was telling Deputy, uh..."

"Krawczak," the short deputy supplied.

"Uh, Krawczak. I'm just trying to h-h-help..." Jim stammered. He wasn't getting such a good feeling about his decision to come dashing in like the cavalry.

The tall deputy looked him over with a practiced eye and motioned him up the weathered steps into the trailer.

"Your cousin is going to need some help. Have you seen this place?"

Jim couldn't ever remember being admitted into the Airstream. Toby spent most of his time in the woods, hunting, trapping, or cutting wood. His eyes went wide with amazement when he stepped through the doorway. Strings of white miniature Christmas lights crisscrossed the living room of the small space. The stale smell of greasy cooking clung to the air although the door was open. A model of the starship *Enterprise* hung suspended from the bottom of a pine cabinet over the kitchen sink. Star charts were taped onto the paneled walls. Several saucer-shaped aircraft were hung among the white lights. Stacks of UFO magazines announcing alien autopsies and human abductions on their covers were arranged neatly along the walls. A few newspaper clippings were on the kitchen counter. Jim picked them up and glanced at the headlines. The articles were on wind farms and the last one was D. B.'s obituary. He quickly put them back on the counter. A box of shells for a .12 gauge shotgun sat on the kitchen table. The stocky deputy picked it up while Jim walked over to the TV. The bookshelves behind it were filled with *Star Trek*, *The X-Files*, and *Battlestar Galactica* DVDs and VHS tapes. He rubbed his forehead and sat down on a dingy sofa next to a large book entitled *The Government and the Secret UFO Projects*.

"I had no idea," he said, tipping back his baseball cap and scratching his head. "No idea at all."

"We need to find Mr. McQuinn, sir. Any idea where we can find him?" The tall deputy, who seemed to be in charge, spoke firmly.

Before Jim could answer, the roar of a truck engine echoed through the trees.

*****

Gracie was still shaking her head when Roscoe's dilapidated Geo Metro finally chugged out of the parking lot.

The shocker was that he was a reporter for *The Sentinel*. Just what she didn't need—an investigative reporter asking her opinion on windmills and UFO sightings. He also had given her the impression that Renew Earth was up to something, and he was trying to unearth some juicy tidbits. Other than the petition that Ben Richter had stuck under her nose, she knew nothing about Renew Earth. Communication Central down at Midge's probably had the scoop, but she didn't mention that to Roscoe. She'd managed to put him off, pleading ignorance on windmills, aliens, and UFOs. She had a nagging feeling he'd be back. Roscoe had always been persistent, so he was probably a good reporter. However, he was still as annoying as a hangnail. To top it off, the Oscar Meyer song was running through her head. What had his parents been thinking the day the poor guy was born?

Gracie sighed and looked at her watch. Jim wasn't back yet. It had been more than two hours since he left her at the kennel. She was finishing the last of the exercise times with two cocker spaniels that required special attention. They didn't play well with others and were a little hesitant around some two-legged creatures. Fortunately, Gracie had hit it off with them, thanks to some irresistible liver treats and her natural likability to the canine set. They wagged their stumpy tails all the way back to their shared run and even licked Gracie's face before plowing into their waiting kibble bowls.

By closing time, Gracie was more than a little worried. She didn't want to call Jim and go domestic on him, but he'd planned on coming back to work.

While she weighed the pros and cons of calling him, the sound of a vehicle turning into the driveway got Haley's attention. She whined at the screen door and then gave three short barks. Gracie let Haley go dashing out while she set the alarm and locked the door. Brushing every color of dog hair from her jeans, Gracie followed Haley to the driveway.

Her father got out of the silver sedan, his face serious and brow furrowed. Her mother was trying to exit without success. Haley had pushed her way past the car door and was practically in Theresa's lap.

"Go on now, Haley. Let me get out. Who trained you anyway?" Theresa shoved Haley's wet black nose away from her pink-flowered Bermudas.

"Haley, come here!" Gracie shouted. "What's going on, Dad?"

Panting and thumping her tail against Gracie's legs, the dog finally sat down, looking demure except for her legs, which splayed wide.

"We thought we'd check on you and Jim. Has Jim gone home already?" Bob Clark answered.

"No, he hasn't been here since right after the funeral. Why?"

"Your father was down at Midge's for the afternoon bull session and..." Her mother hesitated.

"And what?" Gracie began to brace herself for the worst. "What's happened?" she demanded.

Her father frowned. "Dan Evans came in and said he'd heard on the scanner that there was some kind of standoff going on up at Tobias McQuinn's. Some family member was trying to talk him into giving himself up."

"What? No wonder Jim didn't come back to work. Holy cow, Dad! I've gotta get up there. I told Jim that Toby was going off the deep end." She patted her pockets, searching for her keys. "The guy is as crazy as a loon."

Gracie turned to run to the house. Haley whined, begging to get into the Clarks' car.

Bob opened the driver's side back door and motioned for the dog. "Get in, Haley. I'll drive you up there. And Gracie can come too!" he called to his daughter.

*****

Jim sat in his truck, his hands clenching the steering wheel, watching a very large deputy shove a handcuffed Tobias into the back of the cruiser. Toby's goose was cooked for sure now. He'd held six law enforcement officers at bay for an hour, and everyone was more than a little irate. First, there had been a merry chase through the woods in his pickup. After abandoning the truck, he'd run through the brush, hiding in a hunting blind until the deputies and Jim stumbled across it. Toby had punched a deputy, bloodying the guy's nose. Then he'd run again before being treed in his deer stand. There'd been a lot of talk about "they" and D. B. not listening to him, and a lot of other garbage. Jim dreaded telling his mother that her relation (a very distant one, he hoped) had assaulted a law enforcement officer and was on his way to jail and/or the psych ward.

The line of police cars finally began oozing back down the narrow driveway through the thick cover of woods to Jemison Road. Jim put the truck in reverse and carefully backed around to follow them out.

He met the Clark contingent on the way back. Haley's head was hanging out of a rear window. She was thoroughly enjoying the wind in her face. He opened a window and told

Bob to follow him. He'd fill them in and then head to his parents' house. This had made his top-ten list of absolute worst days.

CHAPTER 8

Jim was once again, tinkering with the AC unit that refused to run for more than five minutes at a time. The new system was on its way and none too soon. He'd be busy for the next day or two getting it installed. At least, it would give him something other than Toby to think about. The guy had racked up multiple felonies in the blink of an eye, with assaulting a police officer and first-degree murder topping the list.

Jim would've loved to wash his hands of the whole thing. How he'd become the family babysitter to watch over the crazed and delusional relation was beyond him. His dad was retired. Why wasn't he in charge of Toby? Or even better, where in the world were the man's brothers? He dropped the screwdriver back into the toolbox and snapped the lid shut.

"When does the new AC get here?" Gracie asked as she stepped out the back entrance.

"Soon. No later than two today," Jim answered.

"Good. Having that squared away will be progress. To add to the good news, I hired two more kennel assistants for the summer."

"That was quick. Who'd you decide on?"

"The Stewart twins. Casey and Tracey. They're up for the weekend shift and can start right away. Any word on—"

"No," Jim cut her off. "I'm hoping one of the brothers shows up to take over. I didn't sign up for this."

Gracie frowned. "It *is* a little above and beyond. What's that noise?" She turned toward the sound of a whirring and belching engine. "Oh no," she groaned. "I know who and what that is."

Jim walked around from the back of the building with Gracie trailing reluctantly behind.

"I've seen that car before," he said, wiping his hands on a rag. He jammed it into his back pocket.

"It's Roscoe Myer. You remember him, don't you?"

"You mean Weenie Myer who had that bad crush on you?" Jim threw back his head and laughed.

"The same. And don't remind me," Gracie said through gritted teeth.

"What's he doing here? Shouldn't he be working for NASA or something?"

"No. He's a reporter for *The Sentinel*. He was here yesterday asking about that Renew Earth outfit. I told him I didn't know anything, but I figured he'd be back."

"Reporting on what?"

"I guess the wind farms and that whole controversy. He talked about the UFO sightings too. He acted like he'd talked to Toby about the UFO thing."

They walked back into the kennel. Gracie shuddered. "He's still as ..." she broke off. The bell on the door jangled as Roscoe pushed it open. "Oh, hi, Roscoe."

"Why hello, Grace."

Roscoe sounded professorial and looked the part as he adjusted his glasses. He made an attempt to smooth his wild coiffure with no result. Although he wasn't really overweight, he had a soft, doughy appearance, with a pale complexion to match. It was apparent that he was an indoor sort of guy. The tablet was tucked under his arm, and he had already pulled a stylus from his well-protected shirt pocket.

"You remember Jim Taylor, don't you?"

Jim stuck out his hand.

"Good to see you again, Roscoe. Sorry, I've gotta run and get a couple of parts at the hardware. I'll be back in a bit."

"Can't that wait? Why don't you have some lunch first?" she asked a little desperately. "There's egg salad in the fridge. I'm sure Roscoe would like to catch up with you." Her eyes pleaded with him.

Jim smiled charmingly, shaking his head. His blue eyes danced with humor.

"No can do. I've got to get those parts or we won't have AC, period. I'll get some lunch at Midge's. Nice seein' you again."

Jim was out the door, whistling "We've Only Just Begun."

Gracie knew he was smirking all the way to his truck. She felt her face flushing with temper. She wanted to kick him in the shins for leaving her to fend for herself. Haley was sniffing Roscoe's khaki-colored polyester pants with extreme interest. He edged away from the big black Lab, looking very uncomfortable.

"Uh, this large canine ... He won't ... bite, will he?"

"*She* is Haley. And no, she doesn't bite. It wouldn't be good for business, you know," she shot back. Gracie could hardly wait to get this visit over with. "I really don't know how I can help you with the wind farm article. Like I said before, I'm not involved with it."

Haley had already lost interest in Roscoe. She ambled back to the office, her toenails clicking across the floor. No doubt, she was going to her cushy bed.

"Well, Grace, I need to be honest with you." His voice cracked, and his Adam's apple bobbed wildly. "I'm not an official reporter for *The Sentinel*—yet. I *am* employed at *The Sentinel* in the IT department." He looked down at the floor and pushed his glasses back toward his face.

Intrigued, Gracie motioned for him to take Jim's vacated chair, which he did with some relief.

"So, why *are* you here then?" she asked, tapping a pencil nervously on the oak counter.

Roscoe had always made her uneasy. There was something about him that was damp and clammy. It was hard to put a finger on. Plopping down on the swivel stool behind the counter (and as far from him as possible), she faced the nervous would-be reporter.

"I *want* to be a reporter for *The Sentinel*; however my supervisor just doesn't see it that way. The editor actually laughed me out of his office. Very humiliating." He sighed and balanced the tablet and stylus across his knees. "I decided to take my accumulated vacation leave and come down here to report on the wind farm controversy. Consequently, I found out about the UFO sightings. I've been studying the possibility of intelligent alien life for some time. It's illogical to believe we're alone in this vast universe. Once I thoroughly investigate and validate these sightings, they will have to take me seriously. It is unfortunate that Mr. McQuinn was arrested. He was a very helpful contact with regard to alien encounters. Very knowledgeable man, Mr. McQuinn. I find it difficult to believe that he would be violent in any way." He looked up at her with liquid brown eyes, magnified by his thick lenses.

Gracie bit the inside of her cheek, trying to keep a thoughtful expression on her face.

"What makes you so sure the UFO sightings are legit?" she asked after what she hoped was an appropriately pensive pause.

"I personally witnessed UFO activity. It was in the vicinity of Greerson's Meadow. Absolutely amazing. And there are well-documented cases throughout history that point to visitors from other galaxies." The passion in his voice sounded somewhat asthmatic, and his voice rose slightly in pitch.

"And I can help you—how?" She had no idea where this was leading.

"According to my research on UFO sightings in the Northeast, your property behind your... uh ... canine boarding facility has GPS coordinates in keeping with attracting such visitations. Its proximity to the forest is a classic location for alien activity. I'm seeking your permission to set up some equipment to study these spacecraft."

"You want to study UFOs on my property? I really don't think that's a good idea. Sorry."

Holy cow! Her mind raced with the PR implications. Milky Way Kennels didn't need that kind of publicity. The phone rang, making her jump. Grabbing it, she was relieved to take the reservations for a German shepherd at the end of June. After entering doggie data into the reservation software, she glanced up to find that Roscoe was gone. Grateful that the rejection was accepted without argument, she looked out the front window to see if his car was still in the parking lot. It was. The driver's door was open, and papers had spilled out onto the gravel. Roscoe was frantically trying to corral several McDonald's bags and catch the documents that were fluttering across the parking lot and onto the lawn.

"Unbelievable!" Gracie complained to the empty room.

She'd have to help him corral his trash and get him out of there before anyone came to pick up a dog. Sticking the portable phone in her back pocket, Gracie ran out the front door to assist. Roscoe looked up gratefully as she scooped up several handfuls of paper and deposited them in an open briefcase on the driver's seat.

"Thank you, Grace. I apologize for momentarily littering your property." He shuffled through a mess of clippings and photos that he had clutched to his chest. "Ah, here it is!" He held an eight-by-ten photo in his hand. "This is the personal sighting I spoke about. This was taken at Greerson's Meadow four nights ago." His face was triumphant as he handed her the blurry photo. It showed two blobs of whitish bluish light over the dark tree line. She squinted at the photo, trying to make out any saucer-like shapes. A photographer he wasn't.

"Yes. Very interesting." She wasn't quite sure what to say. The blobs could have been bird poop on his lens, for all she knew.

"As you can see, some spacecraft prefer an open area, and others are consistent in appearing on properties that are also quite wooded. Your property is ideally suited. It meets all the criteria for research on their proclivities."

"Proclivities? I really don't want to attract UFOs, Roscoe. I don't need that kind of publicity."

She turned to watch Jim's truck make its way into the driveway. He must have had second thoughts of leaving her in Roscoe's clutches. She brightened, hoping for a speedy rescue.

"You must realize this research is crucial and could open up communication with advanced civilizations and technologies. I certainly won't damage your property or even mention your business in the research. I urge you to reconsider."

Roscoe's soft demeanor had turned surprisingly obstinate.

"You know what? Ask Jim," she said, beaming at the brilliance of her evasion. She would gladly give him all credit for getting her out of an awkward predicament. "If you can get him to agree to your proposal, then go for it. I've got plenty of other things I need to do this afternoon. You'll have to excuse me."

Before he could respond, she strode to her office, resisting the urge to look back. Within minutes, Jim was in her office, whistling the *Star Trek* theme song. She sat back in her chair, grinning broadly.

"How'd he take it?"

"I agreed with him."

"You what?!"

Gracie took a couple of deep breaths and mentally kicked herself about 50 times. Why had she opened her big mouth?

"Now, hold on before you blow a gasket," he admonished. "There's a method in my madness. He's up there for two weeks and can't mention Milky Way or either of us in his articles. The caveat is that he's going to help prove Toby's innocence in D. B.'s murder. I appealed to his burning desire to be an investigative reporter, and since he likes Toby, he'll work on that during the day and study UFO stuff at night. Toby didn't kill D. B. even if he's off his rocker. He does need some real help or he'll be convicted of murder in a heartbeat."

Gracie shook her head and sighed. "All right. But how do you know Roscoe has any skill at all in investigative reporting? Toby needs a really good lawyer and some medication. I have serious doubts about Roscoe's ability to help."

Jim sat down in his moldering plaid recliner—his favorite seat and the pimple on the office decor. "Roscoe's convinced that Toby had nothing to do with D. B.'s murder. With a court-assigned lawyer in his future, he needs every scrap of help he can get."

CHAPTER 9

The clink of dishes and sizzle of bacon greeted Gracie when she walked through the door at Midge's. The place was filled with farmers enjoying breakfast. A row of men sat at the counter, hunched over heaping plates. They were piled high with pancakes, eggs, bacon, and sausage. You got your money's worth with Midge's version of the big breakfast. Midge was at the grill, working like a madwoman to keep the flow of food steady. Gracie skirted the familiar crowd; her focus was on getting a dozen sweet rolls for Milky Way's growing staff. Both Casey and Tracey were training with Jim today.

She plunked onto a stool at the end of the counter that was notorious for its wobble. It had been that way for years and was almost always empty. Gracie considered it hers, for all intents and purposes, since she was about the only one who put up with its peculiarity. A waitress placed a cup of coffee in front of her without even asking. The wispy twenty-something server, with cropped jet-black hair and red highlights, pulled an order pad and pencil from her apron.

"What can I get for you?" the girl asked.

Setting the mug down, Gracie answered, "A dozen sweet rolls to go."

"Minis or large?"

"Minis."

Midge's sweet rolls came in two sizes. The minis weren't by any means mini, and the large ones were a meal for two.

Anticipating all the brown sugar and the caramel oozing from them, Gracie's mouth began to water.

"I'll see if we have enough left. I don't know." The girl turned to examine the pastry shelf where pies, brownies, and sweet rolls were lined up.

Midge turned from the grill, long spatula in hand. She smiled when she spotted Gracie. Hollering for her assistant cook, she handed the spatula off to the lanky man, who shoveled eggs onto waiting plates. The short, wiry woman hurried over to her.

"Good to see ya, Gracie. How's business at the kennel?"

"Good. Very good, in fact. I've even hired a couple more part-time kennel helpers. The obedience training is filling up, and the search-and-rescue team wants to use the new barn to train too."

"When that other kennel went out of business, I just couldn't believe it. You and Jim have done a good job getting it going again." Midge poured herself a cup of coffee and leaned against the counter.

"Well, the Burrmans had a lot of health problems. They wanted a quick sale. Jim and I got a good deal on that property. It needs a lot of work though. Seems like everything mechanical should be replaced this year."

The waitress plopped two foam containers next to Gracie, just missing the coffee mug.

"Here you go," she said with a deadpan expression.

She pushed back a piece of red hair, exposing an assortment of earrings up to the top of her ear. When the girl disappeared into the back kitchen, Midge began grumbling.

"Sorry about Tabitha. My sister's girl. She dropped out of college and thought she'd just hang around home. Edith wasn't puttin' up with that nonsense, so she talked me into hiring her. I'm already regretting it." Midge sighed.

"Family stuff, huh?" Gracie quickly took another sip of coffee and picked up the roll containers.

"Sure is. And now I'm stuck with her, or Edith'll be down here telling me I'm too hard on the girl." Midge shook her head and then glanced toward the dining room.

"Well, well. Look who's here. He's one slimy guy, if you ask me."

Gracie tried nonchalantly to shift her gaze to where Midge had indicated. Ben Richter sat at a corner table, drinking coffee with the town assessor.

"Which one?" Gracie grinned.

"The one with the beard, not Si," Midge laughed.

"I guess he's not too popular after that protest up in Greerson's Meadow."

"He's a first-class troublemaker. You know he's a lawyer, don't cha? He was really working poor Toby over in here one day. I'd like to know what he's up to."

"I'm sure the police will want to talk to him about D. B.," Gracie responded.

"I don't know about that. They've already got Toby. I've always thought he was harmless, but people snap. D. B. was no picnic to do business with either."

"Jim seems convinced Toby didn't do it. I agree. People can have a breakdown, and I think he has some real mental problems." Gracie drained the last of the coffee from the mug.

"Want a refill?" Midge asked.

"No. I'd better get the rolls back to the troops."

She glanced over at Richter's table. He was standing and shaking hands with the tax assessor. It all looked friendly; however Midge's question was a good one. What was Ben Richter up to?

*****

A message slip lay on her desk when Gracie finally sat down to go through the mail. It was from Kim Jackson. She wanted to stop by and talk to her. Trudy had checked the "Urgent" box. Pursing her lips, Gracie hesitated before making the call. How much did she want to get involved with the situation? Twice she'd let herself get caught up in a murder investigation and twice she'd put herself in danger. But maybe Kim just needed someone to vent to. She picked up the phone and dialed.

*****

The new widow was punctual and pulled into the driveway just as Gracie finished putting the last of her dishes into the dishwasher. Haley barked and whined at the screen door. Grabbing Haley's collar, she held the dog and pushed the screen door open. Kim's face was pale. With no makeup, the dark circles under her eyes were proof of sleepless nights. Gracie knew her pain all too well. You had to force yourself to put one foot in front of the other.

After the red taillights of Kim's sedan disappeared down the road, Gracie took Haley to the now completely fenced backyard for her last potty trip of the night. Kim had blown off a lot of steam tonight. She was frustrated with her kids, the family lawyer, and her husband's partners. Her children just wanted her to sell the farms so they could get their shares. The farm managers, who were all minor partners in their respective farms, wanted time to get financing. The worst problem was the lawsuit brought by Renew Earth. Benjamin Richter, Esq., was the attorney representing his own organization.

Although she really didn't want to get involved in a family squabble, in the end, Gracie had promised Kim she'd do some digging on Mr. Richter. He was pressing the Jackson lawyer to settle the suit and quickly. She thought Kim was wise not to cave to scare tactics, but a suit like this could drag on for years. Maybe she could find something on Renew Earth that would be damaging enough for the activists to back down. Besides, there was something about the man she really didn't like.

She wished that Kim hadn't shared the details of D. B.'s death. Whoever had murdered him used the shotgun with a vengeance. It must have been at close range, because they'd blown a very large hole in his chest with one shot. Kim wasn't convinced that Toby was a killer either.

Gracie stood watching the stars, in her bare feet enjoying the coolness of the damp grass. Death had been instantaneous for D. B. Not so for Michael. He'd lain dying under the tractor. She tried to stop thinking about the scene that replayed so easily in her mind. She should have checked on him as soon as she'd gotten home. Or she should have been home so she could have been with him. But she'd had a doctor's appointment, and the ultrasound had confirmed she was having a boy.

CHAPTER 10

"How do you work in all this ... this noise and odor?"

The tall blond wrinkled her nose with predictable disdain. Her stylish lavender-and-beige capri set and matching wedges were perfect.

Gracie was sorely tempted to "accidently" dump her Coke on her cousin, Isabelle Browne Baker, but she refrained, at least for the time being. Isabelle, a decidedly bottle blond, was the epitome of fashion, social status, and a perennial pain in Gracie's butt. As the only daughter—check that—only *living* daughter of her mother's late sister Shirley, Isabelle had married up and correctly by snagging Tim Baker. His family had owned the Deer Creek Community Bank since the village had incorporated in the early 1800s. Old money and the big house on Crescent Lane were hers, and she never let anyone forget it. Since becoming a widow herself in the last year, Isabelle had been making some significant changes in her life.

"It's a kennel, Isabelle, not a spa," Gracie retorted. "And it's a *clean* kennel." She had to bite the inside of her cheek to keep from saying more. Trudy gave her boss a quick grin and studied the schedule on the desk.

Isabelle huffed, poking through the leashes and collars that hung on a revolving rack in the reception area. She acted like she was afraid they might be infected with some horrible disease.

"First cows and now dogs! When will you outgrow this animal craze? They're so ... so dirty and messy." She shuddered, turning to face her cousin with disapproval. Her layered chin-length cut revealed sparkling diamond studs on her ears.

"So, why *are* you here exactly? I really have an awful lot to do," Gracie inquired with barely controlled impatience.

"Oh, I just finally had time to stop by to see how business was going. It looks like it's ... well, busy."

"And so it is. You always were observant, Isabelle," she answered sarcastically. "Lovely to see you ... as usual. Now, if you'll excuse me." Gracie turned to go back to the office.

"There was one more thing, Gracie. Perhaps I should speak to you in private."

She lamented inwardly. The last thing she needed was a private talk with Isabelle, the family finagler. Trudy pretended to examine the schedule even closer and avoided looking at Gracie, for which she was grateful. Knowing Izzy, some committee probably needed one more person, or she wanted free room and board for a friend's dog.

"All right, but I've got an appointment in just 15 minutes."

An exercise session with a golden retriever wasn't exactly a fib. A time limit should curtail Isabelle's long-windedness though. Gracie led Isabelle back into the office, offering her the uncomfortable plastic folding chair by the desk.

After wiping the chair with a tissue, her cousin sat down carefully. She immediately launched into what Gracie determined was her real reason for descending on Milky Way Kennels. Her eyes widened in surprise when her cousin described a real estate scheme that would've turned Jim's hair gray in mere seconds.

*****

Jim pulled receipts from his pockets, laying them on Gracie's desk. She stashed them in a folder to be entered into the accounting program later. He took a bottle of water from the small refrigerator by the coffeemaker. Settling into his dilapidated green recliner, he unscrewed the bottle.

"I had a visit from Isabelle today, and I have a message for you."

As soon as she mentioned Isabelle, he groaned, closing his eyes.

"What could she want from me?"

"You'd better get comfortable. Now that she's a hot real estate agent and sits on the bank board, she's on a mission to get control of Greerson's Meadow."

Jim straightened and stared at Gracie. "What? What interest does the bank have in the property?"

"Because the Meadow is so important to the wind farm company, which is in line for substantial government grants and some hefty financing from the bank, it is 'imperative'— that's Isabelle's word—that you get a power of attorney or be appointed as conservator for Toby. She wants the property to be conveyed to the bank instead of messing around with D. B.'s estate and that mortgage he held. I was told that time is of the essence. The local economy and the future of the bank are hanging in the balance. Also straight from the queen's lips."

"Doesn't she just beat all!" Jim said with some venom. "Since when is our economy solely dependent on a field?"

"Good question, Jimmy. I don't know. Her panties are in quite a twist about this land deal. Knowing the situation with Toby and all, I have no idea why she'd even bother asking."

"There's something more to this whole thing than meets the eye, and it's a little too complicated for poor old Tobias McQuinn to be a part of it," Jim mused, rubbing his jaw. "Just another reason why I don't think Toby killed D. B." He jumped up suddenly from the chair. "I'm going up to see Roscoe. He'd better have something for me."

Gracie sat cross-legged behind the heavy oak coffee table, stuffing the remains of some cold pizza in her mouth. Typing in "Renew Earth" on her iPad, she watched the search engine generate her choices. Haley lay by her side, stretched out and snoring. The search brought up a few archived newspaper articles from *The Sentinel*. Renew Earth hadn't been around for that long. It looked like the organization had started up maybe two years ago. She guessed that was about the time the Richters moved to Deer Creek. Gracie scrolled down through the article, scanning the information for anything that looked like a red flag. Renew Earth's mission was to preserve the beauty of planet Earth and oppose the overuse and commercialization of rural areas. Petitions, peaceful protests, and education comprised their three-pronged approach to oppose wind farms, major dairy operations, mining, and whatever other commercial business they decided might ruin or otherwise taint the pristine rural environment. They were self-appointed watchdogs and would litigate to achieve their goals. Gracie shook her head. The reports were standard fare, but the violence in Greerson's Meadow made her skeptical. And if there was a connection to D. B.'s death, that didn't make them a friendly environmental group at all.

She stretched her arms over her head and then leaned back against the sofa. Haley stirred and thumped her tail.

Disappointed that there didn't seem to be anything that would help Kim win the lawsuit, Gracie closed her eyes wearily. Maybe Jim was having more luck with Roscoe.

CHAPTER 11

In the moonlight, the campsite looked like something from a "B" sci-fi movie. A couple of battery-powered lanterns hung on poles outside the dome-shaped tent. They cast wobbly shadows around the campsite. The Geo was parked at an angle next to the brown tent. A pile of fast food bags wafted the odors of greasy French fries from the front passenger seat. Jim wrinkled his nose. If Roscoe wasn't careful, he'd have a car full of critters.

A telescope stood at the ready next to two old and sagging card tables that sported an assortment of what looked like ham operator equipment. It reminded Jim of his Uncle Jerry's garage with its radios and antennas. Two laptops sat side by side on another table, with Roscoe studying both screens intently. He looked like a mad scientist with his hair at all angles and his glasses hanging on the end of his beak-like nose.

"Hey, Roscoe. Any luck yet?" Jim queried.

"Oh, why, hello," Roscoe answered distractedly, stepping back from the computers and pushing his glasses back up onto his face. "As a matter of fact, I've not yet been able to ascertain if my GPS coordinates are in error or if our visitors have indeed left the area."

Jim raised his eyebrows and smothered a chuckle.

"I meant any luck with information that might help my cousin."

"Oh. I see what you mean. I have done some research on the wind farm issue. Let me get my notes." He began rifling through a pile of file folders that were under the laptops. "Ah, here it is."

Roscoe adjusted his black-framed glasses again and pulled out several sheets of paper from a tattered manila folder.

"This wind farm company, New Energy Strategies Team, is relatively new. They began as a solar energy company five years ago and have now added wind power to their portfolio. In fact, it appears that Mr. Jackson was one of the first to lease land to them. That's the wind farm in Strykersville." He looked up at Jim, peering through his thick glasses.

"The company president is Mitchell Allen, who was once an executive for T & T Salt Company. He has an engineering background and ..." Roscoe ran his index finger over his tongue and turned the paper over, scanning the contents of his handwritten notes. "Oh, yes. Mr. Allen's company does seem to be in a precarious financial position. N.E.S.T. is relying heavily on government grants and bank financing to get these wind farms established."

"N.E.S.T? Whatever," Jim grumbled impatiently. "That doesn't help Tobias out. I was really hoping you had something that might shed some light on who might want to kill D. B."

Roscoe's face fell. He shifted his feet uneasily, clutching the papers to his chest.

"I apologize if I misunderstood you, Jim. I think highly of your relative. Why, he and I had a very stimulating conversation after the rally at Greerson's Meadow. He described in excellent detail the flight patterns of the spacecraft he observed a few nights before all the ... the rather tragic events ..."

Jim interrupted the extended apology. "You and Tobias met after the brawl at the Meadow?"

Roscoe's brown eyes blinked with bewilderment. "Why, yes. He had some excellent journals of the recent spacecraft sightings. He was quite hospitable, although shaken after that unfortunate incident with the Renew Earth protesters."

"You were with him at his trailer?"

"Yes. That's where the journals are kept, of course." Roscoe's tone became slightly patronizing.

Jim's pulse quickened as he mulled over the possibilities. "What time were you there? Do you remember?"

"Of course. I considered it an interview for my report. I can tell you exactly when I arrived and departed." Roscoe stuffed the papers back into the folder and shoved it in the pile under the computers. Jim reached forward, steadying the laptops, which were hanging precariously on a mountain of paper. Roscoe, already preoccupied with his next task, walked quickly to his tent and disappeared inside. Making sure the laptops were balanced properly, Jim checked his watch. It was just nine o'clock. Maybe he'd have time to call Toby's attorney if Roscoe hurried. The flap of the tent opened, and Roscoe reappeared with his iPhone and flashlight. He held the flashlight under his armpit, while his finger swiped the phone.

"Here it is," he said, looking up as the flashlight dropped to the ground, its light flickering. Jim quickly bent down to retrieve it and looked at the phone.

"I recorded it. The conversation is officially time stamped. I began the interview at 8:35 p.m. and concluded it at 10:52 p.m. I took photos of his journal for verification and some video of Mr. McQuinn. They're time-stamped as well. It's all appropriately documented. Mr. McQuinn was most helpful in explaining alien abductions that evening. Did you know that he was taken as a child? Most extraordinary experience for him," he mused, staring off into the night sky.

"Yes, Roscoe. I'm very familiar with that story. You're sure about the times?"

"Of course. The app is absolutely accurate, as are the other functions. I wouldn't use the phone if it wasn't precise." He seemed offended that the question had been asked.

"Thanks, Roscoe. Keep that phone in a safe place. It's going to be needed." Jim handed him back the flashlight and slapped the bewildered man on the back. "You're a genius."

*****

Jim punched the "End" button on his cell and leaned back on Gracie's extremely comfortable leather sofa, putting his feet on the coffee table.

"So?" Gracie asked, anxious to hear the news.

"So, the lawyer says it's an alibi and basically airtight. I'm going back up to tell Roscoe to hand in his phone tomorrow morning. The medical examiner put the time of death for D. B. between 8:30 p.m. and 9:00 p.m. There's no way he was there. Roscoe took some photos of Toby that night too. Everything is documented. The lawyer had some news too."

Gracie pulled the clip out of her hair, letting it fall over her shoulders. She took a sip from the glass of iced tea, wiping the condensation from the bottom before setting it back on the coaster on the mission-style end table. She curled up in a club chair, with Haley intently chewing on a bone on the floor next to her.

"What else is going on?"

"The shot that was used to kill D. B. was pretty big, as in triple B steel shot. It's bigger than anything that Toby had on hand. The cops found #6 at the trailer, which is for small game. He needs to start assisting in his own defense though. For some reason, he just won't cooperate with his attorney. I need to go talk to him again. Maybe I'll take my mother. Then he'll be sorry." His eyes crinkled with humor.

Gracie laughed. "Take mine too. He'll stand no chance then."

Jim stood to go, tucking in his shirt, which had pulled out slightly. Gracie picked up their empty glasses and followed him to the kitchen. Haley was immediately at her heels with her bone securely clamped in her jaws. Gracie bent down to open the dishwasher, placing the glasses on the crowded top rack.

"I almost forgot to tell you in the excitement of Roscoe's big revelation," she said, standing. "Kim Jackson called me right before you got here with some interesting news of her own. Renew Earth made an offer to settle."

Chapter 12

The air conditioning was now working. Just in time too. The forecast predicted warmer-than-average temperatures for the week. Gracie sat back in her chair to enjoy the cool air now circulating through the office. The familiar whistling of "How Much is That Doggie in the Window" announced Jim's triumphant arrival through the back hallway.

Marian shouted, "Thanks, Jim!" from the grooming room.

"Hold your applause, please," he said, bowing toward reception and then toward the grooming room. "It's just gratifying to know you're now all cool and comfortable because of my outstanding skills."

His boyish grin of satisfaction made Gracie laugh. He leaned against the doorway of the office, looking outrageously handsome. Why Laney, his last girlfriend, had decided to pick a corporate ladder climber over Jim was beyond her understanding. Unfortunately she had nothing good to say about herself. After all, she'd messed up a relationship with Marc Stevens not so long ago at about the same time Laney had broken Jim's heart. Her last email from the handsome deputy, who'd saved her life right after they'd first met, informed her he was entering K-9 training in El Paso after he finished a stint with the Sierra Vista police in southern Arizona. Her feelings lately were that single was okay and relationships required too much work.

"Outstanding skills in dialing a phone, you mean," Gracie wisecracked.

"Huh?" Jim looked perfectly innocent. "I don't know what you mean."

"I saw the Artie's Air Conditioning Service van in the back parking lot."

Jim shrugged and helped himself to a bottle of water from the refrigerator.

"I've learned when to give up," he replied. "You should appreciate that. Otherwise, you'd still be waiting for the AC. That's what matters, right?"

"I agree. I hope it's not going to be a really big bill though."

"Nah. A couple of hours work for Artie. I was just lucky to get him out here so fast."

He took his usual seat on the ratty recliner, which Gracie semi-affectionately referred to as "The Heap." Uncapping the water, he slugged down half of its contents. Gracie refilled her coffee mug while Jim finished off the water.

"So did you call Toby today?" Gracie had been waiting all morning to get the details on the disposition of Toby's sanity and if the D.A. would drop the murder charge.

"My parents actually went to see him with the attorney. Dad just called a little while ago. Tobias does have some problems, which they want to treat, but he's competent. They also talked him into cooperating with the lawyer. He confirmed Roscoe's story that they were talking until late about his abduction and a whole lot of other UFO things the night of the murder. For some reason, he had it in his head that D. B. had been killed the morning he found him. He has this thing about not trusting anybody with the government."

"I guess I can't fault him for that. There's a lot of that going around right now," Gracie said with a vinegary voice. "What about the murder charge?"

"We have to wait and see. If he hadn't slugged that deputy, it would a little better for him. They're checking the time stamp accuracy of Roscoe's phone recording. The lawyer says they really could use a bona fide suspect to convince the

D.A. With what you found out from Kim last night, we might be able to give them one."

"We? Isn't that the police's job?" Gracie asked. "Aren't you always telling me we both have enough to do without getting involved in police matters?"

"All right, Chief," Jim answered. "I see your point. But we're both sort of involved in this mess. You with Kim and me with Toby."

"And that makes a difference? Because we're both involved?" She couldn't resist needling him just a bit more. He'd warned her off both the library case and investigating her own cousin's death. Now he wanted to go whole hog into a murder investigation, dragging her along with him. She wasn't so sure she was up to another one at the moment.

His blue eyes were thoughtful as he rubbed his jaw in contemplation. "You could tell Kim to give that investigator a call and tell her about the Renew Earth settlement offer. There's something very fishy about settling a quarter-of-a-million-dollar lawsuit for twenty-five thousand and assuming the mortgage on the Meadow property. It might get their juices going if there are other possibilities besides Toby."

Gracie chuckled softly. Apparently he was plowing straight ahead despite any of her misgivings. "I guess. I'm not sure if Kim would call. She really wants that lawsuit to go away, and I don't blame her. It could hold up the settlement of the estate forever. However, Kim doesn't think Tobias killed D. B. either." Gracie absently picked at the crumbling eraser on the pencil she twirled.

"Guys! Come quick!" Marian called frantically.

Jim and Gracie jumped from their seats and dashed to the reception area, where Trudy was pointing, her finger pressed against the window.

It was Roscoe. He was running wildly around the parking lot, three raccoons in hot pursuit. Gracie gasped.

"Are they all rabid?" she practically screeched.

Rabid raccoons were not unusual in Wyoming County. The summer months always brought warnings from the health department to watch for unusual animal behavior, especially from raccoons.

"I don't think so. Do you see what he has in his hand?" Jim answered with disgust. "What an idiot!"

She opened the door and yelled, "Drop the food, Roscoe! Drop the food!"

He looked up, startled at the sound of her voice, and ran toward the door.

"Don't come in here. Drop the bag!" Gracie shrieked.

Her worst nightmare would be three raccoons loose in the kennel. She slammed the door and locked it.

Jim opened the window and thundered, "Roscoe, get rid of the bag! They'll stop chasing you!"

A flash of realization came over him, and he released the large fast food bag.

The raccoons dove onto it, shredding it within seconds. Two more ring-tailed companions jumped from the open rear window of the car. Roscoe stood shaking; watching his lunch being devoured by five greedy raccoons. The hamburgers, fries, and packets of ketchup were daintily consumed. They sat up contentedly, their paws holding French fries like seasoned gastronomes. They chattered amongst themselves, as if congratulating each other on their victory.

Gracie unlocked the door, motioning for Roscoe to make his escape. Smelling of sweat, onions, and grease, he stepped gratefully inside.

Receiving the lecture of a lifetime about not feeding wild animals, even if they were cuddly and cute, Roscoe sat properly chastised in a brown vinyl chair, surrounded by three disapproving faces. After the impassioned speech by Gracie, he sheepishly admitted he'd been letting the family of raccoons eat and play in his car since he'd been camping behind the kennel. Among his reasons for letting them become squatters in his car was that they were intelligent and polite.

He hadn't realized they were sleeping under the pile of bags when he'd picked up lunch on his way to see Jim. The hitchhikers had decided to help themselves to lunch just as he pulled into the kennel's driveway.

"You are sooooo lucky," Trudy stood, shaking her pretty head at the exceedingly disheveled man. "Raccoons can have rabies. Oh, my gosh! Did they bite you?"

"No. No, I don't believe they inflicted any bites on me."

Roscoe shoved his glasses back up his glistening nose while inspecting his arms for marks. His usual hair explosion was damp with sweat and lying flatter than Gracie had seen it.

The four gathered around the front windows to watch the raccoons finish the meal and walk single file back to the Geo. One by one they jumped through the open windows.

"I'm calling animal control," Gracie said, grabbing the phone. "They need the witness relocation plan, plus they should be checked for rabies."

The animal control truck rumbled into the driveway 20 minutes later. With Jim's help, the animal control officer rounded up the sleepy Wild Bunch, confining them to cages. They were now headed for the county lockup. They'd be quarantined to make sure no one was rabid. Roscoe was instructed to clean his car and campsite. The officer reiterated that it was not a good idea to allow wild animals of any sort in his vehicle or tempt them to stay around his campsite. A very subdued Roscoe drove out after the animal control vehicle to get checked out by a doctor. Gracie figured it would serve him right if they started rabies shots on him. What a dope!

Haley was obviously disappointed she'd been held captive inside during all the excitement. The windows, however, were covered with her nose smears. Her tail drooping and her head low, she finally gave up trying to get out the front door.

Gracie gave her a butt rub as she went by. "Sorry, girl. A little too much excitement for you to be involved in."

Ignoring her mistress, Haley flopped onto her bed in the office, rolled on her back, and with an irritated snort, went to sleep.

The Clarks were pulling into the driveway when closing time came. Jim had already left to check on Roscoe's status. Haley loped off to meet and greet. Gracie sighed when she saw her mother carrying a casserole dish. It could only mean she was worried that Gracie wasn't eating healthy or something like that. A hot bath and an early bedtime would have been her first choice tonight. Apparently her plans had changed.

"Hey, parents!" she called out.

Haley was slobbering on her father's pants, while receiving a good scratch behind the ears. Her mother held the casserole at eye level, anticipating Haley's interest.

"We thought you might like a little company tonight, and I'd already made this big dish of mac and cheese," her mother started. Gracie decided to accept defeat and save time discussing.

"Sounds good. I can make a salad to go with it."

She pulled a bag of greens from the refrigerator while her mother snugged the foil on the large brown casserole dish. Theresa switched on the oven and bent to slide the dish onto a rack.

Her red hair had now faded to a sedate auburn with prominent strands of gray. Mother and daughter were about the same height, although Gracie was sure she was at least a half-inch taller. Gracie's eyes were her father's, as was her nose. Her brother, Tom, was the spitting image of their father, except for the red hair that their mother had generously passed on to both her children. Theresa was an avid walker, who worked at staying fit. For a woman who had just turned 64, she was in pretty good shape. Bob, on the other hand, was always wrestling with his weight. Gracie understood that struggle herself. A fortieth birthday looming in a month and jeans that were a little too tight were her reminders.

Supper with her parents proved to be informational when the topic got around to Isabelle's strange visit of the day before. Aunt Marlene, who was the family's self-appointed gossip hotline director, had informed Theresa about the difficulties the bank had encountered dealing with D. B.'s estate. D. B. had promised them Greerson's Meadow. The board was feeling serious pressure to make the wind farm deal happen. The land, of course, was the big holdup and a major inconvenience for Isabelle, who was scouting properties for them. Greerson's Meadow was currently the only acceptable property because of the elevation. Nothing on the Jackson farm was remotely in the running.

"Isabelle told Marlene that this Mitch Allen of New Energy Strategies Team made it clear to her in a meeting that N.E.S.T. didn't especially care who they did business with now, it just needed to happen," Theresa finished.

Gracie was still mulling that bit of information over, when her father chimed in with news about the Memorial Day activities.

"This N.E.S.T. company is sponsoring a carnival for the whole village after the parade this year," he offered, pushing back from the table after two generous helpings of everything.

"A carnival? That'll put a different spin on the day," Gracie said, shoving the last bit of macaroni, with the wonderful crunchy breadcrumb topping, into her mouth.

"I guess we'll find out all about it next week," said Theresa. "You *will* be there, right?"

"Wouldn't miss it. It'll be a chance to find out more about this N.E.S.T. mess."

CHAPTER 13

"If he hadn't assaulted a police officer, I could get a bail hearing," the young and earnest Gary Haskins, Esq., told Jim.

"I understand," Jim said matter-of-factly. "I tried to tell you, Toby. I wish you'd listened to me."

Jim threw a worried look at the attorney. Thrusting his hands back in his pockets, he began pacing again. Everything about being in the jail area made him feel like a trapped animal. Toby must be feeling even worse, he reasoned.

Toby, who sat in a straight-back chair in the empty visitors' area, nodded, looking glumly at his feet.

"I know. I know. It's my own fault." He leaned back in the chair to face Jim and his lawyer. His eyes were weary with fatigue and uncertainty.

"However," the attorney continued, "the sheriff's department is continuing their investigation. With the statement from Roscoe Myer and his recording checking out, we stand a good chance that the murder charge will be dropped today. You need to tell me if you saw or heard anything unusual that night. Did you hear a gunshot?"

"Not that I remember. My trailer's a good ways from the field. I guess I could've heard somethin' if I was outside, but me and Roscoe was in the trailer for the whole time, except for when he left. I walked him out to that little car of his, but that was pretty late."

The young attorney nodded, snapping his briefcase shut. "All right. If you think of anything, call me. I'm due in court right now. It was nice seeing you, Mr. Taylor." The sandy-haired man in the navy blue suit stood to leave.

"Thanks. You too." Jim stood to shake the attorney's hand, then quickly returned to his seat by the glass partition. He hoped he could jog something loose in Toby's memory of that night. Before he could ask his next question, a male voice behind him greeted Toby.

Jim turned to see a well-dressed man with a neatly trimmed beard approach them, smiling confidently.

"You must be Jim Taylor," he said, extending his hand. "I'm Ben Richter." Jim stood, hesitantly accepting the extended hand.

*****

Investigator Hotchkiss exited her county SUV, quickly surveying the manicured lawns and gardens. A patrol car turned into the driveway and parked behind her. Giving the deputy a quick wave, she pulled out her notepad. The athletic investigator climbed the broad steps to the front door of the Jackson home, with the deputy close behind her. The doorbell chimed pleasantly when she pressed the ornate brass button. The heavy door, decorated with a simple grapevine wreath and silk apple blossoms, swung open almost immediately. A young woman with long brown hair, who appeared to be in her late 20s or early 30s, stood looking at them with questioning eyes.

*****

Kim's hands trembled as she punched in Gracie's cell phone number. She took a deep breath to steady herself. From the living room bay window, her daughter Sara watched the deputy carry two shotguns and a box of shotgun shells to his cruiser. Investigator Hotchkiss frowned and looked back at the big house as she slid behind the wheel of her car.

*****

"Slow down, Kim. Now, what did they ask you, exactly?" Gracie strained to understand what Kim was telling her.

Between sobs, words piled over the top of one another. She could barely understand what the frantic woman was saying. Gracie bent her head in concentration, pressing the cellphone hard against her ear and shoulder. Pulling a potholder from a drawer, she opened the oven door and pulled out a pan of muffins. Tipping the pan over, the fragrant blueberry muffins tumbled onto the cooling rack. Haley stirred from her bed and trotted to the kitchen door. The dog woofed half-heartedly as Jim's truck rolled in, crunching over the gravel driveway. Gracie, still listening to Kim's tearful discourse, walked to where Haley stood panting and thumping her tail against the kitchen cabinets. She pushed the screen door open, motioning Jim to come in.

"All right, Kim. I'll be over this afternoon. You'd better call your attorney before then. I'm sure you don't have anything to worry about. The police have to investigate everyone. It's just standard procedure. You can't be an actual suspect." She paused, listening intently again. "Yes, I'll be over right after lunch."

She ended the call and stuffed the phone in her jeans pocket. Jim was already in the kitchen, helping himself to coffee and a steaming blueberry muffin.

"Ouch! These are hot!" He dropped the contraband, blowing on his burnt fingers.

"I just took them out of the oven. Give them a minute or two."

Jim scowled in displeasure, opening the refrigerator door to snag a carton of half-and-half. He dumped a generous amount into his coffee before attempting to pick up another muffin.

"I gather that was Kim Jackson on the phone," he said.

"You gathered correctly," Gracie affirmed.

She sat down on one of the stools at the breakfast bar, carefully picking up a hot muffin for sampling. She broke it in half, watching the steam rise before taking a bite.

"The sheriff's department was up there a little while ago, questioning Kim about where she was the night of the murder. They also took two shotguns that D. B. had in his office."

"Well, that confirms what Toby's lawyer said about them continuing the investigation." Jim sat down on the other stool, slurping a mouthful of coffee.

"I can't imagine they'd seriously consider Kim a suspect. It's just ridiculous."

"We might think so, but you don't know what's really going on with people."

"There must be other suspects, like that Ben Richter. Kim tried to tell them that. Her impression is they're not too interested." She took another bite of the cooling muffin.

"Funny you should mention him. He offered his legal services to Tobias today while I was there."

"Really," Gracie said. "I just heard he was an attorney the other day from Midge. Why would he want to represent Toby? He doesn't have any money to pay him."

"Toby and I asked him the same thing. He says he'd work out a reasonable payment plan to make it easy on him. He went on about defending the rights of the little guy and noble ideals—things like that. Of course, there was a mention of protecting the Meadow too. It's a bunch of hooey, if you ask me, but Toby's thinking about it. He's just not very comfortable with the public defender guy."

Haley's wet nose suddenly appeared on Gracie's thigh, sniffing hopefully.

"Hey! No begging. Scram!" Gracie pushed the disappointed dog away.

Haley merely switched humans, locking her sights onto Jim.

"This Richter could end up being investigated, so I'd let Toby know that," Gracie continued. "He and D. B. had a couple of pretty heated arguments. Of course, D. B. started the first one."

"How did he do that?" Jim asked, slyly slipping a piece of muffin to the waiting Haley.

"Kim told me that D. B., apparently being in jerk mode, 'accidently' dumped a load of manure on the Richters' front yard."

Jim shook his head. "Sounds like D. B. Was this before or after the lawsuit?"

"It was the day D. B. was served with the lawsuit papers. Richter was up to the farm in a flash, yelling and carrying on. He even took a couple of swings at D. B. Threatened to ruin him and take him out."

"D. B. did love a good fight." Jim brushed the crumbs off his hands, showing Haley that there were no more sneaky treats to be had. "Sounds like Mr. Richter has a bad temper too."

"It does look that way," Gracie agreed, finishing her coffee. "Kim also said that Dean and D. B. were pretty sure someone tampered with the temperature on the bulk tanks. They had to dump a lot of milk because of it. D. B. naturally went ballistic, which isn't surprising. I would have too. But he and Richter got into a shouting match outside of Midge's. Dean had to break it up before they went at it."

She got up to put the dishes in the dishwasher. Jim stood, looking out of the kitchen window toward the kennel. His brow was furrowed.

"D. B. wasn't an easy guy. In fact, he could be a downright ... well, you know. Michael and I had a few disagreements with him," he added thoughtfully.

"I know what you mean," Gracie replied. She began wiping down the counter. "Michael was pretty upset about that equipment sale. D. B. really did pull the rug out from under us."

"Exactly. We needed that front loader and had worked out the deal with him. When we went up to get it, he'd taken it to one of the other farms. Told us it was no longer for sale." Jim scowled, remembering the incident. "I think if the cops start digging, they'll find quite a few people who may have had it with D. B.'s antics."

Gracie glanced at her watch. "I'd better check on a couple of dogs before I go see Kim. We've got two who need meds right now."

"Good. I'll make sure Tracey is doing okay."

*****

Kim and Gracie finished looking over the settlement papers from Renew Earth. Kim's attorney recommended that she accept the settlement and fast. He didn't want it withdrawn from the negotiating table. Gracie's head was swimming with "whereofs," "heretofores," and "forthwiths."

"I don't feel right about accepting this. There's something hidden in all of this legalese if you ask me." Kim stood next to Gracie at the kitchen counter, staring at the blank signature line. "Dean and the kids want me to sign it too. What do you think I should do?"

Gracie had no intention of supplying an answer. There was no way she wanted to be responsible for Kim signing or not signing the document. She drummed her fingers on the counter, stalling for time.

"I really can't tell you what to do, Kim. I have the same concerns as you do. I'm not a lawyer though. Is there a time limit on the offer?"

"I don't think so, but Nolan wants me to sign it soon. By the end of the week, he said, and that's tomorrow." Kim twisted the rings on her left hand nervously. Her face showed the strain of the mounting pile of decisions along with the earlier police visit. "I just don't know what to do," she half-sobbed.

Gracie's stomach went cold, remembering she'd said the exact same thing when she and Jim had discussed selling the farm.

"What if it's the wrong thing, and somehow the farm is harmed by my signing it? I can't make a mistake on this."

"I'd stall for more time, if you're really not sure," Gracie said, chewing her bottom lip. "If there's no real deadline, maybe a few more days will give you time to think."

Kim pulled a tissue from the box on the counter, wiping her swollen, red-rimmed eyes.

"Maybe," she said finally, blowing her nose on the sodden tissue. The exhausted woman sat down heavily on a spindle-back chair next to the broad farmhouse table. "But what if I'm in jail by then?"

CHAPTER 14

Theresa stood in the Blooming Idiot, Deer Creek's only florist, waiting for the urn. Every year without fail, either Theresa or one of her siblings brought the urn to be refilled that stood guard by their parents' headstone from May to October. With the loss of her sister, Shirley, and her brothers living in another county, it would be her turn every year, most likely. Esther Smith, the proprietor, came from the back of the greenhouse, hauling the heavy pot. It was filled with bright red geraniums, vinca, and the obligatory spike. A small American flag was stuck in the center. The short, round woman heaved the urn up onto the counter with a heavy sigh.

"Another beautiful job, Esther. It's perfect," Theresa said, smiling as she wrote out the check. "Has Gracie called you for anything yet?"

"No. I don't think so. How's she doing anyway?" Esther's cheerful ruddy face, glistening with perspiration, smiled up at Theresa.

"Just fine. She's awfully busy with the kennel, which is a good thing." Theresa tore out the check, handing it to Esther who placed it in the cash drawer.

"Poor girl. She and Michael were such a good couple. It's just a rotten shame. And then the baby too."

Theresa nodded. "She's on track now. But it's still hard."

"Yes, it is," Esther said, as if waiting for a bit more information.

Theresa stuffed the checkbook back into her large, leather-patchwork hobo bag. "I'll remind her about the flowers. You're pretty busy, so I'd better get going." Theresa glanced over her shoulder toward the display areas around the parking lot. All of Esther's workers were occupied with customers. Flats of pansies, begonias, and phlox were going like hotcakes.

"It's always our busiest weekend. Thanks again."

The bell on the door jingled brightly as Theresa lugged the urn to the car. She saw Isabelle pulling in the driveway with her cherry red Mustang. The top was down, and her daughter, Anna, was in the passenger seat. Theresa felt tears pricking her eyes, a wave of sorrow overwhelming her. Isabelle had a lot of flowers to purchase today. At least, she had her children though. Something Gracie would never have.

*****

Haley was in the second minute of the long-down stay. Her tail wagged tentatively, anticipating the release signal from Gracie, who was studiously avoiding eye contact with the dog. Haley was notorious for breaking on this obedience exercise about 30 seconds from finishing. The last two obedience matches had been lost because of Haley's eagerness to get up and stretch. Gracie watched the second hand sweep around another minute on her watch. Almost there. The sound of a vehicle entering the driveway distracted Haley. The black Lab flew to the fence, woofing a greeting. Gracie shook her head. It was practically impossible to get the dog to just relax. Some dogs even went to sleep on this exercise. She'd seen it plenty of times. Haley unsuccessfully strained to look over the fence. She heard her mother call out when Haley barked again.

"We're in the back, Mom. Come through the gate."

Theresa stepped through to the shady backyard, looking around at the flowerbeds that enjoyed the morning sun, and mostly shade in the afternoons. Day lilies were budded heavily, and tall phlox scented the air with sweetness.

"I just stopped by to remind you to get flowers for the cemetery. Esther didn't have an order from you yet."

Theresa patted the panting Haley's head. Greeting completed, the dog trotted off to sniff the trunk of one of three ancient maples that sheltered the large backyard.

Gracie swallowed hard, frantically trying to come up with an excuse to not make the annual trek to the family plot. She really wasn't sure she could do it without falling to pieces, especially after her recent conversations with Kim. The freshness of death clung to her again.

"I know. I'll try to call this afternoon."

"She's awfully busy there, so don't forget. The parade is at ten, so be there by 9:30. We'll all go up to the cemetery before the parade and the ceremony. Everybody is going to the carnival after that."

"Sure," Gracie answered softly.

She bent down to pull a few random weeds that had made an appearance between the peonies and iris. Throwing the weeds into the small wheelbarrow next to her, she decided that it was probably easier just to agree, rather than inform her mother of her real plans. When she stood up, her head began to throb, and she rubbed the back of her neck, hoping to find a pressure point that would give some relief.

"Does 'everybody' include Isabelle and her boyfriend, what's-his-name... Kevin?" There was a bit of a petulant tone to her voice.

"Of course, it does. Don't be a no-show because of them." Her mother's mouth was pressed into a firm line.

"All right, all right. I was just asking. I may have to get back to help with exercise sessions and other things. I *am* running a business, holiday or not."

"I'm sure you won't be missed for a couple of hours," her pokerfaced mother said, not letting her daughter off the hook.

The Memorial Day tradition was a big deal with her mother's family, the Fergusons. It used to be that Aunt Shirley, her mother, and their three brothers all trekked to the cemetery to place flowers on the family graves. Any available children were expected to join their parents. Available was defined as in "be there." Besides her grandparents' graves, there would be flowers for Charlotte, Aunt Shirley's daughter and Isabelle's sister, and then there were two sets of assorted great aunts and uncles that she barely remembered. Now it included Michael, and their son Andrew, Uncle Stan, Aunt Shirley, and Tim, Isabelle's late husband. Her stomach lurched at the thought.

"I'll see how it goes. Thanks for stopping by."

Gracie wanted nothing more than for this conversation to end. She wanted to get back to work anyway. She whistled for Haley who ran toward the two women. Theresa glanced at her watch.

"You probably need to get back to work. We'll see you for supper tonight then."

"Right. Six?"

"Six is good. Your Dad is picking up the food, so don't worry about that. Is Jim coming too?"

"I'll check. He's probably booked though. I'll call you if he's coming."

*****

Jim was refilling kibble bins when Gracie walked through the noisy corridors, checking to see who needed playtimes. She stopped to scratch the heads that pressed against the gates, vying for her attention. Jim folded up an empty 50-pound bag and tossed it in the blue recycling box in the corner.

"Looks like everybody has been taken care of today," she remarked.

"The girls are working out. They're really staying on top of things."

"Good to hear. Oh, my mom stopped by."

Jim looked at her. "And?"

"Well, she wants to know if you're joining us for dinner tonight."

"Sorry. I can't make it. I've got plans," he said, grinning at her.

"I figured," she said and then hesitated.

She leaned against the gate of an empty run, hugging herself.

"All right, Chief. What is it?" he demanded.

"I guess I might as well just come out with it." She took a deep breath, and plunged ahead. "Would you go to the cemetery with me tomorrow? I can't do the family thing on Monday, but I need to go." The words tumbled out, her voice quavering.

His face momentarily hardened and then relaxed.

"I'll go," he told her, his voice taut with emotion. "We both need to do this."

CHAPTER 15

Gracie lugged the large Grecian style resin pot from the shade of the garage and put it in the back of the SUV. Michael hadn't ever been big on flowers. However, she thought he'd approve of the elegant Stargazer lily surrounded by small ferns. It was a custom arrangement that had met with some silent disapproval from Esther. Geraniums were tradition, but Gracie didn't like them much. She brushed stray bits of dirt from her hands once she'd shut the door. The first part was over. The second part would be much more difficult.

*****

She always loved driving down into Deer Creek, or D.C. as some affectionately called it. Anyone would be hard pressed to dispute the rich beauty of the Genesee River Valley. The fields were lush and green. Besides alfalfa, wheat, oats, and corn, just a few miles away there were acres of potatoes growing near the tiny village of Gainesville. She passed one of the many apple orchards as she turned off Simmons Road and onto the state highway toward the village. Maples, oaks, and white birch were thick in hedgerows between the fields that led down the steep hill to the small village. The S-shaped curve kept everyone's speed honest. Those who disregarded the sharp turns sometimes found themselves in the hospital or worse. She could attest to that after last winter's library scandal.

There wasn't too much in the way of retail in D.C. All the essentials were on Main Street. Deer Creek Community Church was at the south end of town—an old brick church with stained glass windows and a graceful red-shingled steeple. Her family had always attended there. The Harwood Funeral Home was only a block further down on the right. Its Doric column façade intimated the solemnity of the business. Interspersed between businesses were colonial two-story homes. Most of them were painted white. A few Victorian homes, some restored to their former glory, gave Main Street a little bling.

The center of Deer Creek boasted a small grocery store, the fire hall, a gas station, the bank, and Midge's Restaurant. The post office, library, Stroud Insurance Agency, and the small Baptist church were a little further down. Evans Hardware sat on the corner of Genesee Street and Main, the only modern storefront in town, besides the grocery store. The old, deteriorating storefront had been refurbished when Dan Evans had gone with a hardware franchise in March. The Blooming Idiot greenhouses were nestled between the hardware and Tice's Garage, a little ways down Genesee Street.

Just before Park Street, a bridge spanned the meandering Deer Creek, which flowed eventually into the Genesee River. The creek had plenty of trout and a few deep swimming holes. There was even a small waterfall that could give you a wild ride in an old inner tube when there was enough water running. The creek was a wonderful place to disappear to in the summer if you were a kid. Gracie smiled, remembering many summer afternoons spent swimming and hiding out from doing chores around the house.

The feed store was at the north end of the village near the railroad tracks. A milking equipment repair company had recently remodeled an empty commercial building next to Hillside Feeds. A fleet of repair vans now filled the fenced-in parking lot behind the renovated building.

Crescent Lane was hands down the best neighborhood in D.C., full of large homes, some Victorian and others,

Craftsman style. The lots were large and deep. Landscaping reached a whole new level for homeowners on Crescent. Rose arbors, wisteria trellises, and elaborate water features were just small components of well-tended and well-designed flower gardens. Driving down Crescent was a pleasure, but there was no way Gracie would ever feel at home in such a perfect environment. A weed or two was not something to stress over in her book. She imagined it *was* for the residents there. Besides it was Isabelle's environment. She couldn't envision being Izzy's neighbor. Isabelle had been a boil on her butt since they'd been kids. Gracie's childhood home was two blocks over on Ash. The houses in that neighborhood were a mixture of styles, but mostly colonial. Her parents had been in the cedar-shingled cottage-style house since they had married almost 47 years ago.

The dappled shade offered by the long line of sugar maples that stood like sentries along the sidewalks was refreshing. She inhaled the fragrance of lilac and lily-of-the-valley from her open window. Haley vainly tried to push her head through the narrow opening between the back of the driver's seat and the window. Gracie hit the button to lower the back window slightly, so the dog could enjoy the smells too. The Lab immediately stuck her nose in the crack, leaving a trail of saliva across the window.

Taking a left turn at the corner of Goldenrod Avenue, she decided to drive around to the village's park. Little girls were playing T-ball on one of the softball fields. The petite blonde at bat slugged the ball out past the shortstop. The stands erupted into cheering. Gracie couldn't help but laugh when the girl sat down on first base, refusing to go on. It was easily a double. What was it like watching your daughter or son play? It had been so close for her, and now it was impossible. Tears stung her eyes. She unconsciously placed a hand on her stomach. Turning around in the parking lot by the picnic pavilions, she decided that she'd stalled long enough. It was time to meet Jim at the cemetery.

Jim lugged the heavy flower container across the neatly trimmed grass. Small flags waved proudly next to every headstone that honored a veteran. Gracie strolled through the sea of stone. Haley's nose was pressed to the ground, sniffing and snuffling. A gray squirrel suddenly appeared on a large rose-colored granite marker ahead of them. Haley's eyes fastened onto the surprise quarry. She wasted no time in giving chase. The squirrel, spotting imminent danger, agilely jumped from the stone. He chattered at Haley while sitting on the branch of a nearby oak before the big dog had even reached the headstone.

"Getting a little slow there, Haley," Jim teased the disappointed dog.

"I'll say," Gracie agreed, rubbing Haley's silky ears. "Come on, girl. That squirrel is out of your league."

They both stopped when they came to the sunny clearing in the newer section of the cemetery. Most of the headstones were smaller, although there were two elaborate markers that resembled tree trunks. An intricately carved grapevine twined its way up each trunk.

"Ready?" Jim asked, looking at Gracie.

She felt like Jell-O inside. She wasn't even sure her legs would work at all. Jim's face belied his own churning emotions. Gracie nodded, willing her legs to carry her forward.

The stone was not too big and it was simple, which suited Gracie just fine. "ANDERSEN" was carved in an arch at the top. Underneath on the left side, it stated, "Michael John." The next line was "December 9, 1974 – August 26, 2011." On the right side, it read, "Andrew Michael born in heaven, August 30, 2011." The final line on the light gray granite was: "The heavens declare the glory of God."

It had been a favorite Bible verse of Michael's since he was a child. Always fascinated with the night skies, it hadn't been a stretch to name their farm The Milky Way Dairy. Both she and Jim had decided to keep the moniker for the kennel. The beauty of their small dairy had been the ability to name and know their cows that had been more than mere numbers. Michael had made sure each name was always astronomy-related. Their prize bull had been Jupiter Rising, and their best cow was Celestial Mama. Jim bent down to place the container to the right of the stone.

"It's nice, Gracie. Michael would be happy with it." His voice broke as he straightened the urn's position. He avoided her eyes and stood studying the gravestone intently. He had stoutly refused until now to visit the cemetery.

"I think so too." The tears poured down her cheeks. She knelt to run her fingers over Michael's name and then Andrew's. Jim knelt down next to her, his arm protectively around her shoulders.

Haley whined with concern, pushing her nose under her mistress' arm. The pair finally stood, and Gracie pulled a tissue from her pocket to blow her nose. Haley looked at both of them, wagging her tail with anticipation. Jim smiled and scratched behind the dog's ears.

"Haley keeps life a little lighter for everybody," he commented, his voice rough with emotion.

"I guess so," Gracie finally answered, wiping the dampness from her cheeks and chin. "It's a good thing God left Haley and you with me. I was mad at Him a good long time for taking Michael and the baby. The anger is mostly gone ..." She bent to check the soil in the pot once more to make sure it was thoroughly wet.

Jim rubbed his jaw, his face impassive. "I still have a ways to go in that department, Chief."

He took one last look at the stone and strode back to his truck. Gracie watched him leave, knowing Jim and Michael's friendship hadn't ended with Michael's death. Jim had supported and cared for Gracie every day since then. Maybe that explained their relationship failures. She contemplated the thought as she and Haley strolled through the sea of granite to the Ferguson section. She stopped suddenly, spying Isabelle with both Greg and Anna in tow in front of their father's headstone. She had to give her cousin credit for that move. A wave of thankfulness for a good husband, who would've been a great father, washed over her.

Tim had certainly been neither. She made a one-eighty and walked back to her vehicle.

CHAPTER 16

The school band blared a boisterous rendition of "My Country 'Tis of Thee" followed by "The Battle Hymn of the Republic." The sidewalks were lined with spectators, some standing and some sitting comfortably in lawn chairs. The Memorial Day weather was cooperating at the moment, although thunderstorms were predicted for the afternoon. The American Legion, Girl Scouts, Boy Scouts, and a few small floats straggled behind the band. One of the floats promoted Renew Earth and another New Energy Strategies Team. Renew Earth members tossed granola bars from the wagon pulled by an electric pickup. She could see that Ben Richter was the driver. He smiled and waved at the crowds, looking slightly uncomfortable. She caught sight of one of the signs around the large revolving globe in the center of the wagon that stated "Keep Our Earth Beautiful." N.E.S.T., whose wagon was clearly a professional creation, was covered with flowers, grass, and miniature wind turbines. Two teenage boys held ropes for a calf and a couple of baby goats. Several younger kids on the float tossed small chocolate bars, which were scooped up by kids and adults.

Gracie had to smile at the obvious competition, and then frowned, hoping that it wasn't a precursor to another brawl. She stood in line at the fire hall, waiting to buy a cup of coffee and a doughnut to help support the volunteer fire department. Her parents were already settled in with Aunt Marlene, her father's sister, and Uncle Beau on the walk across the street. Isabelle and her boyfriend were nowhere to be seen at the moment.

Her hands full, Gracie carefully maneuvered through the crowd crossing the street, finally making her way to the line of lawn chairs on the grass. She'd forgotten to bring a chair on purpose. Standing or sitting on the ground afforded an easy escape should the family conversation get too difficult to handle. Her mother and Aunt Marlene were talking nonstop, so no additional conversation was needed from Gracie. Her father and Uncle Beau sat next to each other in their green nylon web chairs, waiting for the whole affair to be over. Haley lay sleeping by her father's feet. Bob held the leash out to Gracie when he caught sight of his daughter. Stuffing the rest of the doughnut in her mouth, she took it and settled herself on the grass.

The end of the parade came quickly. The commander of the American Legion, Congressman Streeker, Reverend Minders, and a bagpiper, jammed into someone's classic convertible, brought up the rear.

After the welcome, Reverend Minders prayed his annual invocation over the proceedings. The Legion commander, Mike O'Connor, introduced the congressman, who droned on about the economy and his innovative solutions to fix the whole mess, with a brief statement about Deer Creek's fallen heroes tacked onto the closing. Light applause segued to the school band playing "America the Beautiful." Mike regained control of the microphone, inviting everyone to join the honor guard and band in the cemetery. When the congressman's attractive aide caught his attention, he nodded, adding that everyone should enjoy the carnival in the park afterward. Rides for the kids were free, which produced a much more enthusiastic response from the crowd. Reverend Minders took the microphone again, closing the whole affair with a gentle benediction for peace. The bagpiper wheezed the pipes into action and played "Amazing Grace." Shouldering their weapons, the honor guard turned toward the cemetery, marching in place, awaiting a "forward march" from the sergeant. The band followed the small group of men, with the Girls Scouts trailing behind, their hands full of lilacs to place at the graves of veterans long departed.

Before her mother and Aunt Marlene could corner her about the cemetery, Gracie had melted into the crowd headed for the park. She didn't dare turn back to look for them. She thought she could feel their laser gazes burning a hole in her back already. She gave the leash a quick tug to get Haley's flagging attention. The three blocks to the park would do them both good. She was anxious to see what this carnival was all about.

CHAPTER 17

A merry-go-round, two jumping castles, and a couple of other kiddie attractions were just gearing up for the crowd taking advantage of the free rides. Food vendors were already set up. The smell of fried dough, hotdogs, and cotton candy made Gracie's mouth water. Haley strained at the leash, pulling Gracie toward a stand that was serving Italian sausages, hamburgers, and onion rings. The Masonic Lodge was happily serving up instant heart attacks today. It would sure be a wonderful way to go, she decided, inhaling the enticing aroma of good grease.

"No way, Haley. Come on now." Gracie firmly steered the stubborn dog down the row of promotional booths near the small midway.

She mentally ran through the story she'd worked out for her mother and Aunt Marlene. The visit to Michael's grave had been very personal and not one she intended to share with anyone, except Jim. She was contemplating leaving the Jim part out. It might give Aunt Marlene ideas. Her aunt had very set opinions about mourning periods, and Gracie's time had expired a year ago. Gracie pressed her lips together, remembering that particularly awkward conversation with her aunt just before the kennel had opened.

Haley tugged at the leash again, sniffing along the ground. It looked like the dog was searching for the right spot, which was not in front of the tents they were walking past.

"Come on, girl. We're heading for high weeds. Just hold it until we get there."

Haley trotted eagerly after her mistress toward the hedgerow of small saplings and bushes bordering a field at the edge of the park. She let Haley meander back toward the activity of the fairway. She stopped to tie her dragging shoelace before re-entering the carnival between the tents.

Two shadows were having an animated discussion in the festively colored tent that housed N.E.S.T. information. Haley sat correctly on her left, cocking her head from side to side as if she was listening too. Gracie had already seen the piles of giveaways on several tables. They had all sorts of literature about the safety of wind turbines, along with balloons, key chains, and piles of other promotional junk that everybody took home and threw out.

A female voice rose over the lower-pitched male voice. "I understand your concern, but now that Mr. McQuinn has a valid alibi, it is in our mutual interest to get a bail hearing."

"It's a bit of stretch, don't you think?" the male voice growled. "I can't even have a hint of anything that's questionable stopping this project. Getting a murder suspect out on bail might raise some eyebrows."

"You need him out of jail to get this deal done. He won't be signing a thing sitting in Warsaw. His lawyer will see to that. We'll do our part and you do yours." The woman's voice could vaporize dry ice.

"Maybe. There's still the estate angle."

"That's not an option. The widow is not cooperating as we thought she would. She ..."

A group of people drifted past the tent. The conversation stopped abruptly. Gracie could hear the man explaining the benefits of wind power, while offering balloons to the children. The woman exited the tent, quickly entering the black–and–silver tent next door.

Haley whined expectantly. Gracie released a grateful Haley from sitting. They walked briskly up onto the midway, avoiding the tents and their occupants.

*****

The family was staking out tables for lunch. Isabelle and Kevin made an appearance with Isabelle's son, Greg, and daughter, Anna. Both teenagers looked pained or embarrassed. Maybe both. Their faces lit up when they caught sight of Gracie and Haley.

"How's everything?" Gracie asked cheerfully.

"Better now," Anna said with a hint of a smile. She was a pretty girl, with long, straight blond hair that reached the middle of her back. "I hate holidays. It's weird and awkward." She frowned, clutching her iPhone.

"I understand completely," Gracie agreed. "How's school?"

Anna shrugged, and her brother spoke up quickly. "Okay. Finals were last week, and I'm home for the summer."

"How was your first year of college? I know I was homesick for the first semester," Gracie said.

"It's been a tough year, and I wish I'd been around to support Anna," Greg began.

"It's all right Greg," Anna replied. "I'm going to private school in Pennsylvania next fall to finish. I can't stand everybody whispering about what happened with Dad. Mom made me go to counseling with her, which was stupid. Now she has this boyfriend who's 10 years younger than she is. The counseling didn't do anything for her." Anna frowned. Her gaze darted back to her phone.

"I'm really sorry that both of you have had to go through so much," Gracie said.

"I can't wait until August," Anna blurted out. "I'll finally be able to get out of this dump of a town. It's suffocating here."

Before Gracie could respond, the pair hurried toward a coed group that was alternating between texting and talking to each other. She caught sight of Jim's profile in the crowd moving toward the picnic tables. A wave of her arm managed to catch his attention. The plan was to eat lunch and then go back to work. They wanted to let kennel employees have at least a half-day off. It was also a valid excuse not to stay long.

Jim was to initiate the movement from lunch to kennel to let Gracie off the hook with her mother.

Plates of barbecued chicken, sausage, grease-soaked French fries, onion rings, and burgers made it to the tables. Jim and Gracie managed to squeeze through the milling humanity to where Bob and Theresa Clark were already eating. The other Clarks, Marlene and Beau, along with Isabelle and Kevin, were eating at the table next to them. Theresa kept searching the crowd, probably looking for Tom. He was supposed to be there with Kelly Standish, but they hadn't even turned up at the parade. Kevin plowed through a heaping plate of chicken and potato salad with hardly any effort. Isabelle picked at hers daintily.

No comments were made about Gracie's absence at the cemetery, although her aunt remarked that the headstone and flower arrangement were "very nice." With any luck, that would be the end of the conversation on the cemetery.

The hubbub of the crowd grew, and the music blared from the rides, making it hard to carry on a normal conversation. No controversial subjects were broached, much to Gracie's relief. They all agreed the carnival was a great success. Jim finally mentioned they needed to get back to the kennel to allow their employees to enjoy some of the afternoon, after Gracie's sneaker had reminded him with a quick tap on his shin. Her dad nodded in agreement with Jim.

"We need to get going too, dear. I've got the backyard to mow yet."

"Okay. I guess Tom and Kelly aren't coming," Theresa said.

She began picking up empty plates for the trash when Ben Richter strolled past with his wife. Gracie watched them slip into the shade of the Renew Earth tent located three tents away from the N.E.S.T. display. She couldn't figure out who else from the area was involved with the organization. The organization wasn't dairy-friendly, and dairy farms were the main employers around Deer Creek. The only local at the protest had been Toby. Everyone else had been people she didn't recognize. They couldn't be from Deer Creek, since she knew just about everyone.

"I think Haley needs a stroll after everyone has slipped her something under the table," she said, excusing herself.

The dog must have consumed an entire sausage and the skin off two chicken halves. Theresa had peeled the beautiful crispy skin from each of their barbeques, much to her husband's disappointment. Gracie just knew her father had made sure Haley got most of it.

"That poor dog. She puts up with a lot. I know that for a fact," her father teased, his hazel eyes twinkling.

"Yeah, yeah. I'll be right back."

She grinned at her father and nudged Haley's backside with her foot to wake her. The pair moved with the crowd coming from the cotton candy trailer, taking a quick exit next to the Renew Earth display. Gracie stood out of the flow of foot traffic, watching the activity in the Renew Earth tent. A few locals picked up pamphlets and some of the promotional materials, like the tiny solar flashlight with the logo printed in equally tiny proportions. A woman who appeared to be somewhere in her 30s wore a flowing caftan that fell mid-calf. Her earrings were simple large gold hoops, and she had a small rose tattoo embellishing her ankle. She looked very 1960s. Scanning the small crowd in the tent, Gracie determined that the Richters must have already left. They were nowhere to be seen at the moment, anyway. Without Ben Richter's pushy presence, Gracie decided to chance it and take a peek at what the mysterious organization had to offer.

The caftan woman was friendly enough. She introduced herself as Summer and offered brochures on greenhouse gases and water table contamination. Gracie decided to take all the information as some further research for Kim. She casually asked about the history of Renew Earth as she studied the chart showing how many birds were killed each year by wind turbines. The woman's expression changed in an instant from friendly to reticent.

"Renew Earth is fairly new, and we're growing," she offered with some hesitation.

"Oh," Gracie said, looking at one of the brochures. She struggled to keep her tone even. "So, what are your membership numbers?"

Summer retreated to a chair behind a card table in the rear of the tent, her eyes wary. A salad in a foam container lay open, a black plastic fork stuck in the middle of the greens. An unopened bottle of water sat next to it.

"I don't remember right off the top of my head," she said, taking a drink from the bottle.

A group of teens crowded noisily into the tent, most likely looking for freebies. Summer quickly got up to greet them, leaving Gracie and Haley standing alone. Turning to leave, Gracie saw Kevin across the midway next to Congressman Streeker's campaign tent. He and the congressman's aide were engaged in a lively conversation.

CHAPTER 18

Jim impatiently looked through the milling people for Gracie and Haley. For someone who hated crowds, she sure had enjoyed today's events, he decided irritably. Her parents had already left, along with her aunt and uncle. He was anxious to get to back to work.

Cleaning up the remains of his Italian sausage-and-peppers sandwich, he walked over to the trash barrel next to the pretzel stand. He wanted to visit Toby late in the afternoon to see if a bail hearing was possible and if he'd decided to change lawyers. He sat on the edge of the metal picnic table seat. He finally caught sight of Gracie and Haley coming his way. Just as he started to stand, Kevin slid onto the long metal seat next to him. There was no way to avoid a conversation without being exceptionally rude. He mentally crossed his fingers for Gracie and Haley to hurry.

"Jim. Just the guy I wanted to talk to," Kevin said, grinning a little too broadly. "I think Isabelle may have stirred up some misunderstanding, and I wanted to straighten it out. You know how women are."

Jim decided to give the guy a lot of rope. It might be interesting. Besides, Izzy's love interest had just been hired as the new commercial lending officer at the bank. Isabelle apparently had a thing for bankers.

"What misunderstanding is that?" Jim asked.

"Isabelle spoke out of turn to Gracie the other day. She heard me talking about the problem with the wind farm property leases."

"Oh, right. Gracie did mention that. So ... what about the leases?"

Kevin licked his lips, looking anxious. "D. B. promised New Energy and the bank he'd get Tobias to sell the land to him, so that the turbines could be built up there. Of course D. B. couldn't close the deal. Now he really can't." Kevin flexed his hands nervously, clenching and unclenching his fists.

Jim let the silence become awkward. Kevin stumbled on to get to his point.

"I'm hoping, as is the bank, that you have some influence to ... well ..." Kevin chuckled nervously. "To persuade Tobias to sell the property to the bank. We're prepared to offer him a very fair price."

Jim watched a bead of sweat trickle down the side of Kevin's sunburned face. Fortunately. Gracie and Haley appeared with a bag of fried dough in hand. Haley leaned against Jim's leg for attention.

"Gracie, I've been looking for you," Jim said with relief.

"Jim," Kevin interrupted. "We really need to talk about this."

"Sorry, not right now, Kevin. Real soon, though. I'll get back to you."

Gracie looked at both men, who looked like they'd been sucking on a dill pickle. She was glad to have missed this particular chat. She was sure she'd hear about it anyway.

"Sorry about being late. I'm ready to go," she said quickly.

*****

Jim met Gracie in the kennel office after they'd finished bed checks. Haley woke from her people-food coma and lapped a generous amount of water from her ceramic bowl. She flopped down at Gracie's feet, ready to join the nightly debriefing session. Gracie took her sneakers off, sighing with relief. She rubbed her feet over Haley's shiny back. The dog groaned, her back leg thumping against the tile. Jim laughed and sat down in the recliner. He pulled the long wooden handle to recline. A crack and the sound of breaking wood startled them both. The chair started back and then stopped abruptly. Jim sat dumbfounded, the wooden piece in his hand.

"Dang! How did that happen?"

Gracie couldn't help giggling. "I told you that chair was on its last legs and as you can see, I was right."

"Great. Just great! I can fix it though. Shouldn't be too hard," he said, bending over the side of the chair to examine the mechanism. "I know what I'll be working on tomorrow."

"You could get a new chair. A leather one would be nice, with massage. How about it?"

"No way. This chair fits me perfectly. It's broken in just right," Jim said firmly. "Don't get any ideas."

"All right. We'll see if you can actually fix it first," she teased, knowing as sure as the sun was coming up, the chair would be repaired first thing in the morning. "Forget about the chair right now. Did you hear anything about a bail hearing for Toby?"

"Funny you should ask. My dad called a few minutes ago and said they had one scheduled for Wednesday. How does that happen on a holiday?"

"I might have the answer on that," Gracie said, leaning back in her chair and propping her feet on the desk.

Jim listened to Gracie's eavesdropping report, his jaw working in agitation. He leaned forward, hands on his knees.

"I'd like to know what the real deal is on this property. We've got this Richter guy who's working an angle to get it because of his lawsuit. The bank wants it, and obviously the windmill company wants the leases on it. Now you're telling me there's actually political interest in it?"

"That's what I heard. I don't know who the chick is that was talking to the windmill guy. Her name, that is. I did recognize her from the parade. She's the congressman's aide or something. Whoever she is, she's pretty sure of herself."

"You're right about that." Jim ran a hand through his hair. "I need to find out what the sheriff's department is doing on this investigation. Are they looking into the possibility that the Meadow is why D. B. was shot up there?" He stood and whacked his Yankees cap against his leg. "Toby doesn't have a clue about what's really going on. I don't either, but we need to find out. Are you game to do some more investigating?"

"Why not," Gracie answered impetuously.

D. B.'s murder was creeping her out. No murder weapon had been found, and Lord knew if the killer might try to take someone else out. The hair on the back of her neck prickled.

CHAPTER 19

Roscoe decided it was time to break camp. He hadn't seen a single UFO since he'd set up a week ago. After the raccoon attack, the charm of the outdoor life had evaporated. The visitors from space had, for some reason, decided on new territory, so he was wasting time and effort. He hadn't even seen a twinkle of one in Greerson's Meadow either. The groundbreaking report that would assure his future as an investigative reporter never made it from his notes to a paragraph. His shoulders slumped in defeat and he began packing away the ancient equipment he'd picked up on eBay. It had been a stellar deal, but, unfortunately, of no use in attracting UFOs here. His theory about GPS points had been a disappointing failure.

Shoving the last of the boxes in the back of the hatchback, a small piece of paper, half-dried in the muddy ruts behind the car, caught his eye. Picking it up, he rubbed the caked-on mud from what appeared to be a mangled business card. A green globe with stars surrounding it appeared after the dirt flaked off. Roscoe stared at the card in his hand. Where had it come from? He hadn't picked up a Renew Earth business card anywhere. Only Jim had visited him here. Puzzled, he walked around the campsite to see if any sign of other visitors was present. Finding none and feeling both relieved and disappointed, he finished dismantling the small tent. He shoved it into its canvas storage bag and strapped it down with bungee cords to the carrier on the top of the car. He leaned against the beat-up, rusty vehicle, deciding whether to go back to Rochester or stay somewhere in Deer Creek.

Since the UFO research had proven unsuccessful, perhaps he needed to focus on the investigation of the murder and establish Mr. McQuinn's innocence by uncovering the killer.

Two weeks of paid leave were still available. Now was the perfect opportunity to prove his capabilities by testing his intelligence-gathering skills on Renew Earth or New Energy. Perhaps he could go undercover as a volunteer with Renew Earth or apply for a job with N.E.S.T. It would require some additional reflection, which was difficult, at best, when his stomach was growling. The Geo, for the first time ever, didn't have food of any sort in it. The first order of business was getting something to eat at Midge's.

*****

"I am so happy, I could just ...!"

Tobias burst through the doors of the courtroom, his face beaming. The public defender, wearing a wide grin, followed behind his client.

"Hey, slow down there, Toby," admonished John Taylor, Jim's dad. The tall man with steel gray hair put a calming hand on the Toby's bony shoulder. "We need to show some respect. We're in the courthouse."

"Yeah. Okay, John. Man, I'm happier than a dog at a fire hydrant convention! Ya done good, there, young man," he said gleefully, pumping the attorney's arm up and down. "I didn't think ya had it in ya. No offense, of course."

"None taken. I'm a bit surprised it all went so fast, but I *am* pretty pleased." A fleeting half-smile crossed Gary Haskins' sun-starved face. "Now, don't do anything, and I mean *anything* foolish, Mr. McQuinn." The lawyer's expression turned deadly serious. "You must make your next court date on time and be dressed appropriately and stay on your medication."

"My wife and I will make sure of that, counselor," John interjected. "I'm sure Toby understands the serious charges he's facing. Right, Tobias?"

Toby swallowed hard, looking at the two men.

"Sure thing. I understand. I'll be there, and I won't do anything foolish. Got it."

"Of course, I'll be talking with you before the court date. I'll have my secretary call you for an appointment," the lawyer said.

"Uh, I don't have a phone, Mr. Haskins." Toby's face creased with worry.

"Just call us. You have our number. We'll make sure he gets to the appointment," John Taylor filled in quickly.

"All right. Thanks. Remember Mr. McQuinn, nothing foolish and take your medication." The young lawyer stowed the red wallet file under his arm and hurried down the stairs.

*****

The long driveway to the Airstream had a few mud holes left over from the rain that had soaked everything the evening of Memorial Day. The pickup splashed and bounced through them to where the ground leveled off in front of the mobile home.

"Have you got everything you need for tonight, Toby?" John asked, pulling a bag of paper goods from the back of the club cab.

"Sure thing. Thanks a lot, John. I appreciate all your help today. You and Jim have really helped me out. I won't forget it. I still can't figure out why that windmill company would post my bail though," he said, hefting a bag of groceries from the truck.

"I'm not sure about that myself. If you should get any visitors who want you to sign something, you'd better let me take a look at it before you do anything."

Toby nodded gravely. He walked over to a large white pine next to the tool shed and tipped over a small rock with his foot. Setting the groceries down, he picked up a key. The key worked easily in the lock, and the door opened. Tobias almost dropped the bag of groceries when he saw papers scattered everywhere. Furniture was overturned. The once neat stacks of magazines were strewn across the floor. His spacecraft models had been ripped down, tossed carelessly with the rest of his outer space memorabilia. Before Tobias could say anything, John dialed 9-1-1 on his cell phone.

*****

Jim sat with his father and Toby on an old, blue tweed upholstered sofa, while the deputies finished up their report. It didn't look like anything had been taken, but then Toby wasn't really sure. The place was an absolute disaster. Toby's lawyer promised to check out the report and possibly stop in tomorrow.

"That's about it, Mr. McQuinn," the tall, reedy deputy said, holding out his clipboard. "Just read that over and sign at the bottom."

The man's hands were trembling slightly as he clutched the clipboard, squinting at the report. "Looks all right to me. Where do I sign now?"

"Right on that line at the bottom. Put the date by your signature."

"Any chance you can catch whoever was in here?" Jim asked.

"Probably not. Might have been kids, playing a stupid prank. It doesn't take much to pick a lock like that, although most break-ins around here start with a rock through a window. Of course, a lot of people knew Mr. McQuinn was in jail."

"True, but he's never had any trouble up here before," John said with a tinge of anger in his voice. "I don't have a good feeling about this."

"We'll take a run past here later tonight and check things out. That okay with you, Mr. McQuinn?"

"No need. I'll be fine." Toby was already straightening the magazines.

"I'd feel better if that happened," John said, looking at the deputy.

A light knock at the door startled the group. Toby opened the door, his eyes widened with surprise.

"Good evening, Mr. McQuinn. I just heard you'd been released from incarceration," Roscoe said, smiling broadly. He looked around at the questioning faces staring at him. "How very considerate of the police to escort you home."

CHAPTER 20

Gracie yawned and rubbed the back of her neck. The iPad screen was blurry. Her eyes stung from fatigue. She'd spent the whole evening updating the kennel's website and Facebook page, plus doing a little Facebook stalking on the activities of her niece, Emma, along with those of Greg and Anna.

Haley stood whining at the door. A glee club of peepers sang with abandon when she opened the French doors to the patio. The Lab raced out to the far end of the fenced yard. With her inky camouflage, she instantly disappeared in the darkness. The flagstone was cool on Gracie's feet. She looked up at the sparkling sky. The sound of Michael's voice was in her ear, pointing out the constellations, explaining the gases that made up stars and how to find the planets.

The cell phone in her pocket ended her reverie when it buzzed insistently. Investigator Hotchkiss asked for a quick interview in the morning. The police were looking for more information about the rally in Greerson's Meadow. She pushed the phone back into her pocket and hugged herself, suddenly chilly in the warm night.

*****

The alarm clock woke Gracie easily from a fitful sleep. After struggling with her problematic curls, she decided a braid was her best option for hair control. The makeup brush smoothed on a dusting of foundation, and a smudge of taupe eye shadow completed her toilette. Haley raced down the steps and stopped mid-dash to the kennel to bark at the sheriff's SUV pulling into the house driveway.

Investigator Hotchkiss, with Haley sniffing at her shoes, made her way up the walk. Gracie opened the screen door and offered the policewoman a cup of coffee.

"Good morning, Mrs. Andersen. This is getting to be a regular occurrence."

The woman was dressed in navy blue slacks and a white shirt. Gracie glanced at her sidearm and wondered if it ever got uncomfortable carrying a gun around all the time. Did she remove it to go to the bathroom? It couldn't be convenient.

"I guess so," Gracie answered and took a seat on the stool at the kitchen counter. "I'm not sure how I can help you on this one though."

"We're trying to piece together the altercation up in the field the night Mr. Jackson was killed. A lot happened quite fast, and you've always been a good observer." The investigator paused. A slight smile crinkled her face before she continued. "I'd like your take on what happened. Especially anything you might have noticed about Mr. Richter or Mr. Allen."

"Mr. Allen?"

"He's the New Energy Strategies CEO. He was there to speak about the wind farm construction."

"Right. Well, it was like you said. The whole thing happened pretty fast. I did see Ben Richter with his group, and I'm pretty sure that's where the rocks came from. I was almost hit by one. The Allen guy, I don't know. I guess he probably got in one of the SUVs when it all started."

"Did you see Mr. Allen talking with Mr. Jackson afterwards?" The investigator scribbled a few notes and looked up for Gracie's response.

"You know, I'm not sure. Jim was dealing with Toby, and I was talking with some of the guys from town. Sorry."

"That's fine. We're just checking on a few things. What about Dean Jenkins? Did he attend the rally?"

"No. I didn't see him at all. I suppose he could have been there, but no. I didn't see him."

So Dean was still on the list. It made sense, Gracie reasoned. He was, after all, D. B.'s right-hand man. Shooting D. B. in cold blood wasn't his style. Or was it? The investigator seemed to be avoiding Richter though. His group had to have started that fight.

"While we're on the subject," Gracie said, "I'm wondering about Ben Richter. He's pushed Toby to allow him to represent him. He certainly wasn't friendly with D. B. Have you taken a hard look at him yet? Kim is very concerned about what he might do, especially with this lawsuit."

The investigator's dark eyes met Gracie's. "We're talking to everyone, Mrs. Andersen. It's nothing for you to worry about. And, as I've told you in the past, let us do the investigating."

She'd certainly heard that before. Why were Mitch Allen and Dean Jenkins of interest now? Why weren't they turning up the heat on Ben Richter?

"Of course. I'm sure it's all under control."

"It is. Thank you for your time, and if I need anything else, I'll let you know."

"Sure. Anything to help."

She really wanted to ask what they'd found out about the shotguns removed from Kim's house. It was a good bet no information would be shared. It was an active investigation. Blah, blah, blah. How the cops could keep the pressure on a grieving widow was awful. Why did this woman get under her skin every time? Gracie rose to send her early morning visitor on her way, forcing a smile. It looked like Investigator Hotchkiss was reciprocating with her own insincere smile.

Haley sat on the steps, watching the SUV back up and swing around to exit the driveway.

"Come on, girl. Let's go to work," Gracie called to the dog.

If the police wouldn't look into Ben Richter, it was time to do something about that omission.

The melee in the Meadow the night of D. B.'s death had been short-lived, and she hadn't been there for all of the action. The question about Dean made her uneasy. He could have been in the crowd. In all of the confusion, it was easy to miss someone.

*****

She was still ruminating about Dean and Ben Richter while rinsing the suds from the matted coat of a cocker spaniel in the tub. The owner, tired of trying to keep the long, curly hair under control (which Gracie could relate to) wanted a short summer cut for poor Mitsy. The cocker had an affinity for the swamp close to home and was particularly drawn to burdocks too. The dog, shorn of the blond tangled mess, seemed relieved and ran in circles, yipping in delight. A pink bandanna completed her new chic look. Gracie had to laugh at the dog's antics.

"I'm glad you're so happy with the new do, pretty girl. Here's a treat."

Gracie threw her a small biscuit in the fenced drying area. Trudy came through the doorway with the next squirming customer, a Yorkie, who smelled absolutely ripe.

"Is this Elmer?" she asked, wrinkling her nose.

"I'm afraid so. He got away from Pat on the way to the car and rolled in some road kill. Whatever it was, it's pretty bad." Trudy held the tiny dog out at arm's length, her nose wrinkled in disgust.

"Okay, tough guy, let's get you cleaned and trimmed up. Holy cow! You *are* smelly!"

Elmer didn't seem to mind how bad he smelled in the least. He licked Gracie's face and whined excitedly.

A break in the schedule came after the deodorizing and trimming of Elmer. With Trudy and Casey handling the playtimes, Gracie was impatient to do a little more research on the Richters. Even if they weren't on the police radar, maybe there was something worth pursuing. She needed to learn more about New Energy and Mitch Allen too. Both men had a bone to pick with D. B.

She heard Jim come in the rear entrance whistling "How Much is That Doggy in the Window?" An immediate chorus of barking and howling echoed through the hallways.

"Thank you, thank you very much, ladies and gentlemen," he said in his best Elvis impression. "For my next number, I hope you enjoy 'Hound Dog.'"

Gracie stood outside the office, hands on hips, trying her best to look disgusted.

"You know, it was relatively quiet until you showed up."

"Chief, you gotta give the customers what they want," he joked.

It looked like he hadn't had time to shave and his five o'clock shadow was already showing at eleven.

"Not shaving today?" she asked, smiling.

Jim rubbed his face. "I'm thinking about a beard. We'll see how it goes or grows, actually."

"I'd say you probably got up late and didn't have time."

He shrugged. "Uh, well, you could be right."

"As I thought," she said, turning to go back to her computer. "I had a visit this morning from Investigator Hotchkiss."

"Funny coincidence. I did too. Wanna compare notes?"

After a few minutes of discussion, the pair decided the investigator was definitely interested in Mitch Allen along with the farm manager. Jim shook his head in concern.

"I can't see Dean doing that to D. B., even though he's been jerked around by D. B. for years. I guess he could've gone off the deep end." He sat on the edge of the recliner, his fingers interlaced. "Maybe ..." He paused, a quizzical expression in his eyes. "I've heard some rumblings about D. B. and Carla. If that's true ..."

"Who's saying that?" Gracie asked, leaning back in her chair.

"Yeah, well ..." Jim's voice became dull. "Harry." He looked at his feet, avoiding her eyes.

"Are you kidding?" she snapped. "Harry is the most unreliable source of gossip in the county. Midge will tell you that. He just loves getting the rumor mill working overtime. The truth has no relationship with Harry."

"You're right," Jim admitted. "But Harry *does* see stuff."

Gracie huffed. Harry, the driver for Hillside Feeds, always had the lowdown on the next extramarital affair or financial debacle. He lived for scandal and getting people upset.

"And puts his own spin on it."

"Yes, he does. It was just something I heard. You don't have to bust a gasket over it."

An uncomfortable silence filled the room.

"Sorry." Gracie attempted to smooth it over. "I guess I just have a problem with Harry."

Jim muttered that he was buying lunch for everyone at Midge's and went to take orders. Gracie grabbed a Diet Coke from the refrigerator and tapped away at the keyboard, sipping the cola while she waited for the search engine to populate her choices. There were about a half dozen sites for information on Ben Richter. Her eyes widened when a link to a Vermont newspaper came up. She couldn't believe she hadn't seen this before. Clicking on the link, she waited impatiently for the page to appear. The headline read, "Freak Auto Accident Claims the Life of Burlington Woman." Scrolling quickly through the story, Gracie skimmed the details about the untimely death of Samantha Richter three years ago. She leaned toward the monitor; her index finger tracing the story on the screen to avoid missing a single word. Samantha had been the estranged wife of Tyrone B. Richter, Esq. After leaving a fundraiser dinner for a fine arts foundation, she'd been killed as she sat in her car parked on a deserted road outside of Burlington. A large branch from a tree fell on the car roof, crushing her and the car. The body wasn't found until the next day when a farmer discovered the wreck. No one knew why she was on the road, and her estranged husband, overcome with grief, declined to comment much. He said they were trying to reconcile, and that he "couldn't believe she was gone."

Gracie sat back in the swivel desk chair. She drummed her fingers on the desk. It had to be the same person. The "B" must be for Benjamin. She wondered if Investigator Hotchkiss knew anything about this part of Ben Richter's history. Of course, it might not be the same guy. She went to the newspaper's online archives to check for a follow-up story or obituary. The obit popped up three days later. She perused the contents for surviving family members. There were no children, but Tyrone B. Richter was listed as the surviving spouse, along with Samantha's parents of West Bridge, New Hampshire. She had two brothers, Eric and Stephen, who lived in Burlington. They were both married with families. Samantha's parents, Arthur and Deborah Harrington were apparently part of the old New England aristocracy. The obituary implied they were well-heeled: "The Harringtons are generous supporters of the arts and major donors to Ivy League higher education."

What an odd statement to put in the obituary. Who had written it anyway? Sounded like it had been Samantha's parents. She scrolled through another week's worth of newspaper reports for Burlington. A small article finally appeared, stating that the death had been ruled accidental, although the police had pursued another line of questioning at the request of the family. She jotted down the names of the brothers and parents on a yellow sticky note. It might bear further examination. Should she hand it off to the investigator or do a little research on her own? Slipping the paper in her jeans pocket, she decided on the latter.

*****

"Oh, Lord, won't you buy me a Mercedes Benz!" Jim sang at the top of his lungs.

The dogs launched into another refrain of barking and howling.

He plunked a pile of white clamshell containers on the reception desk and called out, "Lunch everybody! Get it while it's hot or cold, depending on what you ordered."

Gracie grabbed a walkie-talkie to let Trudy and Casey know that lunch had arrived. They were finishing up the morning exercise times and sounded grateful for the break. The dogs began to quiet down. She could hear Jim walking down the corridors and speaking sweetly to each one. She shook her head and had to laugh.

"Hey, Chief," he called out to her as she stepped into reception to grab the containers.

If any dogs were dropped off, they didn't need the added distraction of a pile of food on the desk.

"Yes, Janis," she chirped. "You're so darn melodious, I'm sure you must have a new ... well, friend."

"Not hardly. I don't need my life any more complicated than it already is," he said and changed the subject. "Now, listen to this." He sauntered back down the hallway to the office.

"Okay, what?" Gracie called after him.

She separated the containers on her desk, found the chicken finger salad, and located utensils. Jim opened his container, looking reverently at a Philly cheese steak sandwich. He obviously was having a special moment over the aroma that immediately filled the room. Trudy, Tracey, and Casey appeared, gratefully grabbing their lunches. They took off for the picnic table in her backyard when Gracie offered the shady spot.

"Jim and I will handle the phone and reception. Go eat."

The twins and Trudy headed for the outside.

"All right, what were you going to say?" Gracie asked after the back door slapped shut.

"Well, while I was waiting at Midge's, that wind farm guy, what's his name, Allen came in with Kevin. They both looked a little sickly. I turned my back, hoping Kevin wouldn't see me. I didn't want to get into the land thing again. I considered thanking the windmill guy since he put up bail for Toby, but like I said, I didn't want to end up talking to Kevin."

"And?" Her leg was jiggling impatiently. Jim was taking the long way around the barn with this story.

"Just wait. I'm getting there," he said, taking a bite of his sandwich. He chewed slowly and methodically just to further annoy her. He swallowed and continued. "They started talking, in the dining room, fortunately at the table closest to the counter."

Gracie's eyes were beginning to glaze over. "And?"

He gave her a slow smile. "All right, all right. They were obviously trying to be discreet. Then Investigator Hotchkiss comes in and walks right up to their table."

Gracie stopped mid-bite, looking expectantly at Jim, whose blue eyes twinkled with twisted humor.

"She asks ever so politely if Mr. Allen would accompany her to Warsaw for questioning."

"You're kidding!"

"Not kidding, Chief. He never said a word, just got into his Mercedes and followed the sheriff's car." He sat back, took a huge bite of the dripping sandwich, and watched for her reaction.

"Did Kevin say anything?"

"Nope," he said, shaking his head. "He just looked like he was going to puke and walked out of Midge's. Walked right on down the street, back toward the bank."

Gracie played mindlessly with the salad, finally taking another bite.

"Did Midge have anything to say about it?"

"When doesn't she? She said she wasn't surprised. D. B. and this Allen guy had a very public display of animosity just a week before the murder. D. B. took a swing at him, and Mr. Allen told D. B. where he could go and how he could look forward to the trip. Happened in front of the bank, according to her."

"Things that make you go *hmm*. I never heard anything about it at the time."

"You don't get out much, remember?"

She gave him the hairy eyeball while taking another bite of salad. The phone rang, interrupting her glib comeback. Gracie washed down the salad with more cola before answering, "Milky Way Kennels."

She made reservations for two dogs for the weekend, which included baths. Before she could finish the phone call, the bell jangled up front. Jim jumped up to answer. Seconds later, a collie, making a mad dash for the reception area with Jim at the end of the leash, sped past the door. She tossed the container in the wastebasket, smiling to herself that Rocket was aptly named.

Rocket's owner, Margie Hurlburt, stuck her head into the office with the collie straining at the leash. Margie, a short and stocky woman, was Isabelle's competition in the real estate business. Her sharp brown eyes and dark, cropped hair were set off by her neat wheat-colored linen pants and short matching jacket. She'd just returned from a real estate seminar in Albany.

"Thanks, Gracie. He looks great. You're doing a wonderful job. I told Jim that we've needed a kennel like this for a long time in D.C."

"Thanks, Margie. Rocket's a fun dog." Gracie scratched the dog's ears. "Bring him back again."

"I will. There's always some training deal I have to travel to. Oh, and I wanted to tell you that Kim really appreciates all the support and help you've given her. I'm afraid she still has a lot to go through with this terrible murder investigation. I don't know how they can think Kim would shoot her own husband," she snorted.

Rocket shook his head as if on cue to agree. He sat down and scratched enthusiastically before standing again.

"I don't know either. Hopefully the sheriff's department is smart enough to realize that."

"They'd better. Dean and Carla told me she's really stressed. They're pretty worried about her right now." Margie shook her head sorrowfully. "She's got a lot to handle with the farm. I told her she'd be better off getting Dean to buy her out. He's wanted to do that for years."

"She did mention something about the partnership agreement with Dean. I think the lawsuit might be the sticking point, but I don't know."

"That crazy environmental guy. My Lord, he's a pain! I'd sue the pants off that weasel myself just for aggravation. He's made my life a misery looking for the 'right' property." She made quotation signs with her hands in the air.

"The right property?"

"Whatever *that* means. He finally went with another agency. I said good riddance." Margie looked at her watch. "Sorry, Gracie. I gotta dash. I have two houses to show to a buyer in an hour."

Chapter 21

Kim Jackson sat twisting a Kleenex in her hands. Nolan Schmidt looked over his drugstore reading glasses at his client, who sat rigid as a fence post in the brown leather wingback chair in front of the massive mahogany desk.

Nolan was an XXL guy, bald as a cue ball. His florid face was most likely indicative of high blood pressure and a fondness for good Scotch as the smudged shot glass behind him on the credenza attested.

He tapped a sausage-like index finger absentmindedly on his open appointment calendar, waiting for his client to answer.

Gracie sat uncomfortably next to her friend, still wondering why she'd agreed to come along for this appointment. Kim had practically begged her. She didn't want her children advising her on anything at the moment. Gracie had steadfastly told her she'd go for moral support only—no advice. Kim had readily accepted the terms.

"I can't prove I was at home all evening or all night. How could I, Nolan? It was just me in the house that night," Kim said with exasperation. "I talked to him on the phone about the flat tire. He said he'd be home as soon as he'd changed it."

"Did he say anything, anything at all about someone hanging around or staying to help him?" Nolan stopped tapping the calendar and leaned back in his oversized leather desk chair.

"No. No, I don't think he did. I went to bed ... in my bedroom. I had a terrible headache. D. B. and I decided on separate bedrooms when Duane went to college. I suppose that's terrible, but his snoring was awful. He got up early and it just wasn't ... ." Her voice quavered.

Nolan waved his hand understandingly. "All right, Kim. My wife kicked me out years ago for the same thing. It's not a crime. But you do need a better alibi, or I'm afraid you're still a good suspect. Now, think. Did you make any calls or see anyone? Anyone come in from the barn to see D. B.?"

Gracie re-crossed her legs in an effort to get comfortable. The whole situation was surreal. Kim glanced at Gracie as if she needed reassurance that her answers were the right ones. She tried to look supportive but knew her smile was weak. Nolan had told them the sheriff's department had matched up the shot size with shells D. B. used for goose hunting. Two shells were missing from a full box in the gun cabinet D. B. kept his office. Kim didn't have a soul who could confirm her whereabouts other than D. B. The house was far enough from the barns to keep vehicle movement at the big house hidden from those finishing up the milking that night. If she'd driven off to shoot her husband, no one would have been the wiser.

"No. I don't remember any calls or seeing anyone. I don't even know how to shoot a gun, Nolan. I hate them. I just hate them." Kim's voice was strangled. Her face was as white as a sheet. She tugged at a pearl earring anxiously as she struggled to regain control.

Nolan rubbed his bald head with a meaty hand. He sighed, staring blankly at the yellow legal pad in front of him.

"What about D. B.'s cell phone?" Gracie asked suddenly.

"What about it?" Nolan grumbled. He rummaged through a drawer and found a roll of Lifesavers. He offered the candy to the women, who shook their heads. He shrugged and popped two into his mouth.

"I was just wondering what time he called exactly. If he called the house phone, then Kim obviously had to be home.

How long would it take her to drive to the Meadow if she'd left right after he called her?"

"I hadn't thought about that, Gracie. He *did* call me on the house phone." Kim's plump face showed relief. "So I can prove I was at home."

"It doesn't take very long to get from the house to the Meadow, unfortunately," Nolan said stoically. "Maybe 15 or 20 minutes, but it might help." He scribbled a note on the legal pad. "The investigator still has D. B.'s phone as evidence. I'll ask for a log of calls on that date, or we can get it from the phone company. It might give us something." He leaned back in his chair, sticking his thumbs under wide red suspenders. "Now, what's the deal about the mortgage on Tobias McQuinn's land?"

CHAPTER 22

Jim followed Toby through the underbrush behind the trailer toward the Meadow. The scrubby maple saplings quickly sprung back into place as they pushed through the stringy branches. Toby had found ATV tire tracks that crisscrossed several woodcutting trails he'd developed.

Toby hoofed it pretty fast through the woods with no effort, while Jim felt a stitch in his side coming on, trying to keep up. He thought he was in better shape than this. Maybe he should start running again.

"See, they're right here," Toby said, pointing to the set of deep tracks in the mud near one of his stacks of wood.

Jim attempted to work the cramp out, rubbing it with his hand as he bent down to examine the marks in the soft ground. The tire tracks were definitely from an ATV. He walked around the impressions to get a sense where they led. They disappeared in the spongy layers of leaves and became invisible in the compost of the woods.

"You're right. Could be a couple of kids that were up to no good," Jim said after closer examination, removing his baseball cap and scratching his head.

"I found more tracks over where I'm cuttin' up that old elm." Toby waved his arm toward the south.

The terrain dipped over a gentle slope, where Jim could see a large tree was lying, partially sawn. A small stack of firewood stood a few yards away from a pile of sawdust.

"They might be takin' some wood, but I'm not sure. Could've left the ATV up here some place and walked down to break in." He brushed the back of his hand across his forehead and wiped it on his jeans.

"I guess there are a lot of possibilities," Jim responded. "We'd better let the sheriff know. Maybe they'll come up and take a look."

Toby frowned. "I don't need no deputies up here. I can take care of it myself."

"Now, that's not a good idea," Jim said. "They're investigating the break-in, and they need to know about this. I'll call it in. You can't afford any more trouble right now."

Toby spat with contempt against a large rock that jutted out of the layer of old leaves.

"I guess, but they won't do nothin'."

"We'll see. I'll call your attorney first though."

Jim pulled out his cell phone and searched through his contacts. He left a voicemail for the public defender, then shoved the phone back into the holder on his belt. As long as he was already close to the Meadow, he wanted to see the scene of the crime. It wasn't as close as he thought, and they trekked up the well-worn trail for at least another mile before the woods ended. Crumpled beer cans littered the edge of the trees, along with a small pile of cigarette butts.

"Looks like kids were havin' a little party," Toby remarked.

He kicked at the cans; water sloshed out of couple. The trash had been there through a couple of rainstorms at least.

"Maybe they're the ones with the ATV," Jim said, glancing around for any tracks.

Seeing none, they moved from the trees to the alfalfa, which needed chopping.

"Who's got dibs on the feed up here?" Jim asked.

"It was D. B. Part of our deal on that mortgage. It counts as monthly payments during the summer. I guess I'd better tell Dean it needs cutting." Toby brushed the top of the long green stalks with his hand.

The sound of a vehicle caught their attention. Jim shaded his eyes against the sun as he walked down the hill toward the road. Both men stayed in the shelter of the trees that edged the field. A black SUV came to a stop at the edge of the property. Toby swore under his breath.

"It's that government woman again. I'm tellin' you, she's up to no good."

"What government woman?" Jim squinted and saw there were two people in the SUV.

"It's that congressman's assistant or somethin' like that. She yanked me aside before that rally the night D. B. got himself shot, tellin' me I needed to do my civic duty and sell the property to D. B. I told her I wasn't lettin' no stinkin' windmills up here. D. B. was gonna hafta foreclose on me before I'd let that happen." Toby's fist clenched and unclenched, anger etching his face. "If she trespasses on my property, I'll git the cops up here to arrest her butt. She can't miss those new signs down there."

Jim put a hand on the man's shoulder. "Just take it easy, man. I'm interested to know who's with her."

Toby huffed and muttered something unintelligible. He backed away into the trees, keeping his dark eyes focused on the SUV. Jim continued his stroll down the hill to get a better look at the visitors, staying well into the camouflage of the trees. The long-legged woman got out of the driver's side. She stood with her hands on her hips, looking up the steep incline of the field. Her body language was a good indication that Toby was probably right about her. She was used to being in charge. The woman turned back toward the SUV, motioning to the passenger. A man wearing a cowboy hat stepped down from the vehicle and joined her. He looked familiar. He watched the couple continue an animated conversation. It had to be the windmill CEO. He now stood with the leggy woman, gazing at the large piece of land. His hand rested on the small of her back or maybe it was a bit lower. The woman jerked away, returning to the vehicle.

*****

Gracie dashed into the kennel, frustrated that the meeting with Kim and her attorney had taken up half the morning. A deposit was waiting, and payroll was tomorrow. She also had to check on inventory. The first week of the month was her time to do any ordering. Why had she gotten herself in this fix? She wanted to be a friend to Kim, but she'd never intended to get this involved. Advice on how to avoid a murder rap, especially the murder of your husband, was not high on her list of skills.

Marian and Trudy assured her everything was under control. Casey and Tracey were scheduled to handle exercise times and feeding for the afternoon. Runs were clean, all the dogs were exercised at the moment, and Marian had just two more appointments for grooming. Gracie sighed with relief and sank into her desk chair to check the deposit. Everything was in order. She grabbed the blue canvas bank bag and stuffed it into her large tote bag. The pile of invoices that needed mailing was neatly rubber banded; she jammed those into her bag. As she dashed out the door, she promised the bemused Trudy and Marian that she'd be right back.

*****

The line at the bank was long for some reason. Only two tellers were available; everyone else must be at lunch, Gracie surmised. She caught sight of Kevin pulling a folder from one of the large black filing cabinets that lined a dark-paneled wall. Wondering who his victim was, she craned her neck to look around the large silk ficus tree next to his desk. You didn't see the top-gun loan officer unless you were behind on your mortgage or begging for a big loan. She smothered a laugh when she saw a red-faced Ben Richter, writing furiously. He tore a check out from a black binder and threw it on the antique walnut desk. Kevin sat back comfortably in his chair with a look of satisfaction. He caught Gracie's gaze and quickly looked back at his customer. The bearded man stood, pushing his way past a secretary carrying a load of files in her arms. She stumbled and caught the slippery folders before they escaped. The Renew Earth CEO, who evidently couldn't have cared less, pushed through the double glass doors without looking back.

Gracie's cell phone began ringing "Who Let the Dogs Out" just as she reached the window. Placing the bank bag on the counter for the teller with an apologetic look, she rummaged in her bag to drag the phone out. The caller was Kim. She shut the ringer off and tossed the phone back into the bag. Once she finished at the window, she stepped out on the sidewalk in the warm sun. Hitting the call back button, she couldn't imagine what had happened so soon to warrant a call. Kim really needed to get a grip.

A young male voice answered the phone. It was Kim's son, Duane. His voice sounded shaky as he told her the news. The sheriff's department had returned his father's truck right after his mother had come home from seeing the lawyer. When he and his mother examined the truck to make sure everything was intact, he'd noticed that the .20 gauge shotgun that should have been hanging on the rack in the truck was missing. His father had carried a shotgun in the truck for years. When Kim asked the deputies if they were holding the gun, they informed her they hadn't found any gun in the truck.

Chapter 23

The counter at Midge's was almost empty. The lunch hour rush was over. Midge stood facing the grill, ready to flip the last burger onto the toasted bun that sat waiting on the thick blue plate. Perfectly sautéed onions and mushrooms were piled up next to the burger.

Roscoe sat at a corner table where he had an unobstructed view of the counter and grill. His tablet had finally connected to a random wireless network while he waited. He scrolled slowly through pages of articles about N.E.S.T. They'd been around awhile and were experts on applying for and receiving government grants for renewable energy projects. Roscoe pulled a mechanical pencil from his shirt pocket and scribbled a few notes in a small notebook.

A plate clattered on the table, startling him. A server with curves in all the right places positioned the plate expertly next to the iPad. Crispy fries and a burger joined the glass of iced tea he'd been sipping.

"Thank you, Miss," he said, grabbing the burger. He groaned with happiness, biting into the huge sandwich. Allie smiled and peeked at his screen.

"I'm Allie. "Whatcha doin' there? Playing games? I love computer games."

Roscoe quickly swallowed, washing the burger down with tea. He was momentarily speechless in admiration of Allie who was a petite brunette with sparkling brown eyes.

"No games, just some research." He patted his disheveled hair, sat up straight, and pushed his glasses back into place.

"What kind of research? Are you in school or something?

"No," he said, looking myopically at her. "I'm assisting some friends about inquiries into wind turbine farms. I'm a reporter for *The Sentinel*." His chest puffed out with importance.

"Wow! A reporter," Allie said with surprise. "I don't think I've ever met a real live reporter."

"Well, I'm ... I'm ..." Roscoe stammered, "I'm just a neophyte reporter."

Allie gave him a questioning look. "A caveman reporter? What are you talkin' about?" She turned on her heel and made for the kitchen.

"No, no, miss. That's 'neophyte,' not 'Neanderthal!'" the confused Roscoe called after her, his face flushed red.

Sighing, he turned back to the screen. The sound of male voices coming through the door distracted him from the lines of text in front of him. He glanced up, seeing N.E.S.T.'s CEO claim an empty table. Dean Jenkins joined the squarely built man with glasses and thinning brown hair.

Dean looked nervously at the reporter. He looked around the dining room repeatedly, as if uncertain whether he should stay or leave. Mitch Allen looked cool and in charge. The attractive waitress who'd served Roscoe the best burger he'd had in some time was already taking their order. She quickly returned, depositing two slices of pie and coffee in front of the men.

Roscoe only caught odd snatches of the conversation. "Tobias McQuinn," "foreclosure," and "bonus" were the words of interest.

*****

Gracie and Jim finished bed check and turned off the lights in each corridor. Every bone in Gracie's body felt weary tonight.

Haley trotted through ahead of them to the reception area, as anxious as her mistress to get to the house. Her otter-like tail whacked loudly against the door, while her tongue, long and pink, hung goofily from her mouth.

Jim's cell sang out the opening notes of the "Twilight Zone" theme just as he punched in the security code to lock up. He pulled the phone from the belt holster.

"Good. It's Roscoe."

"You told him to come over?"

Gracie stood with her hands folded across her chest, vainly trying not to sound irritated. She leaned her back against the kitchen counter, mentally calculating whether she had enough bread and peanut butter for supper. Her head hurt, and she really just wanted a long, hot shower with no interruptions, especially from Roscoe.

"Yes, and I know you'd rather not, but he's got some updates. Besides we need to put all our information on the table. Toby's still in trouble, and so is Kim."

She had to admit that was true. Since Tobias' release and Kim's becoming the focus of the investigation, everything had been happening so fast. They needed to regroup. Gracie shrugged. If this pow-wow would help Kim, then she could survive a Roscoe invasion. At the moment, there was no doubt: Kim was knee deep in cow poo.

"Let me change," she sighed. "I'll cowgirl-up to face Mr. Myer."

Leaving Jim standing in the kitchen, she went to her bedroom to peel off her hairy clothes. Every dog seemed to be shedding, including. Haley. Dog hair covered every inch of her clothing. She heard Haley bark as soon as she closed the bedroom door. Roscoe never wasted any time.

Pulling her mass of red curls back tightly and clipping it in a tortoise shell barrette, Gracie took a quick look in the mirror. Clean shorts and a T-shirt would have to do.

Her cell phone rang where she'd laid it on the bedspread just as her hand touched the doorknob. She picked up the iPhone and squinted at the read-out. It was her mother. But the caller turned out to be her father. He'd just gotten back from his card night at the Legion Hall. Her mouth dropped open in surprise as he filled her in on the events of the evening.

*****

"She said *what?*" Jim asked incredulously.

"Unbelievable, don't you think?" Gracie answered, sitting back on the big leather sofa with her legs pulled up to her chin.

Jim claimed the repaired recliner, while Roscoe sat doodling in his notebook, apparently in his own world, on the large ottoman near the coffee table. Haley was snoring on her back, comfortable in her bed next to the fireplace.

"Streeker's aide was very persuasive. Of course, in a re-election year, aren't they all? But my dad said she flat-out promised that all kinds of money could find its way to Wyoming County if the wind farm was built in Greerson's Meadow. She wants everybody's support to convince Toby that it's crucial to the local economy. It'll mean jobs and additional financial support for dairy farms. She said there were lots of ways the congressman could make sure Deer Creek got the bulk of the "help." Ms. Harkness also played the vet card. She's an ex-Army sniper. Served a couple of tours in Iraq and Afghanistan. The guys were impressed with that."

"No doubt," Jim said, closing the recliner.

He laced his hands, put them behind his head, and leaned back against the chair. He closed his eyes. Gracie could tell the wheels were turning.

She stretched her legs out on the coffee table and took a sip of coffee from her mug. "A couple of them even asked her to go to the club to shoot. And she agreed."

"Really?" Roscoe jumped in, breaking his unnatural silence. "I actually researched Ms. Harkness today. Quite a versatile person. I imagine she's invaluable to the congressman."

"I hope you've got more than that," Jim said scowling.

CHAPTER 24

What Roscoe had was quite a bit of information. Between the three of them, the sketchy outline of N.E.S.T., Renew Earth, and the personnel involved with both was starting to take shape.

The would-be reporter pushed his glasses back onto the bridge of his nose and confirmed that Cynthia Harkness was a sniper in her former life. She'd worked with Congressman Streeker for five years and had been his chief of staff for the last two. Ms. Harkness was single, about 40, and very ambitious. She had built a substantial resume with her military service and political interests, and as a liaison for the government grants and N.E.S.T. Jim shared what he'd seen from the woods, and the three concluded maybe there was a reason for that exclusive connection.

Roscoe had managed to download the previous year's balance sheet for the wind farm company, which appeared to be cash poor. It looked like Mitch Allen was counting on the construction of this last wind farm for a generous influx of grant money straight from the taxpayers.

Gracie uncurled herself from the chair and went to collect glasses and the pitcher of lemonade chilling in the refrigerator.

"I guess my time with Kim wasn't wasted today then. I'm afraid Mr. Allen is going to get a shock when he has no leverage to get the land."

"Whaddaya mean?" Jim quizzed.

"The mortgage isn't under the farm's name," Gracie answered, filling the glasses and carrying them carefully to the living room.

"So, Mr. Jackson held the mortgage personally, and not the farm?" Roscoe asked as he reached for the lemonade.

"That's the story. The attorney said she could do what she wanted. Kim plans on just discharging it and calling it paid in full. She's the executrix of the estate, so it's her choice. She told Nolan to write a letter to Toby about it and get the paperwork done. She's never been happy that D. B. held the mortgage over his head. I don't think she was happy with D. B. in general and this whole windmill business." Gracie resettled on the couch. She set her glass on the cork coaster on the end table.

"I guess you'd have to get in line on *that* cause. D. B. wasn't known for his warm, fuzzy business dealings." Jim rubbed his jaw and smiled. "Toby's going to be happy to get that letter, but that may not be the end of things for him. There are at least four people who want that land pretty badly. Your cousin's boyfriend is one of them too."

Gracie narrowed her eyes and grimaced. "I'm sure Isabelle knows exactly why Kevin's pushing to get the land. I can't believe it's just about a loan to N.E.S.T. Maybe I can do a little more snooping on that."

Roscoe looked up from his iPad, his spider-like fingers finally motionless on the screen.

"Now, do you want me to pursue any further information regarding Mr. Richter?"

"Yes," Jim and Gracie answered together.

"I'm wondering if he's trying to hide his identity," Gracie said.

"Why do you say that?" Jim asked, surprise in his eyes.

Gracie explained the hit on the news article of Samantha Richter's death.

Jim gave a low whistle, shaking his head. "Definitely check that out."

Roscoe nodded gravely and promised to look into the Vermont connection to Ben Richter. He sat cross-legged on the floor, focused on the iPad. He tapped the screen and typed furiously.

Gracie drummed nervous fingers on the arm of the sofa, wondering if Investigator Hotchkiss would take any of this seriously enough to let Kim off the hook.

Roscoe seemed exasperated with his Internet search, making some odd grunting noises. She glanced at the mantel clock, surprised that it was already 10:30. Looking over at Jim, who had fallen silent, she saw he was dozing in the chair. He suddenly jerked wide awake, startling himself.

"Sorry, but I've gotta go home. It's been a long day," he said sheepishly. He stretched his arms overhead and yawned.

"I agree," Gracie said, rising from the sofa. She yawned dramatically with the hope Roscoe would get the hint.

"I feel quite invigorated. I can continue all night if necessary with the research," Roscoe responded.

"Great idea, but we'd better let Gracie get her beauty sleep," Jim said, giving Gracie a wink.

"Oh. Right." His pale face flushed with embarrassment. "Uh, I can certainly continue my research elsewhere." Roscoe stumbled to his feet from his cramped, cross-legged position on the floor. He snatched up the tablet and stuffed it in a battered messenger bag.

Sighing with relief, Gracie locked the door after the two men. Haley whined at the French doors to the patio, and Gracie hurried to oblige. The dog bounded ahead of her, happy to investigate the night smells. Finally, she raced back to the patio and pushed the unlatched doors apart. Gracie followed, feeling zombie-like. The dog made a beeline to the coffee table, sniffing the phone that was vibrating insistently. She had a text message. "The UFOs are back."

CHAPTER 25

"You saw them this time?"

Gracie shoveled dog food into stainless steel bowls, while Jim put fresh water in for each canine guest. Everyone seemed eager for breakfast; muzzles immediately plunged into bowls.

"Well, sort of. I saw lights or something, I guess. Roscoe is going to stay at the trailer and set up his equipment. He and Toby are hatching some plan to catch it all on video, create a website, the whole nine yards."

"How did Toby get a hold of you last night? I didn't think he had a phone."

"My parents talked him into a cell phone. It wasn't easy though. They got him one on their plan. Reason finally won out."

Gracie nodded. "It's a good idea. He's gotta have a phone with everything that's going on. So, what did you see?"

Jim gave a belly rub to the golden retriever, who begged for one any time a human walked by. The dog panted and whined for more attention.

"All right, Jasper. Just a minute more, buddy." He turned back to look at Gracie. "I saw some lights over the woods on the other side of the Meadow. They kind of hovered and then just disappeared. It could have been some kind of small airplane, I guess, but Toby's all over this. He's convinced they're UFOs, aliens, whatever. He could be right. It was pretty weird."

"Who owns the woods past the Meadow?"

Jim rubbed the dog's belly once more and closed the gate. Jasper stood, disappointment in his gentle brown eyes.

"Sorry, boy. We'll be back later." Jim pushed his Yankees cap back and scratched his head. "I'm not sure who owns the woods. It used to be Hansen's. Seems like I heard they sold it off a couple of months ago."

"Maybe I can find that out or maybe our super researcher can," Gracie said as she dumped the last of the kibble into a bowl.

"I'm not sure what that'll do for us though."

"I'm not sure either, but it might help," Gracie answered, absorbed in thought.

The walkie-talkie clipped onto her waistband crackled into life. Marian informed her that a Mr. Richter wanted to talk to Jim. He was waiting in the office. She raised an eyebrow, smiled, and watched Jim head to the office.

Ben Richter paced impatiently in front of Gracie's desk. He was in business casual attire, khaki Dockers and a crisply pressed white button-down shirt. The sleeves were rolled up to his elbows. The man was fit and Jim could see that Mr. Richter worked out regularly. He held out his hand to Jim, who shook it reluctantly.

"What can I do for you?" Jim asked in clipped tones.

"I'm here on a business matter." Ben said smoothly, stroking his dark beard. "Do you mind?" he asked, pointing to one of the uncomfortable vinyl chairs.

"I can't imagine what business we might have." Jim's eyes narrowed, and he motioned for the visitor to sit, while he took a seat behind the desk.

"Actually, it's about your cousin's property. I'm here to make an offer to purchase the back 30 acres. Not the whole piece, but the area behind the pond."

"Why ask me? Toby's the owner." Jim watched the man carefully.

"I have. In fact, I just left there. Your cousin is a rather difficult person, and I don't believe he's competent. He's talking about UFOs and space visitors."

"Tobias is competent. He must have told you 'no.'"

"He did. Unfortunately, he did it with a shotgun. I'm sure you understand what that might mean in his particular situation." A look of satisfaction crossed Richter's tanned face. His dark eyes flashed with triumph. The trump card had been played.

Jim groaned and stood, wishing he'd never heard of Greerson's Meadow.

"I'd be happy not to press charges if he'll agree to sell the back portion of the Meadow property. I don't want the entire piece, just that acreage. You might want to tell your cousin that it's in his best interest. Otherwise ... " He paused and then continued, "He could lose the entire property easily enough while he serves his time. I can then pick it up for the back taxes."

Jim took off his cap, curling the bill in his hands. Toby had done it this time. He sighed and replaced his cap. "Let me get back to you, Mr. Richter," he said coldly.

"I'll give you 24 hours, Mr. Taylor."

Richter stood and pulled a folded contract from his back pocket. He threw it on the desk before making a confident exit toward reception. He barely missed running into Gracie, who led an overweight yellow Lab to a run at the end of the corridor. Jim glared at the unwelcome visitor's back, the contract clutched in his hand. Richter was out the door and striding across the parking lot to the waiting yellow car.

"Trudy, I'll be back later," Jim said through gritted teeth.

He stalked out the front door and let it slam. The bell jangled raggedly. Trudy nodded, looking puzzled. She shook her head and answered the ringing phone.

*****

The big pickup bounced and growled its way through the woods to the silver trailer. Toby was loading the back of his rusted, beat-up truck with Roscoe's UFO equipment. Roscoe squatted on the ground, tapping on a black box with a screwdriver. Jim had run through at least four scenarios for his confrontation with Toby as he jostled up the long driveway. He still wasn't sure what approach to take. He stepped down from the black F150 and sauntered over to Roscoe, his hands thrust in his pockets.

Roscoe finally looked up, apparently oblivious to the fact a truck had pulled into the driveway.

"Why, good morning," he greeted Jim.

"Hi. What's happening?" Jim asked.

"We're loadin' up this research equipment to haul up to the Meadow," Toby said, wiping his hands on his jeans.

"Anybody besides me drop by here today?" Jim went on, biting back further comment.

"Just that lowdown weasel, Richter," Tobias groused. "Why?"

"What did he want?"

Tobias stooped to pick up another box of miscellany.

"He wants my land. That's what he wants. It's the same garbage he was sayin' to me before D. B. was killed. Except now I wised up to his game." He heaved the box over the rusted tailgate; the parts clattered when the box hit the truck bed.

"What garbage is that?" Jim asked with interest. He squatted down with Roscoe to examine whatever the black box was. Still uninformed, he stood and looked at his extremely distant cousin.

"He wants that back piece behind the pond." Tobias jabbed a thumb over his shoulder. "Says he wants it as a wildlife preserve with the land he's bought next to it. I don't believe a word of it."

"He owns land up there?"

"Yup. He bought three pieces on Jemison Road. Hansen's woods and a couple of other parcels. About 75 acres, all told." Tobias wiped his forehead with the back of his hand and leaned against the truck. "What are you gittin' at anyway?"

Jim hesitated. He didn't want to set the volatile man off, but he had to know. "Did you threaten him while he was up here today?"

"Threaten him? Did he say I did? How do you know all this?" Tobias' eyes narrowed into slits. Color rose in his creased, unshaven cheeks.

Roscoe stood, holding the black box, his eyes as big as saucers. Without comment, he took it to the pickup and placed it gently into the front seat.

"Well, did you?" Jim demanded. "You do know you're out on bail, right?"

"I didn't threaten him. He threatened me though."

"You didn't happen to have a shotgun out here?" Jim just wanted to get to the bottom line.

Richter was a smooth operator, and it'd be easy for him to spin Toby's reactions any way he pleased. Jim could picture the sly and malicious man working Toby over.

"It's up there on the porch." Toby pointed toward the small, roughly constructed overhang on the trailer. "I'm keepin' it there when I'm workin' outside. We've got a lot of rabies this year. Shot a skunk just yesterday that was sick."

"Ahem, if I might interject, Jim." Roscoe cleared his throat nervously. "Mr. Richter was rather verbally threatening to Mr. ... uh, Tobias. He was merely standing next to the shotgun. I was working in the shed over there." Roscoe nodded toward the rusty roofed storage shed. "I don't believe Mr. Richter saw me."

Jim smiled sourly and shook his head. "You always seem to be around at the right time, Roscoe. How do you manage it?" Inwardly he blew out a sigh of relief, hoping it was true.

*****

Kim signed her name with a flourish to the discharge of mortgage that lay on her attorney's desk. Her face was flushed with triumph when she looked up at the portly man. Dean sat next to her, stony-faced, his jaw working slowly in agitation.

"It's done. Please do whatever you need to do to make this official," she said, handing the pen back to Nolan.

He signed beneath her signature and put his notary stamp on the document.

"I'll have it recorded today. Don't worry," Nolan said, snatching up the paper. He checked it over and seemed satisfied. "I'll get Christine to take this right over to the clerk's office." He punched in his secretary's intercom number. A heavyset woman, with frizzy, short gray hair and reading glasses that hung from a gold chain around her neck, plodded in to take the document.

When the door closed, Dean leaned forward, his jaw set. "Now I want to talk about the partnership agreement. I'm not going to be cheated again. Not this time."

The secretary ambled to the reception area. "I'm going to the clerk's office," she told the receptionist. "I'll be right back."

*****

Christine had just settled back in the chair to check her email when she heard the front office door slam, and a loud male voice demand to see Nolan. The receptionist was doing her best to calm the man, but Christine grudgingly hauled herself up to see if she could assist.

"Is there anything I can help you with?" she enquired.

The man whirled around to face her. "I need to see Mr. Schmidt immediately. It's about his client, Mrs. Jackson. It's vital to settling our case."

The voice suddenly clicked with her. She'd heard the condescending voice plenty of times. And now she got to meet the irascible Ben Richter face to face. Good looking, well sort of, but what a pain in the ear!

"Mr. Richter, if you'll have a seat, I'm sure Mr. Schmidt will want to see you. *After* he finishes with his client, of course. He has a very heavy schedule today." The big woman smiled and easily led him to the large black leather couch in the waiting room.

"Oh, right. Of course." Richter seemed momentarily disarmed by her coolness.

"Let me get you some coffee while you wait. Cream? Sugar?"

"Uh, no ... yes. Black is fine. Thanks." He stroked his beard and perched on the edge of the sofa.

The young, attractive receptionist sighed, rolled her eyes, and went back to her computer screen. Christine handed the man a white foam cup, which he practically grabbed from her.

"How long do you think he'll be?" he demanded, regaining his arrogant tone.

"I'm not sure, but let me know if you need more coffee."

She returned to her desk and brought up the instant messaging software to warn Nolan. The lawyer's suite had a convenient back door, which had assisted many a client in disappearing to the parking lot before there was a scene in the office. She and Nolan hated scenes, and she had a bad feeling Mr. Richter rather enjoyed them.

CHAPTER 26

Gracie wasn't sure how it happened, but she was going to Isabelle's house for tea. In the back of her mind, a vague recollection of Isabelle mentioning the afternoon soiree nagged at her. For all she knew, she'd pitched the invitation. Isabelle had swept into the office, alternately chastising and begging her to attend. Gauging her cousin's insistence, Gracie's best guess was that Isabelle had forgotten to invite her and just realized her error. So, by rights, she should've been thoroughly insulted by such a last-minute summons for what she knew would be an uncomfortable and formal affair. It was just to show off some redecorating Isabelle had done. Why it was so urgent was unclear. But Isabelle had verbally bludgeoned her with guilt—how she needed Gracie's support during her grief recovery, which was unlikely, and then warbled about how fabulous Carla Jenkins was as a decorator. However, the deciding factor was who else was on the guest list.

She smoothed back a few stray curls that always managed to escape her ponytail. Teatime was at four o'clock. She could only hope Jim would be back, and she'd have time to shower and change. The familiar diesel rumble of his truck caught her attention. She shuffled a stack of papers together and dumped them into her in-box for later. Haley trotted out to reception to greet Jim.

He strode into the office, his eyebrows knit over stormy blue eyes. Patting Haley's head, he stood by his recliner as if deciding whether to sit or stand. Haley flopped down by

Gracie's desk chair. Gracie clicked the shutdown on her computer. She looked up, surprised by his surly expression.

"Whoa, what's going on?"

"Toby's done it this time. He'll be back in jail by tomorrow." Jim tossed his baseball cap onto the desk and grabbed a Coke from the refrigerator.

"What's he done now?"

"Threatened Ben Richter with a shotgun or *possibly* threatened him. He says he didn't. Who knows? Between Toby and Roscoe, I don't know who's lost more marbles." He slumped into the recliner and took a swig from the can.

"Why would Toby threaten Richter?" Gracie locked her desk drawer, dropping the key in a paperclip container.

"It's that stupid land. Richter is bound and determined he's going to get it. Today he only wants the back portion, which is a new twist."

"What's the big deal with that land? There's something more to the whole thing."

"I don't know. Toby's lawyer called while I was up there. He told me that Kim discharged the mortgage today."

"I knew she wanted to do it. I guess she didn't waste any time. The land is his free and clear now. That must be a relief."

"Ha! Not likely. Toby will do something to ruin his good fortune. I just don't know ..."

She swiveled the chair, back and forth, looking at the wall clock. "Well, I hate to break up this meeting, but I received a royal summons for afternoon tea."

Jim looked at her in surprise, pushing his baseball cap back from his forehead. "Really? What brought that on?"

"Isabelle just *has* to show off some redecorating project, which needs to be properly oohed and aahed over. It'll probably be a real snorer except that she told me Ms. Harkness, Streeker's aide, would be there along with the wife of the New Energy guy. Knowing Isabelle, she's got something up her sleeve with these women. It might be an interesting intelligence-gathering opportunity."

"Might be," Jim agreed. "We need to find out the real story soon, because Toby isn't going to sell that land to anyone. He told me today. They'll have to pry his cold, dead fingers off the deed." Jim finished the Coke and tossed the can in the wastebasket.

"You be careful," he warned.

*****

Cars lined the one side of Crescent Lane you could park on legally. No parking signs guarded the other side of the street. And parking was at a premium for this event. Gracie was late and not fashionably so. It was almost 4:45 by the time she walked up to the heavy oak door of the huge arts-and-crafts style house. A large wreath of fresh peonies hung on the front door. Her stomach churned with nerves. She hated these kinds of social gatherings. She'd rather be throwing tennis balls for dogs.

A caterer's van sat under the shade of the maples that stood in the middle of the circular driveway. A black Mercedes was parked in front of it. The door opened, and Gracie was greeted by a frazzled looking woman wearing a white shirt with "Kate's Katering" embroidered on the pocket. Isabelle hadn't messed around with this tea event.

The sound of voices came from the dining room, which was to the right of the foyer. Steeling herself for disapproval, Gracie smiled at the caterer, smoothing her French-braided hair. She could only hope that her navy blue Shantung silk-cropped pants with the matching short, fitted jacket passed muster. The chatter in the dining room momentarily stopped when she stepped through the doorway.

Her mother, who'd predictably been looking for her, scurried to greet her and whisper, "You're late. Really late, Gracie."

"I know, Mother. It just couldn't be helped. I found out two hours ago I was coming," she hissed back.

Theresa frowned. "You should have gotten the invitation weeks ago."

Gracie shrugged. "What do you think?" she asked, motioning to her outfit.

"It looks perfect on you. I told you that was a good buy."

Gracie nodded distractedly. She was more interested in looking around to make sure her targets were in attendance.

The wives of the deep pockets in Deer Creek were present and accounted for, but she didn't see Cynthia Harkness anywhere. Everyone was dressed to the nines, mostly in pastel dresses or suits. It was a good thing she hadn't come in what she really wanted to wear.

Petit fours, scones, shrimp, mushroom caps, and tiny sandwiches were on fine china tea plates. There wasn't much tea to be found, but most were enjoying what looked like pink champagne. Silver trays of graceful champagne flutes were staged in strategic places. She looked toward the large living room, which was a straight shot from the dining room. Isabelle was in deep conversation with Carla and another woman whom she didn't recognize.

Theresa touched Gracie's elbow and whispered, "Go get some food. It's wonderful. And mingle."

She rolled her eyes at her mother, who was already talking to her sister-in-law, Marlene. Her aunt glanced over at her and smiled. Aunt Marlene was looking downright spring-like in a linen lavender suit. Her father's sister was tall with wavy steel gray hair that brushed her shoulders, and she had a bosom you could park a casserole on.

Gracie turned her attention back to the food. Darlene Evans buttonholed her as she picked up a napkin and plate to start through the buffet line.

"Isn't this a great room?" she gushed. "Make sure you get Carla's card." She flashed a black and gold business card from her jacket pocket. "They're at the end of the buffet."

Gracie nodded and saw a silver dish with a pile of cards near a teapot. She hadn't even noticed the room when she walked in. She had to admit it was a beautiful dining room. A bay window had been inserted in place of the old picture window. A border of stained glass trimmed the top and bottom of the window. The trim and crown molding looked properly arts and crafts. The hardwood floor gleamed with an aged patina. Gracie wondered if it was reclaimed flooring or new. The area rug under the obviously custom table was deep red. The rug pattern had been picked up tastefully in the stained glass.

"It is beautiful," Gracie admitted.

"Isabelle spent some serious money on this room," Darlene said appreciatively. Her eyes swept over the elegant peony centerpiece and candles on the long dining table.

"No doubt. She never does anything halfway."

Most of the women were gradually moving to the large patio area at the rear of the house. Darlene and Gracie went with the flow. The warm afternoon was inviting, and Isabelle's HGTV-perfect gardens were the envy of many. Isabelle, of course, had a gardener who came weekly. She'd ruin a perfectly good manicure otherwise, Gracie ruminated tartly. It seemed everyone ahead of her was commenting on the landscaping. The waterfall was the real attention grabber. Gracie filled her plate with cucumber sandwiches and a delicate pink-iced petit four. She caught sight of the caterer, who looked exhausted. She leaned against the kitchen counter with her eyes half-closed. Gracie slid into the kitchen, a grin on her face.

"My cousin can wear you out in no time," she joked.

The woman looked startled and backed away from the counter.

"I'm sorry. Was there anything you needed?" She was plump, with rosy cheeks, a straight short nose, and a neat pageboy cut that just brushed the collar of her shirt.

"Not a thing. I'm trying to avoid the crowd, but appear social at the same time. I'm Gracie Andersen. The hostess' cousin."

"Nice to meet you. I'm Kate." Her face remained guarded.

"I know from long experience that Isabelle is a challenge to work for," Gracie said, stuffing another sandwich in her mouth.

"Well, 'challenge' is a good word for it. Plus one of my assistants called in sick just before the party. It's been a wild day."

"Ooh. That *is* tough. Everything is delicious though. Have you been doing this long?"

"Thanks. I was working at a restaurant in Geneseo and decided to strike out on my own last fall. Even with the bad economy, I've been pretty busy. Mostly political fundraisers and some weddings."

"Political fundraisers. Really?"

"Surprising, right? A friend of a friend got me hooked up with Congressman Streeker's aide, Ms. Harkness. I've done several for them, which has made getting my business going pretty smooth ... so far."

Gracie stopped mid-bite. She wiped the corner of her mouth with a white linen napkin. "Cynthia Harkness? Is she here today? I think Isabelle told me she was going to be around."

"She's been outside on her cell phone for the last few minutes."

Kate pointed through the kitchen windows. Gracie peeked through the brown tab curtains and caught a glimpse of the tall, athletically built woman, talking intently on her phone.

"How is *she* to work for?" Gracie picked up a stuffed mushroom from a silver tray on the counter.

"Tough, but okay. She definitely knows what she wants. Ms. Harkness got me a job with New Energy too, so I can't complain." The caterer turned to grab trays of sandwiches and skewered shrimp. "Excuse me. I've got to replenish the table."

Guests were filtering back into the house for more food and drinks. Isabelle caught sight of Gracie in the kitchen and immediately made a beeline for her. Gathering her intestinal fortitude, Gracie pasted on a smile and walked from the kitchen.

"Where have you been?" Isabelle demanded. "Your mother said you were here, but I haven't seen you anywhere."

Her blue eyes were blazing. She was perfectly dressed in a watery blue nubby silk skirt and creamy silk blouse. Pearls adorned her ears and neck. Her blond hair was pinned in an elegant French twist. She was like June Cleaver on steroids.

"Sorry. I was hanging out by the food. I really wanted to meet Cynthia Harkness, but I guess she's not around." Gracie tried to get the focus off herself.

"She's got a business call, but come and meet Ann Marie, Mitch Allen's wife."

"The windmill guy's wife?"

"Yes." Isabelle said curtly, and then her expression softened. "She could use a little company right now," she added. "Maybe you could show her the gardens. I really could use some help with her."

"Sure. Why not?"

Isabelle looked at her cousin in surprise, one eyebrow arched doubtfully.

"Really?"

"Yes. Anything wrong with that?"

Gracie picked up a glass of what she hoped was lemonade in an attempt to look nonchalant. She wanted a clear head, so none of the pink stuff for her.

"Why, no."

Isabelle regained her composure and led Gracie to a short, mousy-haired woman, who looked well into middle age. She held an empty champagne flute in her hand and had a slightly silly smile on her face. After appropriate introductions, Mrs. Allen was immediately chummy, a sure sign that she'd had more than one glass of bubbly. Gracie felt sweat begin to seep into the underarms of her jacket. She'd reached the limits of her socialization for at least a week but she had to carry on. She reminded herself that amidst this torment was a treasure trove of information just waiting to be discovered.

"I love your hair. Is it natural?" Ann Marie asked a little giddily.

"Why, thanks. Yes. I grew it myself. I understand your husband is the CEO of the wind farm company." She couldn't waste any time. A few women had already left, and it wouldn't be long before they'd all be heading to their cars.

"Yes. It's my dubious claim to fame." The woman frowned and grabbed another glass of champagne from a nearby tray. "I'm a windmill widow. Business is demanding ... very demanding." Her gaze went to the gardens outside, and she took a sip from the glass.

"I can imagine. New Energy has had quite a time trying to get that wind farm built on Jemison Road. There's been so much controversy. It must be hard to deal with it all." Gracie was surprised at how easily she'd slipped into the role of Ann Marie's confidant.

"Terrible, just terrible," she said with a slight slurring of her words. "That awful D. B. has made life a misery. I can't say I'm sorry he's ... well, gone. Mitch is certainly happier. But it hasn't worked out the way we thought." Her voice trailed off as a tray of miniature scones and tiny slices of cheese cake were placed on the wicker-and-glass coffee table by the caterer's assistant.

"Why don't I get a plate of these, and we take a stroll in Isabelle's gardens? I'd love to show you the gazebo," Gracie urged.

Ann Marie was perfectly fine with that idea and followed Gracie out onto the lawn. They met Cynthia Harkness, who was talking intently to several women about the local economy. Gracie steered the unsteady Ann Marie on the path toward the gazebo at the back of the yard. Ann Marie tripped along beside her in her pink sheath dress that was a tad too short and too tight. She was definitely more than a little wobbly. They took a seat in the gazebo for safety reasons. Gracie was sure the woman was going to fall flat on her face if they kept walking. Plying Ann Marie with the goodies, the conversation resumed. Maybe with some food in her stomach, they'd make it back to the house. Gracie placed the plate of sweets between them.

Without much encouragement, Ann Marie continued sharing the woes of the windmill business. D. B. wasn't anywhere near being the Allens' favorite person and neither was Tobias. D. B. had asked for an outrageous amount on the last lease agreement, and he didn't even own the land. Tobias, in her opinion, was mentally defective and should be made to lease the land to New Energy. It sounded like financial ruin was just around the corner if the last wind farm, along with the government grant, weren't forthcoming. It also appeared that Cynthia Harkness was working day and night to make sure the last wind farm happened. Gracie couldn't help but wonder why it was so important to the congressman's aide.

Ann Marie struggled to pull her dress toward her knees in an effort to cover a well-exposed thigh. "I've got to stop eating at these awful parties," she said disgustedly. "I used to be a size 6 and now ... oh, shh—shoot," she finished awkwardly with a crooked smile. "I've got a run now." A gaping hole in her pantyhose snaked into a wide run to her ankle. "I hope there's another pair in the car. I'd better go change."

Brushing a strand of hair out of her eyes, she stood a little more steadily. After setting her glass on the seat cushion, Ann Marie made her way to the house from the octagon-shaped gazebo.

A few cars were pulling out and making their way down Crescent. Cynthia, who wore her hair closely-cropped in an almost military style, was on her cell phone again, watching Ann Marie half-stumble to the Mercedes in the driveway. Her foxlike face was pinched with concern and Gracie was quite sure she wasn't pleased. Politics must be an unhappy career. With any luck, she'd at least get an introduction to the woman. Cynthia turned her gaze toward Gracie and seemed to look right through her as a cat does its prey. The feral eyes gave Gracie a chill, and the hair on the back of her neck rose, tingling. No doubt the woman had been an excellent sniper.

Cynthia glanced at the departing guests and turned her back to Gracie, walking toward the shade of a maple. Gracie meandered in the same direction, pretending to study the back lawn. The sharpness of the woman's voice made her conversation distinct.

"It's plan 'C' now. I can't believe it's all falling apart. We've got to get this done. I was sure when the first problem was solved, it would go like clockwork."

Gracie kept strolling and then turned back to the house hoping that Cynthia hadn't noticed her.

Carla came from the patio out into the sunshine, with Isabelle in tow. They were both smiling. It must be official. The redecorating and the tea were a success. Gracie took a deep breath. She needed to be on the right side of Isabelle to conclude the afternoon's activities on a high note. Plus, after what she'd seen today, it might be a good idea to talk to Carla about her own master bedroom. The woman had a real eye for color and putting accessories together. That wasn't always Gracie's forte. Her bedroom needed repainting, the carpet was in terrible shape, and one wall sported floral wallpaper from the 80s. It needed help, and she was fresh out of creativity. It wouldn't hurt to get her ideas on the upstairs too. But, after that, she needed to go home. Her fun meter had been officially pegged. Within minutes, she and Carla had made an appointment to get together on the weekend, Isabelle was properly congratulated on a beautiful dining room, and Gracie, still mulling over Ms. Harkness' phone conversation, was seated in her RAV4 headed for home.

CHAPTER 27

Saturday morning proved to be rainy. Gracie finished up last-minute pick-ups and drop-offs before walking back to the house. The light rain was just a mist, and the clouds were beginning to clear. Haley waited at the kitchen's screen door. Gracie wiped her wet sneakers on the mat before she opened the door to receive the dog's wiggly greeting.

Casey and Tracey were handling the rest of the exercise times and the afternoon mealtime. Gracie had almost a whole day to herself, but most likely it would be spent housecleaning and doing laundry. Checking the clock on the gas range, she realized that she had barely enough time to put on a pot of coffee before Carla arrived. The smell of coffee filled the kitchen just as a dark gray sedan pulled into the house driveway.

The decorator arrived with bangs damp against her forehead, but smiling. The gangly woman in navy blue capris and a yellow camp shirt carried an iPad in a black-and-white polka-dotted neoprene sleeve. Haley woofed and then wagged her tail furiously, anxious for attention. Carla obliged good-naturedly.

"Hey there, big dog," she said, giving the Lab a quick head pat.

"That's Haley. She'll suck every ounce of attention she can get. Come on in and look at my disaster area," Gracie said, laughing. "How about some coffee?"

"That would be great. I've been up since four today. Some emergency with milking equipment. When Dean gets up, I might as well too. He's the noisiest person I know."

Gracie smiled and nodded knowingly as she poured two mugs of coffee. "Michael was the same way. Even if he managed to slip out of the bedroom without waking me up, he'd drop something or slam a door."

They proceeded to the bedroom, and Carla quickly took measurements, studied the windows, and pulled up a corner of dingy carpeting to take a peek underneath. She asked about colors and furniture preferences, making notes in a black leather notebook. Her long, plain face was in deep concentration as she wrote down Gracie's preferences. After a tour of the rest of the house, they settled in on the stools at the kitchen island. Carla swiped the iPad screen and quickly brought up her CAD program. She punched in the bedroom's dimensions and displayed samples of several paint colors and hardwood flooring. She began clicking on pieces of furniture and arranging it.

"Do you want to keep the original character of the house?" she asked, tapping the screen.

"That's my goal. I've always liked the farmhouse, country look. It's simple, homey, and you can use some great colors."

"I like it myself. Your taste is very similar to your cousin's. She said almost the same thing before I worked on her dining room."

Gracie choked on the mouthful of coffee, grabbing for a napkin.

"Are you all right?" Carla asked as she pulled several fabric swatches from her bag.

Gracie wiped her mouth and tried to compose herself. "Yes," she rasped, coughing again. "It went down the wrong way."

Carla spread out the swatches. "Look through these and see if you find anything you like. I'm thinking restful colors, muted greens, maybe grays. We'll need to talk proposed budget too."

A calculator appeared from the cavernous bag and was placed on the brown granite countertop. Gracie peeled each swatch back, testing the texture of the fabric. The stack of decisions was suddenly overwhelming. Waves of second thoughts about the whole project rolled into her mind. It might be too soon to think about another change in her life. All she had hoped for were some thoughts about paint color and whether she should re-carpet or go with hardwood flooring.

"I'm not really sure I want to change all the furniture in there or even the bedding," she said finally.

The furniture was hers and Michael's. The old comforter had been a wedding gift.

Carla's face fell. "Maybe we got our wires crossed. I'm sorry. I thought you ..."

"No. No. It's my fault. I thought I was ready. Maybe I am, but now I'm not sure. I'm sorry, Carla. I don't want to waste your time."

Gracie felt terrible. She hadn't intended to lead a fellow businesswoman on. The whole idea was a mistake.

"You know, you might want to take a look at the bedrooms I've redone for Kim. Since both the girls are on their own, she had me redecorate Amanda's and Sara's rooms. They were in desperate need of updating. That house has so much potential." Carla paused, as if considering her words carefully. "I hate to say this—Kim is a friend and all—but she just doesn't have a knack for decorating. Anyway, the bedrooms might give you some ideas," she finished. "Of course, you don't have to make any decisions today." She forced a smile, and Gracie knew Carla was doing her best not to look disappointed.

"That sounds like a great idea. I guess I'm still trying to get used to the single life. Just like Kim is too."

"It must be hard," she said sympathetically. "Dean and I have been married for 22 years and, well ..." She suddenly stopped, staring at the iPad.

"Kim's got it especially hard with D. B.'s murderer still on the loose and the police looking at her as a suspect. It just seems crazy." Gracie finished the coffee and wrapped her hands around the cooling white mug.

"True. But maybe not. She and D. B." Carla arched her eyebrows, her dark brown eyes full of meaning.

Gracie looked at her in surprise. "What do you mean?"

"They weren't exactly close, if you get my drift." Carla twisted her wedding ring uneasily.

"They were having trouble?"

"They have for years. Separate bedrooms since Duane went to college. D. B. planned to retire in the next year or two. He'd said as much to Dean. I'm not sure what that meant for their marriage. There were some rumors about D. B. and his extracurricular activities." She looked down at her coffee cup. "I'd better not say anything more. It's just barn gossip." She pressed her thin lips together firmly.

"I know about that," Gracie replied with an edge to her voice.

There had been two farmhands who had tried to start rumors about her and Jim right after Michael's death. They'd even had the gall to call the accident "convenient." She'd fired them on the spot after overhearing the conversation.

"I do worry about Kim." Carla rubbed her forehead and brushed back strands of straight dark brown hair. "She's not herself, and she doesn't have experience with the farm business, although Dean is trying to help her. He is the manager after all *and* a partner. We have the first option to buy out D. B.'s share of the farm, but who knows if that'll happen now. Kim seems to be a little erratic. The lawyer is trying to get her through the paperwork. It's a really difficult time for her *and* us," she said.

"I'm sure Kim appreciates Dean's expertise. I was glad for Jim's help and my attorney to sell the farm. It's not easy at all."

Carla nodded and took a sip of coffee. "Oh, this is cold. Do you mind?" she asked, pointing to the coffeemaker.

"Help yourself," Gracie answered.

She leaned over to get a better view of the drawing that Carla had begun on the iPad. She liked what she saw, and the lump in the pit of her stomach didn't seem quite as heavy. While Carla sipped at the coffee, Gracie thumbed through the swatches. There were some nice choices and a deep chocolate and burgundy print caught her eye.

"Let me look at the bedrooms you've done for Kim. Maybe I'll get enough nerve to do this."

Carla's face brightened. "The bedroom has a lot of possibilities, and I know I can do it using the furniture you have. Let me work up something for you. A few unique accessories, a hardwood floor, an area rug, and new paint. No obligation, of course." Her words were rushed, and Gracie could see her excitement.

"I guess.... Go for it then," Gracie said. "A breath of fresh air is probably what I need."

She stood at the screen door, watching Carla drive off, still chewing on what D. B. and Kim were planning when he retired. Did they really have marital problems? It all seemed a little vague. And whom would D. B. be seeing? There was Kim's lack of an alibi. But did everyone else have one? She wished she'd asked Carla if the police had questioned Dean about his whereabouts. They must have. If Kim was under suspicion, then D. B.'s partner must be too. He sure wanted the farm badly enough from what she'd heard today.

In the distance, she saw Jim walking from the kennel toward the house. The noise of a car chugging down the road with hardly any muffler caught her attention. Gracie craned her neck to catch a glimpse of the noise polluter through the trees. Sure enough, it was Roscoe's wreck of a car. Jim was already walking toward the noisy vehicle.

Jim spent the next half hour wiring the disintegrating muffler underneath the rusty car. Haley lay close to Jim's feet, looking vaguely interested in the proceedings. Roscoe was given firm instructions to get it properly fixed before he got a ticket or worse, as Jim slid out from beneath the car. Nodding solemnly, Roscoe promised to have it repaired at Tice's Garage.

He held a sheaf of papers in his hands that Haley became fixated on, sniffing and trying to ruffle the pages. Gracie snapped her fingers at the dog, telling her to stop. Her

ears drooped for a second and then she began sniffing
Roscoe's shoes with greater interest.

Jim brushed off his hair and grabbed a rag from his
back pocket to wipe off his hands. A smudge of dirt or oil or
maybe both was on his forehead. Gracie caught his eye,
pointing to her own forehead. He took the hint and managed
to scrub the mark off. His expression was unreadable, but
Gracie calculated he was severely annoyed.

"I do appreciate your expert assistance with my car
issue. I dropped by today with my research on the Renew
Earth organization. I think you'll find it as fascinating as I did.
I've already sent an article to my editor. I believe he's going to
assign me do an exposé on Mr. Richter's rather, well—" He
cleared his throat and continued, his chest puffed out a little.
"Highly questionable organization. I've got it all right here," he
finished, patting the papers he held tightly against his chest.

"Well, then let's take a look at them," Jim said
enthusiastically.

"Come on in. I'll make some lunch," Gracie offered. She
scrambled up the steps and opened the kitchen door.

"None for me. Thank you anyway," Roscoe apologized.

Gracie gaped at him, shocked that he'd actually refuse
food.

"I have a luncheon engagement a little later," he
explained, as a blush of color rose from his neck to his
forehead.

He studied the shoelaces of his black hi-top sneakers.
Gracie noticed that Roscoe looked less rumpled, and his
sneakers were exceptionally clean.

"Oh, no problem. Chicken salad sandwich, Jim?"

"Nope. I'm meeting Pete and Dan. We're looking at a
tractor for Pete. Now, let's take a look at whatcha got."

Gracie shrugged, and they went to the living room,
where Roscoe sorted the papers carefully. If *The Sentinel*'s
editor wanted Roscoe to do the story, he must have found
something substantial, she reasoned.

After Roscoe finished his windy synopsis of Ben Richter and his conman past, Jim and Gracie looked up at each other, both grinning broadly.

"So, our Mr. Richter is in the intimidation and litigation business," Jim confirmed. "He's sure no friend of the farmer. D. B. was his next litigation victim."

"He was also a suspect in his first wife's death," added Gracie. "D. B. may have been more than a lawsuit victim."

"You're quite right. Mr. Richter says he went to the Lake Luster Grill for dinner with his current spouse in Perry after the protest. However, no one at the restaurant corroborates his story, except Mrs. Richter, of course. Also, he maintains he paid cash for dinner, so there is no financial record of them dining there," Roscoe stated.

He pushed his glasses back into place and looked at his large watch with a too-long black strap. He scooped up the papers hurriedly, explaining and apologizing that he had to leave forthwith for his luncheon engagement.

"Well, this explains Richter's empty threat to Toby," Jim said, rubbing his jaw as he watched Roscoe's car depart in a belch of exhaust. "I had Toby's attorney leave a message for him, saying that we knew there was no threat of violence against him, and there was a witness to his visit. No response and no arrest. That speaks for itself."

Gracie sat staring at her wedding picture on the fireplace mantle, wondering what Michael would say about it all. Then she thought of Marc and their brief romantic entanglement. And then Kim's tearful face came to mind.

"We need to find out who killed D. B. It's got to be connected. I wish I knew what the sheriff's department was doing. Why haven't they arrested Richter? He's a big bully and a scammer. Once Roscoe's article is published, they'll have to do something about him," she spouted.

Her gaze left the wedding picture, which bespoke lovely memories. Maybe Kim didn't feel about D. B. the way she had about Michael. What kind of marriage had they had? Maybe she should call Marc and get his perspective from the law enforcement side. It would be good to hear his voice and find out how life in Arizona was going.

CHAPTER 28

Gracie slipped into the last pew to avoid parading down the center aisle to join her parents, who were in the third pew from the front. The group of teenagers who'd parked in the back to escape their parents gave her wary looks. She smiled at the uneasy teens and turned her interest to the week's announcements. The Strawberry Social was only three weeks away, and as always, lots of volunteers were needed. Her mother would be hulling strawberries for that, and no doubt, Gracie would help serve shortcake. It was an annual tradition.

The organ trumpeted out the introduction for the opening hymn. Everybody stood without prompting and sang three vigorous stanzas of "Holy, Holy, Holy," complete with the "amen" at the end.

Once the sermon was in full swing, Gracie looked around to check out who was in attendance. She caught sight of Duane and Kim on the other side of the church near the stained glass window of Joseph dressed in his "coat of many colors." Duane towered protectively over his mother. His young face was hard as he stared straight ahead at the pastor. Duane had short, dark hair and was built like his father, although he was in great physical shape. Gracie imagined that D. B. had once been fit like his son, but that hadn't been true for many years. As the pastor's voice rose in volume to make his point, Gracie swiveled her neck back to turn her attention to the pulpit.

"Are you only a Sunday Christian? Are you pretending to be someone you're not?" Pastor Minders thundered uncharacteristically.

Even Fred Barnes, who typically fell asleep during the first sentence of the sermon, jerked awake. He sat with his wife directly behind her parents. His surprised half-snore brought snickers from the teenagers next to her.

After the benediction, the congregation straggled back to the Fellowship Hall for coffee time. Gracie caught up with her parents to check on Sunday dinner logistics. A roast was in the oven, so Theresa asked her not to be long. Tom and Emma would join them for dessert. There was no mention of Tom's girlfriend and her best friend, Kelly Standish. The fact that Kelly's veterinary skills had saved a poisoned dog during an awful winter also made her a hero in Gracie's eyes. She'd have to call Kelly today and find out what was happening between her and Tom. The reappearance of Tom's ex-wife had slowed down what Gracie believed was a sure trip down the aisle.

Kim and Duane got their coffee and chatted with Dan and Darlene Evans, owners of the hardware store. Kim's face showed a deep weariness. The dark circles under her eyes that makeup wasn't going to cover were a dead giveaway. Duane left his mother's side when he caught sight of a couple of friends home from college. While he talked with them, Gracie made her way to Kim. She was more than happy for Gracie to check out the redecorated bedrooms.

On her way out the door, Gracie noticed Autumn Richter in an animated conversation with Si Silverbrandt, the town assessor, in a corner behind the table of pastries. She hadn't seen Autumn in the worship service. Where had she come from, and why was she there?

*****

Clouds were building for another rainstorm as Gracie parked her SUV in Kim's driveway. Duane answered the door and called for his mother. Gracie stood admiring the sweeping staircase, deciding immediately that it must be fun to decorate at Christmastime. It had a *Gone with the Wind* feel, and she imagined making a grand entrance to a party below. Kim quickly led the way upstairs. Dense beige carpet cushioned Gracie's sandaled feet as she climbed the stairs. The long hallway had five bedrooms, and Kim opened the door to the first one on the right.

"Here's Sara's old room," Kim said, motioning Gracie to enter.

"Wow, very nice," Gracie said with true appreciation.

A metal four-poster bed was the focal point, and the bed design was totally original. The footboard, headboard, and the four posters were crafted to look like bamboo. The dark patina on the metal frame was perfect; it was modern, with an antique look. The windows were covered in buttery colored sheers with delicately woven bamboo blinds to give privacy. The walls were a peaceful green, the crown molding was white, and the bedding was a luscious deep gold with a simple vine embroidered into the silk that picked up the color of the walls. The vine ran diagonally through the middle of the comforter. The accessories—ginger jars and a ceramic Chinese horseman, mounted on his steed—were placed in just the right places in the room. An orchid bent elegantly over the teak nightstand. Its creamy white flowers added to the peacefulness of the room.

"I didn't think I'd really like an Asian theme in this house especially, but Carla really made it work," Kim said. She sat down on the low teak bench near the foot of the bed. It was upholstered in the same bedding fabric and embroidered vine.

"I'll say she did. Where did she find this stuff?" Gracie ran her hand over the comforter and stood back to admire the composition.

"She'll scour every antique and furniture store in Western New York to find the perfect pieces. I think she found most of this furniture from a place near Buffalo. The bedding was handmade by a lady in Castile. She does beautiful work. My sister and her husband have dibs on this room when they visit. Sara just wants to take the furniture to her house." She laughed easily, rising from the bench. "Let me show you my retreat."

They walked to the end of the hallway and the last bedroom.

"This was Carla's first project—right before she opened her business. I wanted to redo the bedroom for D. B., but he was too stubborn to let a decorator in there, even though she came up with a very nice design. I took a chance and let her try out her stuff for me instead. This bedroom has a bathroom too, so it made sense for me to move down the hall." She waved her hand toward the half-closed doorway at the end of the hall. "The master at the other end has a bathroom too. The others share the hallway bath." She pushed the door open.

It was a sunny room with a bank of windows on the east and a double window on the south. Large ferns and white cyclamen in deep red and black ceramic pots were placed on curved floating shelves between the windows. The high ceilings and ornate crown molding made it feel even more spacious. Gracie's eyes swept across the room, attempting to take it all in. It seemed out of character for Kim, whose tastes were quite conventional, as displayed in the rooms on the first floor.

It was a totally modern bedroom. A trim queen-sized bed with an upholstered headboard anchored the room. It had storage drawers built below it with brushed stainless pulls. Cherry hardwood floors gleamed warmly, and a thick, creamy, deep wooly area rug was a huge pool of softness. It spread in all directions from under the bed. A built-in computer desk with bookshelves, all painted in taupe with accents of crimson, provided a simple, but elegant workspace. A modern ebony chaise, upholstered in a print that had the same taupe and crimson, graced the corner where more bookshelves were built-in below a dark wood chair rail. The bedding was a deep chocolate with tiny crimson flowers embroidered abstractly across it. The comforter looked very expensive, and her first guess was it was handmade by the same woman who'd made the other bedding. The walk-in closet with all the built-ins and the spa-like bathroom made her drool with envy.

"Oh, my gosh, Kim! This is absolutely gorgeous. You must love it!"

"I do. I'm glad you like it. This was another case of Carla's creativity. I thought I wanted a frilly, traditional bedroom, and she talked me into this. And I'm glad she did. D. B. hated it, but it wasn't his room," she said with a faraway look in her eyes.

"My guess is that D. B. was heavy on tradition."

"Right. And he was a terrible packrat. I couldn't get rid of anything. Here, I keep just what I need and no more." She stood with arms folded across her ample bosom. There was some fire in her eyes that Gracie hadn't seen before. It made her feel uneasy in some peculiar way. She quickly changed the subject.

"Thanks for the tour. I guess there's no reason why I shouldn't let Carla have a whack at my bedroom." She glanced at her watch. It was already 4:30. It was time to get her canine boarders fed. "I didn't realize it was so late. I need to run."

"I'd love for you to stay for some coffee and dessert. There's homemade strawberry rhubarb pie."

"I'd like to, but I really can't. I need to get back to the kennel. There are 30 hungry dogs right now, and I'm the feeder of the kibble tonight. Thanks again, Kim."

The women padded silently down the long corridor. Gracie's cell phone chirped, announcing a text just as they started down the stairs. She pulled it out of her tote bag and checked the message. Jim was going to help her feed the dogs, and then he had to go look for a missing Toby.

CHAPTER 29

Jim filled the last of the metal bowls with food. Every dog got some lovin' along with a supper bowl. Ears were scratched, tummies rubbed, and hugs dispensed. Reciprocity was a multitude of canine kisses. Both Gracie and Jim were well loved by the time they finished. Gracie wiped her face on the sleeve of her T-shirt. She set the alarm code and then locked up. Jim checked the rest of the buildings, making sure they were secure. Haley plowed through the high grass of the field behind the kennel buildings, easily catching up with the pair walking to the house. She'd been chasing a woodchuck earlier. Since she returned empty-mouthed, Gracie figured the woodchuck had found the safety of his burrow.

"No critter, Haley? You're getting slow," she chided her dog.

Haley didn't seem concerned. The black dog trotted ahead of them, stretching and then lying down on the lawn, panting happily.

"I've got to get over to Toby's," Jim said, brushing the dog hair from his jeans.

"Where do you think he is?"

"I think he's probably hunting up in the woods, and Roscoe's just acting like an old woman. He doesn't know that Toby just takes off sometimes. He hears the call of the wild or something." He frowned, opening the door of his truck. "He left his phone in the trailer, so that's no help."

"Let me know if it's anything serious," Gracie said, turning to whistle for Haley.

"All right. I'm sure it's nothing. See you in morning."

The truck pulled around the driveway and headed south to Jemison Road. Haley trotted toward the backyard, following at Gracie's heels. While Haley busied herself sniffing for stray rabbits, Gracie brought out her iPad and a glass of iced tea. The iPhone on the glass-topped, round wicker table buzzed with an incoming call. She glanced at the readout. It was Isabelle. Steeling herself for the worst, Gracie reluctantly answered the phone.

"Gracie, I'm so glad I caught you," Isabelle said in a dulcet timbre.

The sugary tone could only mean she wanted something, and it was probably inconvenient.

"Hi, cuz. What's up?" she responded coolly.

"We're having a little party this coming Friday, and I was hoping you could attend. It's an exclusive gathering for ..." Isabelle paused as if for effect and continued, "for the business community. Congressman Streeker will be here and available for questions about how he intends to boost the economy in Deer Creek. He's graciously given us the entire evening." She finished dramatically.

An expectant silence followed. "We" were giving a party? Did that mean Kevin was a resident at Isabelle's? That little slip bore further exploration. Maybe her mother had the scoop on it.

"Well?" Isabelle was losing patience.

Gracie knew Isabelle wanted a gushy "yes," but another party wasn't high on her list of priorities. On second thought, it might give her a chance to ask a few questions. Maybe the right people would be there.

"Sounds interesting. Let me check my calendar and get back to you. Anyone else significant going to be there?" She might as well find out ahead of time.

"Of course." Isabelle hesitated slightly. "The Allens will be here, and other influential business people."

"I see," Gracie said brightly. It might be a very interesting time after all, especially if Mrs. Allen knocked back a few drinks. "I just realized I have my calendar right here. Friday looks good. Is it okay if Jim comes?"

It was Isabelle's turn to pause. "Certainly. If you think that's wise."

Gracie closed her eyes, biting her tongue, which really hurt. "What time?"

*****

Jim shoved the gearshift into first and shut off his truck. Roscoe came out of the trailer, hair going every which way, his glasses sliding down his nose. Before Jim could climb out of the truck, Roscoe was standing next to the vehicle.

"Jim, I'm grateful that you were able to come. I've been thus far unsuccessful in locating Tobias. Perhaps you know where he might frequent. I'm not familiar with the surroundings and haven't gone too far afield." Roscoe, more rumpled than usual, looked like an emotional wreck.

"I don't think there's a thing to worry about. Toby goes off hunting all the time. He's probably fishing up at the pond or checking out the best spot for deer hunting in the fall."

Jim jumped down from his truck and walked to the anxious man to the porch.

"You say he was gone when you got up here this morning?"

"Yes, and I've searched the lower forest here and up to Greerson's Meadow. I haven't found a trace of him," Roscoe said breathlessly. "We planned to set up a camera near the edge of the Meadow. Tobias was quite excited about the new equipment."

He motioned toward the Geo and shoved his glasses back into place, swallowing hard, his Adam's apple bobbing erratically.

"Okay, then. Let's take a hike up to the pond. I'll bet he just lost track of the time, or he's fallen asleep fishing."

Jim hoped his guess was accurate. Toby also cut down trees by himself all the time. The man could be lying crushed underneath a tree trunk.

It took the pair a good 30 minutes to trek up the steep slope and navigate the narrow trail that led to the large pond behind the Meadow. Just before they left the filtered sunlight of the woods, Jim caught sight of a man, tanned and hatless, headed toward them through the high grasses. He stopped and pointed at the figure.

"There he is now. I told you he was all right."

Jim quickly called his parents before Toby reached the woods. His mother constantly worried, driving his father crazy. The relief in his father's voice confirmed his suspicion. He shoved the phone back into the holster and waved his hand to get Toby's attention. Roscoe was already trotting out through the grass.

A deep frown bent Toby's expression into borderline surly when he joined Jim on the trail. The sun was low in the sky, and everyone was anxious to get back to the trailer before it was dark. The pace quickened, although Roscoe still lagged behind.

"Man, you gave everybody a scare today. Where've you been?" Jim demanded.

He was grateful to see that most of their return trip was downhill after they reached a stand of white birch trees.

"No need to worry about me. Junior here got his shirt in a knot, I guess," Toby glanced back at Roscoe, who looked slightly sheepish. "Somebody's gonna hafta stop that stinkin' windmill guy. He's got trucks and some outfit up there clearin' land. Looks like they're gonna build anyway."

He pushed a branch away from his face and strode ahead of Jim. The branch snapped back, almost catching Jim's cheek. He ducked just in time.

"New Energy is on your property?" he asked.

"They're over on the piece Cranston sold off. I'm not sure if it's that New Energy outfit or not. Couldn't see a name on the truck. Can't believe it. I'm gonna sue somebody. I don't want them white whirly-gigs up there." He swore under his breath and continued down the incline.

"I think the Renew Earth guy bought that land. I can't believe he'd let them build. He's Mr. Environmentally Correct," Jim said.

"Actually the wind turbines are environmentally correct," Roscoe piped up suddenly.

"Not from what he's been saying. He's had petitions out to stop them, claiming they kill too many birds and have some sort of sound that gives people brain tumors," he countered.

"It's money," Tobias spat out. "They'll pay you pretty good. Why do you think D. B. was in such an all-fired hurry to get them in here? That Richter guy almost had me snowed in the beginning. He was all about keepin' windmills outta here. His wife said the Meadow was such a special place, it oughta be kept just the way it is. To top it off, the jerk took me skeet shootin' like he was some big-time good ol' boy. I shoulda known better."

Jim stopped short at the last remark. Roscoe tripped, trying to avoid running into Jim, and slid down the embankment, grabbing a branch to keep from falling.

"Oh, sorry, Roscoe. Say what, Toby? Richter shoots?"

Tobias slowed and looked back over his shoulder. "Yeah. He shoots. Mr. Environmentally Correct is pretty good too."

Jim's brow furrowed, thinking about the possibility of Richter getting D. B. out of the way to get to Toby and his popular piece of land. It was beginning to look like it wasn't a farfetched idea at all.

Toby picked up the pace again, and Jim lengthened his stride, as Roscoe scrambled up the muddy slope to the trail.

The shadows deepened in the trees. The trail leveled off just as they passed by the edge of the Meadow. Jim peered over at the woods on the other side of the wide field. The sun was fast disappearing, and twilight was settling in comfortably. The glow of dim blue lights over the woods caught his attention, right before the trio made a sharp left turn toward the trailer site. Nobody else seemed to notice, so he decided to keep quiet.

CHAPTER 30

Kim sat in front of Gracie's desk. Her plump, tear-stained face was streaked with makeup running in different directions. In hiccupping speech, she explained that Renew Earth had withdrawn the settlement offer now that she'd discharged Toby's mortgage. Dean, who was usually pretty laid-back, told her in no uncertain terms that she'd irreparably damaged the farm's interests and that she needed his say-so before any more decisions were made. He had reminded her, none too gently, that they could both lose everything if the farm lost the lawsuit.

"I thought I was doing the right thing, Gracie," she said, her voice cracking with emotion. "D. B. had designs on Tobias' property. He even forced more money on him. Told him to get a log splitter and fix up his place. He wanted to make sure Tobias was *really* indebted to him."

Gracie was at a loss to advise her new friend. She could see both sides, with no easy resolution.

"I'd talk to Nolan if I were you. There must be something he can do."

"He warned me this would happen, and I was too stubborn to listen. Richter's wife works for the title company, so she saw the discharge go on record the same day. I was so stupid! I tried to do the right thing." She covered her face with her hands. Gracie noticed that Kim had already taken off her wedding band. She'd replaced it with a square-cut sapphire set in the crook of a small "J" on a simple gold band.

Gracie sighed and leaned back in her chair. She drummed her fingers nervously on the desk, trying to come up with a plan. There was plenty about Mr. Richter and his organization that smelled funny. Roscoe now had most of the backstory on Richter's slimy past. She should see how Roscoe was doing on his article.

"You know, I think I'll have a little talk with this old school friend of mine." She stumbled slightly on the word "friend," but recovered quickly. "He's doing an exposé on Richter for *The Sentinel*. If he has all the research on this guy, you might not have anything to worry about."

Kim looked at her in surprise. "Really? What kind of research?" She blew her nose loudly and tossed the crumpled tissue in the wastebasket. Her eyes were suddenly bright and full of interest.

"Let's just say, Richter has a suspicious past. A dead first wife, a history of lawsuits against big farms. He's been buying up property around the Meadow."

Kim's jaw dropped. "Would your friend talk to Nolan about this?" she croaked.

"Probably. I'll ask."

*****

Gracie went out to find Jim after Kim left. He was tinkering with the tractor mower, which gave them problems every other week. He looked up from the scattered parts that waited to be reassembled.

"The Beast is acting up again. We're gonna have to spring for a new one if this keeps happening."

He grabbed a red rag that lay on the grass and wiped the grease off his hands. He tossed it back on the ground and continued working on the tractor engine.

"Hoo boy," Gracie commiserated. "That would stink. I was hoping to get through the summer with it."

The large mower had come with the kennel property, and to replace it meant big bucks.

"Maybe, maybe not. I'll see what I can do. Reverse on the transmission is pretty much shot on the tractor. The mower deck is falling apart. I guess if I don't have go backwards ever, it might make it," Jim grumbled.

"See what you can do, or just use the house mower."

"I'm not touching your mower. Your dad informed me that he has it running in tip-top condition. If something happens to it when I'm mowing that rough area out back, he won't be happy."

"True," she mused. "If you have to, it's okay. Just tell him I said so."

Jim raised his eyebrows and shook his head. "What did Kim want?" he asked, tightening up the mower deck with a ratchet wrench. "She didn't look so good."

After she explained the latest dilemma, he stood, grabbing the rag to wipe his hands again.

"That lawsuit is pretty much a no-win situation. Kim did Tobias a big favor, but I can understand why Dean's mad. That construction activity up above the pond needs to be checked out. If we can get something on Richter, maybe he'll leave everybody alone."

"Maybe," Gracie said, picking at a split fingernail. She chewed off the ragged edge and continued. "I don't understand why he'd sell out to New Energy now. It doesn't make any sense."

"It doesn't, just maybe they made an offer he couldn't refuse. Who knows? I just want to make sure they don't 'accidently' put a wind turbine or two on Toby's property. He's already over the edge about the possibility. We're going up there tonight to check it out. And by the way, Toby told me that Richter is a decent skeet shooter."

Gracie's eyebrows rose with interest. Her hazel eyes brightened. "So, Mr. Richter *does* know how to handle a gun."

"So it seems. Not so much of a stretch to see him ... well ..." Jim coughed nervously.

"Not much at all," she concurred, picking up on his thought. "I'll ask Dad if he's a member of the Valley Gun Club. Maybe he knows something more about this guy."

"Not a bad idea." Jim put a foot on the mower's back tire to tie the laces on his work boot.

"And what about those lights you saw in Hansen's woods? Are you going to check that out when you go up there tonight?"

"No," Jim said, shaking his head. "I think it was kids partying or parking in there. They probably heard my truck and took off." He bent down and tested the mower deck. It seemed satisfactorily attached.

"You're probably right." Gracie's eyes narrowed. "You said you saw something up there before."

"I'm sure it was just a small plane or something like that, not a UFO. Come on, Chief; don't go *X-Files* on me now." He laughed and climbed on the large mower.

Gracie shrugged and grinned. "I'm not so sure. There are things that can't be explained, and the universe is pretty big."

"Sure there are. I still think it's kids messing around. We found beer cans and ATV tracks on Toby's property. Kids most likely broke into his place. Hansen's woods—or, I guess, it's Richter's woods now—are a good place for that kind of messing around. I think I remember you and Michael ..."

"Right, yes. It's a good place for that," Gracie agreed hastily, cutting him off. She put her hands on her hips. "So, when are you going up there?"

Jim looked up, his expression deadpan.

"Toby and I are going to the construction site around 7:30. It'll still be light, and everyone should be outta there by that time. Why?"

"Just wondering."

In truth, she wanted to go up and see for herself what exactly was happening.

"If you need some help, I'm available," she offered.

"Uh ... in a word, no. We don't need any help." His voice was a little sharp, which surprised her. "I mean, we're just looking around at property lines and checking to see whose equipment is up there. It's nothing." He now sounded conciliatory.

"All right," she relented, exhaling slowly. "How about if I hang out at Toby's? You know, like a Command Central, in case you guys get into trouble. Somebody should be there, ready to call in backup."

"Roscoe will be there for that. It's all covered."

"Oh."

This was extremely disappointing. It was a "no girls allowed" situation apparently. There had to be some way she could stay in the loop on this excursion. Jim was making this way too difficult. She plunged ahead with her next proposal.

"Well, if he'll be there, maybe we can do a little more Internet research on Richter and that Cynthia Harkness. He might find something that can help Kim. Plus, I need to see if he'll talk to Kim's lawyer about what he already has on Richter."

"We might as well make Command Central over here. You two can do your surfing, and I'll be back before you know it. Toby doesn't have any kind of web connection up there."

"Oh, that's right. Sure. Have Roscoe come over here. Why not?" Gracie answered dispiritedly.

Seeing relief on Jim's face made her come to a rather impetuous decision. What could possibly go wrong?

CHAPTER 31

Roscoe rapped on Gracie's kitchen door, iPad and steno pad in his arms. Haley offered a half-hearted "woof" at his arrival, and then went back to her dish to finish eating. Gracie had him set up at the breakfast bar. She pulled her notebook from the junk drawer that contained her observations. It was time to get serious about this investigation. Then maybe there'd be time for a field trip she had in mind.

"I have all the names of the officers for Renew Earth," Roscoe said proudly as he plugged his iPad into the outlet above the bar. "It's an interesting cadre. Sorry, my battery is getting low. Do you mind?"

"No. Go ahead," she said. "So, who's on the list?"

"As you might guess, Mr. Richter is the president. Mrs. Richter is the secretary-treasurer. There are two vice presidents; they're Mrs. Richter's sister and brother-in-law. Summer Thayer De Franco and Stewart De Franco."

Gracie plunked down on the stool next to Roscoe to look at the screen.

"See. It's all right here," he said, pointing to the webpage from the Department of State.

"Yes, I see. But what's significant about that? It's a family business. I think I met the sister at the carnival over Memorial Day. She was handing out information in their tent."

"Correct," Roscoe answered officiously. "But now look at this." He clicked to another page from the Department of Corrections for the state of Vermont. "Mr. De Franco was incarcerated for three years for fraud and identity theft. He was also arrested prior to that for assault."

"You're kidding! Really? What about the Richters? Anything on them?"

Gracie's voice rose in pitch, and Haley was immediately at her knee, whining. She absently stroked Haley's head, still reading the public information on De Franco's criminal history.

"Not really, other than they keep an appearance of being law-abiding citizens, but as you can see, their relatives are extremely questionable." He leaned back with satisfaction, forgetting there was no back to the stool, almost falling on the floor.

"Whoa, Roscoe. Careful." Gracie tried not to laugh.

"I ... um ... well, to continue...." Red crept up his neck and onto his face. "I do have one other, rather startling piece of information on Mr. Richter."

"And what is that?"

She sat up straight on the stool and brushed some stray crumbs from the countertop into her hand. She'd forgotten to clean up after eating her sandwich earlier. Sliding off the stool, she tossed them into the wastebasket. Haley looked disappointed and retreated to her bed by the fireplace.

"He has large mortgages on the two properties he purchased. He's also taken out a sizeable line of credit against his residence."

"Through Deer Creek Bank, right?"

The dramatic scene with Kevin and Richter came immediately to mind.

"Yes. I believe he's in arrears, but is working out a refinancing arrangement. He's given the bank a lien on the timber, which he plans to have removed from the wooded property he just purchased to pay off the arrearage."

Gracie gave the pallid, but earnest Roscoe a look of admiration. "How did you find out all this stuff?" She had to admit that possibly she'd seriously misjudged him.

"Well, I have a source at, you know … at the local restaurant," he said with reluctance. "Of course, the mortgages are a public record at the County Clerk's office."

"Yes, of course, they are," she said, tapping her fingers on the granite counter. Her mind was whirling with possibilities. "How long has Mr. Richter owned the wooded property?"

"He purchased it three months ago."

"That's about the right timeframe then."

"I don't understand. What timeframe are you referring to?"

Roscoe adjusted his glasses yet again. Gracie yearned to superglue them to his nose.

"Let's take a ride up to Hansen's woods," she suggested. "It might explain a few things."

Haley was first in the SUV. She jumped agilely over the console and sat panting on the backseat, ready for action.

The sun was well into its descent. Fingers of sunlight retreated into the growing twilight as Gracie hurried down the rutted dirt road toward her goal. Roscoe was silent after he'd heard Gracie's explanation for the trip. He looked as if it didn't sit well, but he hadn't put up any argument.

His cell phone rang crisply with a techno beat tune as they jostled their way down Jemison Road. It was Jim, calling to let them know they'd met up with the project manager at the pond, who would give them a ride back to Toby's. There was no need to worry. He'd explain everything when they got back.

Gracie gave Roscoe a warning look and pressed a finger to her lips. Roscoe obliged, revealing nothing about their current location: pulling off Jemison Road and onto an old farm lane, which split into two one-lane roads that wound their way into the woods. It was the perfect hidden parking spot.

"Do you have a flashlight, Grace?" Roscoe queried.

"Oh, crap! No, I don't. Great!" She was disgusted with herself for forgetting the essential nighttime stealth tool.

"We can use our phones then. Where exactly are we looking for? What kind of equipment?"

Roscoe stepped down from the vehicle, while Gracie put a leash on Haley.

"Jim says and you confirmed," she said, opening the rear door to let Haley jump to the ground, "that the lights were always seen over Hansen's woods. I think, if we do a little scouting around, we'll find it's all manmade by Mr. Richter."

Haley tugged at the leash, ready for a run.

"I believe it would have been more prudent to examine this possibility in daylight. We really don't have much time before it's quite dark." Roscoe shivered in the evening air, clutching his phone.

"Yes, but we may catch them in the act."

The probability of that actually happening hit her full force. She licked her dry lips, tempted to abandon the scheme. But, she reasoned, they were already here. And she just had to find out if her theory was correct.

She peered down the path that led deep into the woods, while Roscoe continued his droning monologue.

"However, there are no vehicles around, and we didn't meet any on the road. From my research ..."

Gracie gave a quick tug on the leash to get Haley to sit.

"I know you've researched that they exist," she groused. "I think it's more than coincidental that sightings started after Richter bought this land. Let's get going before it's really dark."

She instantly regretted sounding so bossy, but they needed to find out and fast. Jim would be back at the house soon. They couldn't waste any more time talking.

She and Haley took off at a trot down the well-worn path. She supposed that Roscoe was dragging along behind them, but she wasn't going to wait for him. A good-sized clearing was her goal, if she remembered correctly from earlier adventures in these woods. It was where the crumbling stone foundation of an old cabin stood, about a half mile into the mostly oak and maple woods. If her suspicion was correct, it was the perfect place to set up a UFO hoax.

Shadows were getting longer. She slowed to a walk, her breathing a little ragged from jogging. She looked back for Roscoe. He was nowhere in sight. It was probably a mistake to bring him, she thought. But, more likely, he'd just turned around and was sitting in the SUV, waiting for her to return.

Walking quickly through the gloominess of the trees, she tried to remember where the turn was to the clearing. Haley, sensing her urgency, pulled on the leash, sniffing the ground constantly. Gracie gave the dog more slack and quickened her pace again. She thought she saw the glow lights off to her left as she pushed through a small grove of pine trees. The ground dipped sharply, and she slid through slippery pine needles, almost losing her balance. She stopped and regained her footing. Reaching into a jeans pocket for her cell phone to give a little more light, it slipped through her fingers and onto the ground.

"Rats," she complained to herself, dropping to her knees to search for the phone. "Come on, Haley, help me find that phone," she hissed to the dog, who could barely be seen.

The sound of voices made her stop. Haley sniffed the ground, then raised her head and rumbled a low growl. Her hackles rose, as did the volume of her throaty growl. Gracie strained to hear where the voices were coming from. She held the cotton web leash tightly, shushing the dog which continued to rumble softly.

Still hunting through damp leaves and pine needles for the missing phone, Gracie's fingers finally found the hard plastic rectangle covered with dirt and leaves. She breathed a sigh of relief, brushed it off on her pants, and wedged it uncomfortably into her bra.

A yellowish light flickered again off to her left and then glowed steadily. Two voices, one male and one female, rose and fell, a faint echo of their unintelligible conversation bouncing through the trees. Haley whined and pulled at the leash. Gracie inched forward, taut leash in one hand, and the other arm stretched out trying to maintain her balance down the slippery grade. The conversation was still too faint to make head or tail of it. Haley panted heavily and growled intermittently. She needed to get closer, but with Haley's unpredictable vocalizing, she wasn't sure what a safe, but audible distance was. Discovery wasn't ideal at this point.

The sharp sound of a snapping twig halted her progress. Hardly daring to breathe, she clutched the leash and put a restraining hand on Haley's muzzle, willing her not to bark. The voices stopped, and the light glimmering through the trees ahead of her went out. Now in complete darkness, Gracie crouched down with her dog. After what seemed forever, the voices resumed in more hushed tones, and the light reappeared. Her leg muscles protested, and it felt like a charley horse was imminent. Rubbing her thigh, she craned her neck toward the voices. It was no use; she still couldn't make out a word. Grabbing the leash, she crept forward toward the light, dragging Haley with her. A strong breeze rustled through the leaves, providing some white noise to cover her movement. She half-ran to a thicket of bushes on the perimeter and crouched down again to peer through the leaves.

The bushes turned out to be a bad choice since they were fully armed. They had to be blackberry or raspberry bushes. Thorns snagged her arms, and she bit back an "ouch" as she carefully tried to disengage herself from the prickly mess. Haley wisely backed away. She'd stopped growling, but still intently watched the movement through the foliage.

Rubbing the long, stinging scratches on her arms, Gracie leaned forward again, her eyes adjusting slowly to the dim light. She struggled to identify the male figure, seated on an ATV. A smaller, obviously female person appeared from behind the deteriorated foundation, carrying an object Gracie couldn't identify. An explosion of light hit the four-wheeler, exposing the pair in glaring whiteness. A deep male voice ordered everyone to stay where they were. Gracie, shocked out of her mind, stood, stepped back, and promptly fell backward over Haley. The dog yelped in surprise and ran toward the lights, jerking the leash from Gracie's hand. Gracie landed onto the ground with a resounding *whump*, knocking the wind out of herself.

The man with the deep voice identified himself as Investigator Markowski of the Wyoming County Sheriff's Department. He was of average height, dressed in a dark shirt and jeans. Several more uniforms appeared from the woods, with guns and spotlights. The large man on the ATV sat motionless, his back to Gracie. The young woman began crying hysterically. Gracie slowly raised herself up, her elbows supporting her upper body. Her breath came in rasps. She felt like her heart was about to explode from her chest.

"Miss, get up and come with me," a stern voice ordered her from behind.

"Let me get my breath. Give me a hand, will you?" she gasped.

A strong arm pulled her up, and she bent over, clutching her stomach and then her back.

"Are you all right?" A tall, gray-haired deputy stood next to her with some concern on his face.

"I th-th-th-think so. I fell and... and... oh, my back hurts."

Actually it was her glutes that were throbbing. That fall was going to leave a mark. At least nobody would see the bruise.

The deputy guided her into the harsh light, where she stood with the couple, their heads hung, while a short, mustached deputy read them their rights.

Gracie shaded her eyes against the glare to get a look at the couple. She brushed debris from her jeans and T-shirt. She gaped, incredulous at the sight.

"Duane Jackson! What are you doing here?"

The young man's look of surprise matched her own.

CHAPTER 32

Gracie sat on the crumbly edge of the old foundation until she realized that sitting wasn't going to be much fun for a while. Her right butt cheek was still aching from the fall. Gracie ran her fingers through her hair, pulling leaves and a small pinecone from the tangled mess. She must look like Medusa, with curly snakes waving all over her head. She'd already explained who she was, and a condensed version of why she was creeping around the woods. A pat down by a woman deputy with the promise to show her driver's license when she got back to her SUV had been satisfactory, so far. Haley had fortunately reappeared from the darkness and now lay panting at her feet.

Duane shakily began explaining what he and his girlfriend, Heather, were doing. She caught snatches of the interrogation amongst her recital of her address and other personal information to the deputy.

The UFO idea had been cooked up by Duane and some college buddies. It was all about how unsophisticated and gullible Deer Creek residents were. Computer images projected into the night sky and a couple of amateur drones rigged with halos of lights had added some more drama. Tobias had been their guinea pig. He'd made it into a real media event for them. Duane had been traveling back and forth between college and Deer Creek for weeks. Heather was helping him clear out the equipment tonight.

Two deputies were searching the ATV and rummaging through the box containing deflated balloons and strings of lights. They shook their heads at the officer in charge, who sternly continued to question the pair about drugs.

"Why are you up here?" Gracie finally asked the gray-haired deputy, who stood next to her.

He was writing on a pad of paper, with a flashlight tucked under his arm.

"I mean," she gulped, "why tonight?"

"We got a tip about some drug runners doing business in the woods. The tipster was sure a big deal was happening tonight."

"Man or woman?" She had her own ideas about who would make a call like that.

"I really couldn't say, ma'am."

"Hmm. Was it the owner of the property?"

"I really couldn't say."

"You're not arresting Duane, are you? He's just played a prank. Nobody got hurt."

The deputy shrugged and said, "It's up to the investigator. They *are* trespassing. Like you, ma'am." His face was impassive.

The guy must be RoboCop, she decided. She stretched uncomfortably and rubbed her lower back.

"How about I call it a night and get back to my vehicle, deputy?" she asked with a touch of bravado, which was pure make-believe. Why hadn't she stayed home?

"Sure thing. Right after I give you this appearance ticket for trespassing. Didn't you see the signs, ma'am?"

She stifled the comment that jumped to her lips and snatched the paper from the deputy's extended hand. This escapade was going to be hard to explain to everybody, and now there was a ticket involved. She'd never gotten a ticket for anything... ever.

"I'll walk you back to your vehicle. I want to make sure you get back there okay."

Gracie nodded. After a few attempts at more small talk with no success, she kept her mouth shut as they trekked up the alternate trail back to where she'd parked the RAV4. The headlights from a parked cruiser shone through the trees as they reached the split in the lane. She pulled the keys from her pocket and unlocked the vehicle. Haley whined anxiously, dancing in circles, so she obliged the impatient Lab and opened the rear passenger door for her. Gracie fumbled through her bag on the front seat and found her license. The deputy merely glanced at it and handed it back. She forced herself to thank him and smile. Sighing with relief, she watched him disappear back down the narrow lane. Just as the key slid into the ignition, it hit her. Her passenger was missing. She'd lost Roscoe within minutes of leaving the SUV and hadn't seen him since. Angrily slamming the steering wheel with the palms of her hands, she pulled the key out and headed back to the woods, leaving Haley in the backseat. Her phone buzzed in her bra, sending her heart into double time. Breathlessly, she answered Jim's call.

"Where are you? I've been at the house for half an hour. Nobody's answering the door!" Jim shouted.

"I'm up in Hansen's woods, looking for Roscoe right at the moment."

"What? What's he doing up there? His car is here. What's going on, Gracie? Why are you out of breath?"

"It's a long story."

She hit "end call" and punched in Roscoe's number. She needed to find him and fast. The phone went directly to voicemail. Not a good sign. Painfully jogging to catch up with the deputy, her body complained with every step.

*****

Even after Jim and Toby joined the search, there wasn't any sign of Roscoe. Investigator Markowski took Gracie's report, and after two hours, she drove home. Law enforcement and some friends Jim had called were still combing the woods. If anything happened to Roscoe, it would all be her fault. Tears threatened, and she wanted to throw up.

Morning still brought no news of Roscoe. Investigator Markowski stopped in before the kennel opened to let her know they were still searching the woods and nearby fields. He wanted information on Roscoe's family, but Gracie had no idea where to begin. The Myers family had long since moved away from Deer Creek. She remembered his sister's name was Nancy, but that was it. It was duly noted. The investigator left, promising to call with an update.

Jim came dragging in at lunchtime. His eyes were bloodshot, and he hadn't shaved. He shut the office door, dropped into his recliner, and looked wearily at Gracie. She attempted to ignore him, studying her spreadsheet intently. She didn't want to talk about anything, but the look on Jim's face told her that they would have to talk.

"Just so you know, I'm out of this investigation business as soon as we find Roscoe," he stated. "You might want to think about that yourself."

Gracie turned from the computer screen to her handsome, albeit ticked-off partner.

"Just a reminder that you're the one who started this. It was all to help Toby. I'm helping Kim," she countered.

Jim held up his right hand. "Guilty as charged. Last night is on you though. It's time to let the police handle it. They know what they're doing. We're the amateurs here."

"You mean *I'm* the amateur," she shot back. "It was stupid. I know that. I guess that's what I get for trying to help a friend."

"A pity party isn't what anybody needs," Jim retorted, rising from the chair. "We both made some mistakes. I'm going back out to find Roscoe."

He stalked off. Gracie wadded up the paper that had just come off the printer and threw it against the wall. She needed to take a walk. Trudy and Marian gave each other knowing looks, which Gracie ignored as she passed through reception.

"I'll be back in a few minutes," she said, not looking at either woman.

She let Haley out of the backyard gate and headed for the field behind the kennel. Maybe the fresh air and the scenery would clear her head.

Haley bounded ahead into the high grass mixed with masses of daisies and buttercups. If she weren't so angry with herself, it might have been entertaining to watch the broad black Lab head disappear and then reappear. It looked like a variation of "Whack a Mole."

She stopped, broke off the stem on a buttercup, and twirled it in her fingers. Where could Roscoe have gone? Was he lying unconscious in the woods? Maybe there had been drug dealers, or something worse had happened. She couldn't bear to think about it. Then there was Duane. A call to Kim was in order, but she didn't want to be too nosey. Who'd made the call to the police? It had to have been Richter. Nothing made sense right now. She tossed the flower away.

Haley began barking wildly, and she looked up. A man trudged through the field toward them, head hanging and shoulders sagging. The hair was unmistakable. It was Roscoe.

CHAPTER 33

Gracie was grateful to see her parents pull in at closing time with supper in hand.

Haley dashed to the car, barking merrily. She followed close on Bob's heels into the house. He set the stack of to-go containers from Midge's on the kitchen island.

Conversation ran immediately to Roscoe, as they popped the tops on salads for Gracie and her mother and a meatloaf dinner for her father. Gracie, relieved beyond understanding, unloaded the whole story, although she did skip over the part about the trespassing ticket.

Roscoe apparently had gotten himself lost immediately and had spent the night wandering through the woods and fields. He was now spending the night for observation at the hospital in Warsaw. He seemed all right, but was dazed and somewhat confused. He had no idea how he ended up in the field, but saw the kennels and headed for them. Gracie had called the sheriff's department and Jim. The ambulance was summoned after that. Now she was sure that everyone with a scanner in D.C. knew what had happened at Milky Way today.

"Everybody'll be talking about this for a long time," she groused, poking a tomato with her fork.

"Don't worry about that," Theresa said soothingly. "Just be glad you're all right, and Roscoe is all right. I wonder, though, why he can't remember much of anything."

"Probably just shock," Bob commented, stuffing the last of the cheesy meatloaf into his mouth.

"Maybe. But I'm worried about Duane too. I haven't heard from Kim today, and I don't know if I should call."

"She might be embarrassed if Duane really got arrested. Kids do such crazy things," Theresa said, shaking her head. "At least no one got hurt."

"I'm pretty sure that Ben Richter had something to do with that setup last night. He's such a vindictive turd. I wish I could figure a way to find out." Gracie finished the salad and tossed the container in the wastebasket. "It's all too confusing."

"So it is," her father said, leaning back in the chair and pulling a toothpick from his shirt pocket.

"I forgot to ask you, Dad. Do you know if Richter's a member of the Valley Gun Club?"

"I don't think so, but I think I saw him up there with Streeker's aide... uh... What's her name, Theresa?"

"It's Cynthia Harkness," Gracie supplied before her mother could answer. "They were at the gun club together?"

"She was showing off her talents for the guys. She's good, that's for sure. She had a 100 percent for skeet and the same for the range. Of course, she had a speech about renewable energy sources and how much they'd improve the economy here." He stuck the toothpick in the corner of his mouth. "I'm not sure why Richter was there, but they talked for a few minutes before she left."

Gracie grew silent. She wasn't sure what to think of that development. It didn't make sense at the moment.

"According to your Aunt Marlene, the bank's got problems with this Richter, serious ones. Then there's that petty lawsuit against Jackson Farms," her mother chimed in. She collected her husband's Styrofoam container and napkin.

"He does have some big financial problems, according to Roscoe," Gracie confirmed. "And there's the construction above the pond. That land is Richter's now too. Jim was up there talking to some project manager last night. The guy wouldn't give him any details, but Jim thinks they're planning to put in windmills. All the guy would say was the owner wanted to do some development up there, and the road was the first step."

"Why would this Richter put windmills on his land when he's been protesting against them? That doesn't make sense," Theresa interjected.

"Beats me. Jim did mention there was some geologic engineer up there too. I really don't know what that means." Gracie wiped down the breakfast bar and rinsed the dishrag in the sink.

"You know, I bet I saw that project manager at Midge's today," her father suddenly added. "His truck said *Resource Management Services* on the door. Midge called him 'Stew.' Seemed like a nice enough guy. Didn't say much from what I saw. Just had some lunch and left."

"As in 'Stewart'?" she asked, her antennae on high alert.

"Could be. Why?" her father asked in a puzzled voice.

Before she could answer, her phone buzzed loudly on the counter. It was Kim. Her voice was stressed. Gracie tried to counteract the tension with quiet and calm responses. When the jumbled conversation about Richter and the lawsuit didn't improve, she asked Kim and Duane to come to the house. Maybe she could figure out what was going on in a face-to-face.

Her parents quickly said their good-byes, with a warning not to get too involved. Nodding mutely, Gracie figured it was way too late for that.

Kim and Duane arrived both ashen-faced. Kim's eyes seemed perpetually swollen and red these days. Duane looked like every ounce of strength had been drained from him.

Haley seemed to sense the emotional storm, and after initial greetings, flopped into her bed with a groan. She slept with one eye open, maintaining surveillance of the situation.

"You'll have to start at the beginning," Gracie said. "I'm sorry, but I couldn't understand what you were telling me. It was something about an email and Cynthia Harkness."

She motioned for mother and son to sit on the couch. Kim put a hand on Duane's arm, nodding for him to start.

"Well, the Cynthia Harkness part is something I just found out a couple of days ago."

"He was using the computer in D. B.'s office when he found the email," Kim added.

"Yeah. I was working on a spreadsheet for Dean," Duane explained. He leaned forward, his hands clutching each knee. "A reminder popped up on the email to call this Cynthia for a date to get paperwork. I started looking at Dad's calendar, and her name was on some meetings he had with this Allen guy."

"Was it about government grants, by any chance?" Gracie asked.

"I'm not sure, but I did find an email that he'd deleted. They were supposed to have a meeting after that protest or whatever it was."

"Just the two of them?"

"No. The email said attendees were Trexler, Allen, and Harkness."

"Trexler? Is that Kevin Trexler at the bank?" Gracie swallowed hard, her stomach churning.

"I don't know. I suppose it could be. I guess Dad was working with the bank on this windmill thing." Duane looked over at his mother for confirmation.

"It's most likely Kevin. D. B. had meetings with him all the time," Kim added.

"Do the police know about this meeting?" Gracie adjusted her hair clip, pulling back a delinquent curl that kept falling into her eyes.

"They should. They had D.B.'s computer for a week," Kim answered sharply. "Not that it did them any good. I didn't know anything about it though."

"You *do* know that she's an ex-Army sniper," Gracie offered.

"D. B. mentioned it to me once. He also told me that Ms. Harkness wasn't someone to mess with."

"Did you tell the police about her meetings with D. B.?"

Kim put her face in her hands. Duane awkwardly put a hand on his mother's shoulder.

"I don't know what I've told them at this point," she cried. She pulled a tissue from her purse and blew her nose. "Added to everything, this situation with Duane, and that Richter character now threatening to get the police to charge him with all sorts of stuff. It's such a mess, Gracie. We've got to find D. B.'s killer. I know he was involved in something. Something really bad." She blew her nose again and squared her shoulders. Patting Duane's hand, she said, "You know, Duane, I need to speak to Gracie alone." Her eyes glanced to the patio.

Gracie immediately jumped in.

"You could do me a favor by throwing the tennis ball for Haley for a few minutes. She really needs the exercise. Do you mind?"

He seemed relieved as he caught the tattered, dirty yellow ball that Gracie tossed from Haley's well-stocked toy basket. Haley ran immediately to the French doors, eager to play.

After the pair exited, Kim smoothed her lavender slacks with her hands and took a steadying breath.

As she plunged into the details of the last weeks of D. B.'s life, Gracie quickly began to piece together his relationship with Ms. Harkness. It was evident that Kim felt D. B. had been spending too much time with her, although he. had insisted it was "just business." Kim had attended a couple of social functions over the winter—a fundraiser dinner for Congressman Streeker and cross-country skiing with the Allens, Ms. Harkness, and her forgettable date. The pressure to seal the deal on Toby's land hadn't come so much from N.E.S.T., but from Cynthia.

Duane and Haley pushed through the doors. Duane was laughing. Haley headed for her water bowl and lay down on the floor in front of it, slurping happily.

"Geez, your dog is pretty funny. She loves chasing that ball."

He tossed the worn tennis ball into the toy basket. Duane looked more relaxed than Gracie had seen him in the last couple of weeks. He looked at his watch and then at his mother. "Mom, I've gotta pick up Heather in a few minutes. Are you ready?"

Gracie glanced at Kim, who looked like she had more to tell, but was torn about staying.

"Why don't you go on? I'll get your Mom home later. Is that all right with you?" she asked, turning to Kim.

"That's fine," Kim answered eagerly. "I have a couple of other things to talk with Gracie about. Just take my car."

Kim stood at the kitchen door, watching her son drive away. She bit her lip and sighed before settling herself on one of the comfortable stools at the breakfast bar. The conversation suddenly turned to Dean and his ultimatum. Gracie, all ears, put on a pot of coffee. It was going to be a long night.

CHAPTER 34

Jim seemed in better spirits. He'd brought sweet rolls from Midge's and had sort of apologized in his own way. He wasn't a wordy sort of guy. Jim was much happier doing something physical than standing around gabbing.

He was whistling "Jimmy Crack Corn" to the dogs as he hosed down runs. They howled and barked like a backup group. It was quite a serenade.

Things were getting back to normal, Gracie decided as she settled in to run the accounts payable. She was dying to tell him about Dean's ultimatum to Kim, but wasn't sure he wanted to talk about anything related to the "investigation." While the checks slid off the laser printer, she got another cup of coffee and decided she could approach it from the business advice angle.

Marian stuck her head into the office to let her know that the dog food delivery truck had arrived. Gracie was glad for the excuse to go out into the warm June day. A pleasant breeze blew from the west, bringing the scent of fresh cut hay. In the distance, she could hear a tractor chugging.

She greeted the feed store driver, who merely grunted his "hello." Harry, who was short and squarely built, with thick salt-and-pepper hair, thrust a clipboard at her. He was perpetually in a hurry and irritated about something. Gracie knew from experience that it was best never to start a conversation about politics or the price of gas. She checked the stacks of kibble and was pleased to find they'd finally gotten it all right this time. She signed off on the delivery and took her copy.

Jim appeared from the kennel and stood by the storage building as Harry backed the truck to the door. The squeaky truck brakes complained until Jim gave him the high sign to stop. Harry jumped down from the driver's seat, and the two unloaded the stacks of bags.

Gracie walked slowly back to the kennel with her face turned toward the sun. It was too bad she never tanned very well. Sunshine usually meant more freckles and sunburn. Haley came trotting from the open door of the reception area. She gleefully smelled the bags of dog food piled up in the storage barn and then joined Gracie. The black Lab managed to place her head under her mistress' hand to get petted.

"It's all about more attention, isn't it, Haley?" Gracie laughed, complying with the dog's demands.

Haley looked up innocently, brown eyes full of satisfaction.

"Hey! Where's your collar?"

Gracie searched the ground for the red rolled leather collar that was Haley's only accessory.

"I'll bet you lost it in the field. How come I didn't notice?"

After looking through the office and around the kennel with no luck, she grabbed a wide red nylon web collar from the rack in the reception area. She buckled it onto the dog's thick neck.

"There. This will have to do for now. At least you're not naked anymore. I'll have to find your extra tags though."

Haley couldn't have cared less, snuggling into her office bed for an afternoon snooze. The dog stretched out on her side. Her tail thumped twice on the floor before her eyes closed.

Marian entered the office and grabbed a diet soda from the small refrigerator in the corner. Gracie glanced up from the computer screen.

"Have a seat, Marian. You need a break." Gracie motioned to Jim's ratty recliner.

The husky woman smiled, sank into the chair, and popped the top of the soda can.

"It's been pretty hectic today," she said gratefully and took a quick swig from the can.

Gracie agreed. The grooming schedule was full almost every day for the next two weeks, and Marian had agreed to put in an extra half day each week to catch up. They chatted about Cheryl's newest family addition—another foster dog from the county shelter. As if on cue, Cheryl entered the office and helped herself to a bottle of water from the refrigerator.

"How's your foster dog settling in?" Gracie asked.

"Easy as pie. I'm really tempted to keep this little girl," Cheryl bubbled as if talking about a new baby.

"What is she? A mixed breed?"

"No. Not this time. Lizzy is AKC. A Pembroke corgi. Just the sweetest thing. Her owner passed away—an elderly lady who lived by herself. No one in the family could take her."

Since Cheryl had received her obedience training certification, she'd been helping the county shelter train a never-ending stream of foster dogs. Cheryl was the kennel's innovator—always a new idea on the horizon. The training facility was now booked four evenings a week by the search-and-rescue team and the local kennel club, thanks to Cheryl. Her puppy class sold out in two days and she was already planning the next.

"I'm glad you rescued her," Marian said, rising from the chair. "Well, I'd better get back at it. One more appointment and I'll be on my way home."

"How many dogs have you had since March?" Gracie asked Cheryl.

"Wow! Good question. Probably seven would be my guess. Elvis, the beagle I had right before Lizzy, was a corker. He'd sneak past you and be out the door before you knew it. He also liked to jump up on the table to lick plates, if you turned your back. Finished off a crockpot of stew one night."

"Did he get a permanent home?"

"Yup. A family outside of Silver Springs took him. They have a big fenced yard and three boys. Elvis never had it so good." She took another sip from the water bottle. "Have you heard how the police are doing finding D. B.'s killer?"

"Not a thing. But Ben Richter ought to be on their radar," Gracie griped.

Cheryl's eyes widened. "Ben Richter, the Renew Earth guy?"

"That's the one. Why?"

"I'd forgotten about this until now. It's been a little busy. But I saw something kinda weird at their office. I was out looking for Elvis the night D. B. was killed. He'd slipped his collar and took off on me. I found him near the Renew Earth office."

Gracie was instantly on the edge of the chair.

"Really? Was there anything going on there?"

"I'm not sure, but there was a big black SUV parked next to the little car that guy drives. It was in the parking area behind the building. Elvis had tipped over a garbage can and was helping himself. While I was picking up what he'd dumped on the ground, a leggy, really serious looking woman came out the back door."

"You didn't recognize her?"

"No. I don't think so. It was almost dark. She didn't look very happy to see me back there. Little Elvis started to howl, and she took off in the SUV. I think it had a special plate on it."

"Like a vanity plate?"

"No," she paused. "I think it was a government plate. A U.S. government plate."

Gracie's heart was pounding. "Do you remember what time it was?" She was almost afraid to ask.

"Actually I do. That dog made me miss the first few minutes of a Tom Selleck movie that started at nine." She frowned with her hands on her hips. "It took me about 10 minutes or so to walk back home, so it must have been right around 9 o'clock." Cheryl glanced at her watch. "I'd better get everyone fed. It's almost quitting time."

Gracie sat pondering why Cynthia Harkness would visit the Richters, when Jim and Roscoe appeared in the doorway.

"What's up, guys?" she asked, while Jim pulled a couple of bottles of water from the refrigerator.

Roscoe stood hesitantly in the doorway, as if he wasn't sure it was safe to enter. She could well understand his hesitation. She felt like a first-class loser. She'd deserted him in the woods without a second thought. The trespassing ticket was no less than what she deserved, but that was still her secret.

"Grab a chair," Jim said, waving the water bottles in his left hand.

Gracie cleared a pile of mail from one of the brown plastic molded chairs. Roscoe silently took a seat next to Gracie's desk. Jim plunked a bottle down next to him and twisted the cap off his own, gulping down half its contents.

"Against my better judgment," Jim began, looking at Gracie and then at Roscoe, "I'll see this 'investigation' of ours through. I started the whole thing with Toby, so I'm the one who got you all involved." He grabbed a plastic chair and sat down on the other end of the desk. "But no one takes any more chances," he finished, his voice decisive.

Gracie, mentally breathing a sigh of relief, went to open the small cupboard next to the refrigerator.

"I'm glad to hear that because I have some new information that may help Kim."

She smiled, pulling out a plate of brownies. Roscoe's eyes lit up, and he grabbed two before the plate made it to the desk.

"I also have some information. Perhaps we should take some time to review all of it," he added, and then shoved most of a brownie into his mouth.

Jim grinned and adjusted his Yankees cap. He helped himself to a large fudgy square, while Gracie resumed her seat.

"Let me tell you first what Kim told me last night," she said.

She unloaded Dean's ultimatum about an immediate sale of Kim's share of the farm to Dean. His reasoning was that the farm couldn't risk any more of her emotional decisions. He'd work out his own settlement with Renew Earth, and Kim wouldn't have to deal with it. She was free to choose whatever plan suited her fancy, but the farm had to be out of her hands. Whichever she chose, it meant cash in her pocket, but it also meant she needed to move. The residence was part of the farm property.

"Does he have the money?" Jim asked.

"He says he does."

"Well, it would make things easier for Kim and definitely for Dean," Jim said.

"Except for her moving out of the house she's lived in for the last 20 years," Gracie responded. "She really doesn't know where to go. Whether to rent or buy."

"Isabelle can fix her up with something. You have to admit Kim's not handling things—"

"I wouldn't either if I was a suspect in my husband's murder, and my son was in trouble for a UFO hoax."

Roscoe's face fell. "A hoax? What do you mean?" His voice was high and nasally.

Gracie and Jim looked at each other in astonishment; his outburst neatly derailed their argument. The realization hit them both at about the same time: They hadn't told him about Duane.

Jim spoke first. "Sorry, Roscoe. I guess we forgot to mention that... uh... well, Duane Jackson and some friends set up the whole UFO thing." He hurriedly explained the rest of the story to the devastated reporter, who looked like his life was over.

"I can't believe it. I was so sure," Roscoe murmured. He went over to the window and stood gazing toward the field.

"It was just a prank, Roscoe. That's why I wanted to go up there. Except I thought it was Richter." She snapped her fingers and groaned. "It had to be him."

"What are you talking about?" Jim quizzed her.

"The UFO thing. Duane said he hadn't been up there since the night before his father was killed. Richter must have found the equipment. He set up that little raid," she finished tartly.

Roscoe stood looking at her with an owl-like expression. "Is there some significance?"

"Well, I don't know, but I'll bet it's possible he found it the night of the murder. You know, as in he was hiding out in there until D. B. was alone." Her eyes shone with satisfaction.

"I guess it's possible, but that old house is back a ways," Jim countered. "You can't watch what's going on in the Meadow from there."

Gracie felt momentarily deflated. That was true, but it was a great hideout and great place to stash a shotgun. Maybe another trip up there was in order.

"You're not thinking about going back up there, Chief?" Jim's face was stern, his voice steady and even.

She shook her head. "No. I'm just saying it's a possibility."

She couldn't risk getting another citation for trespassing. It wouldn't be good to run into Richter up there either.

Jim looked skeptical. Reaching for the last brownie, he asked, "Any luck with an alibi for Kim?"

"No. She was home by herself. But maybe a couple of other people don't have such hot alibis either."

Gracie leaned back in her chair and commenced to fill them in on Cheryl's recent revelation.

"Why would this Harkness chick be seeing the Richters? I thought they were mortal enemies?" Jim asked.

"I'm thinking Ms. Sniper and Mr. Litigation had opportunity to be up there. They certainly weren't on the best terms with D. B."

"It would be a pretty tight timeframe to get from Greerson's and into town," Jim remarked thoughtfully. "I'm not sure it's possible. We don't know what time they left. I'm not sure I remember when *we* left."

"I can Google it and ascertain it immediately," Roscoe offered, looking longingly at Gracie's monitor.

"I don't trust those maps, Roscoe. It's better to actually drive it and find out," Jim said, finishing off another brownie.

"I agree," Gracie said. "Didn't you say that the Richters told the police they were at a restaurant for dinner that night after the protest?"

"That's correct. If they had a meeting with Ms. Harkness, that would explain why they couldn't prove they were in Perry. My source at Midge's reports that Mr. Allen and Ms. Harkness both said they had a meeting with a Kevin Trexler after the incident."

Gracie's eyes widened. "Your source at Midge's?"

She fought back a grin, forcing her face back into a mask of seriousness.

The rumpled reporter made no reply. He folded his arms and looked properly non-committal.

"So, D. B.'s email was right."

Gracie quickly explained Duane's discovery on his father's computer.

"You know, I'm going to call Kevin and just make sure of that."

"What I don't understand is why this Harkness chick would be visiting the Richters." Jim rummaged through the refrigerator for another bottle of water.

"I believe I'll try to interview Mr. Richter about my exposé," Roscoe said enthusiastically. "I should give him the opportunity to respond before I file the entire story with the editor. I could mention this information even."

"That may not be such a great idea," Jim cautioned. "He's not going to be happy about your article at all. We really don't know what he's up to or capable of. He's apparently lied to the police about his alibi."

"I agree with Jim. It could be dangerous, Roscoe. His first wife died under suspicious circumstances after all."

After the debacle in the woods, there was no way Roscoe could do this on his own.

"As a member of the press, I want to give him an opportunity to give his side of the story. I could also inquire about his newest development behind Greerson's Meadow."

Roscoe's just-rolled-out-of-bed personage took on a surprisingly noble look. He stood, squared his shoulders, and tucked his wrinkled red plaid short-sleeve shirt into the tight waistband of his worn black jeans. He was a man on a mission.

"Please let one of us know if you get the interview. You really shouldn't go alone," Gracie admonished him.

"Just call me. I'll tag along as your sidekick or something." Jim grimaced.

"I am sure there is nothing to be concerned about, but I will call if I think it necessary."

He practically marched out of the office, while Gracie and Jim stared after him, speechless.

"I don't like this, Gracie. I'm getting a bad feeling." Jim brushed brownie crumbs from his jeans.

"I agree. Richter and the company he keeps are dangerous. We need to keep an eye on Roscoe. I don't want him getting into any more trouble."

Jim stood in the doorway with his thumbs hooked through the belt loops.

"I also don't like that look in your eyes, Chief. You're staying away from Hansen's woods and Richter, right?"

"Of course," she said innocently, her heart beating double-time in her chest.

CHAPTER 35

The Renew Earth office was deathly quiet. A sign in the front window said "CLOSED" and "Call Again." Ben Richter stuck another sheaf of documents into the shredder, while his wife boxed up office supplies and a calculator from an old metal desk.

"I told you this had gotten out of control." Her voice indicated severe irritation. "You've got too many irons in the fire." She glanced at her watch. "I wish Summer would hurry. She's always late."

He glared without comment at the attractive woman with whom he'd fallen in love, or, more accurately, in lust. He knew she was right, but he'd been sure he could hold it all together. Who could have known that D. B.'s widow would throw a monkey wrench into the whole deal? D. B.'s death had resolved so many things at the outset and now... Well, it was time to pack up. He could only hope that the Jemison Road project wouldn't fall through. Everything depended on it and the check that was waiting for him at Jackson Farms. The stupid kennel woman was sticking her nose in things, and that wasn't good. Maybe the cops had scared her off after the trespassing incident, but he couldn't be sure. An insistent tapping at the front door made the pair freeze.

"The sign's in the window. They'll go away," hissed Richter.

He tied up a black garbage bag full of document confetti and set it by the rear exit.

The tapping continued. It was joined by a muffled voice calling out, "Reporter for *The Sentinel!*"

Autumn swore angrily.

"What does *he* want?" she whined.

"I'll find out," Ben snarled, his eyes dark with temper. "Stay here."

He pasted a smile on his face and strolled from the back office to the front door.

*****

The phone rang twice before Isabelle said "Hello." Gracie broke the ice by asking for more information about Friday's cocktail party. She listened impatiently to her cousin prattle on about the menu and the important guests. She prayed for the woman to take a breath. Gracie wedged in her first question, which she hoped sounded solicitous enough.

"How's Kevin making out with the wind farm deal? I know it's been difficult for him since D. B. was killed. Even Aunt Marlene mentioned it's been a real trial. I'm sure it's been doubly hard with the police investigation and all."

Isabelle was silent for a moment as if considering her sincerity. She couldn't resist the bait, however.

"Of course, it's been difficult. If that crazy Tobias McQuinn had just sold his land to the bank, it would have been fine. Kevin will figure something out. He's very clever at arranging things."

"I'm glad to hear that. It's been so stressful for everyone. Of course, if the police could find the killer ..."

"If you ask me, they really don't need to look any further than Kim. I know that sounds awful," Isabelle said quickly, her tone surprisingly softer. "D. B. mentioned to Kevin he was selling out to try and fix things with Kim. They were having trouble, you know." Her voice took on a conspiratorial tone.

"So I've heard. Kim mentioned that D. B. was supposed to have a meeting with Kevin and Mitch Allen the night he was killed. I guess the police have probably questioned him about that."

"That awful detective, that Hotchkiss person, asked about it last week. D. B. was supposed to be here right after that stupid protest or rally. He called and said he was fixing a tire and would be about a half an hour late."

"Do you remember what time that was?" Gracie asked with excessive sweetness.

"I told the police it was a little before eight. At least he called. Of course, he never got here." Isabelle paused and then continued in an aggravated tone, "I don't know why Cynthia didn't call. Kevin and Mitch waited forever and finally she showed up. She looked a sight too when she finally got here."

Gracie's stomach dropped to her sneakers at the mention of Cynthia's lateness.

"Didn't Mitch and Cynthia leave the protest at the same time?" she probed.

"How would I know? Mitch was here right at 8:15 for the meeting, and Cynthia didn't get here until after nine."

"It was awfully confusing when that rock throwing contest started. People left in a big hurry."

"I'd forgotten that you were there. We didn't attend, of course. Much too political for us."

Gracie wanted to pound her head against the wall. What was Isabelle talking about? They were hosting the incumbent candidate for Congress at a party, for heaven's sake. She closed her eyes, sighed, and asked meekly what time she should arrive on Friday.

*****

It wasn't until six o'clock when Gracie finally locked up the kennel. Haley was already out the door, trotting toward the house. No doubt the dog was anxious for her supper. She had to admit she was too. The rumbling of her stomach was constant. She was pretty sure there was nothing except a peanut butter sandwich on the menu for tonight. Maybe she'd head to Midge's and at least get something to go.

The distinctive wheezing of the Geo coming down the road caught Haley's attention first. She detoured to the driveway to greet the sputtering car. Gracie felt an actual sense of relief as Roscoe got out. He was obviously none the worse for wear after his encounter with Ben Richter. But maybe he hadn't tracked him down yet. The somber look on the usually friendly face gave her pause. Maybe it hadn't gone well. The steno pad was in Roscoc's hand as he walked purposefully toward her. Haley was sniffing his pant legs, which didn't seem to faze him this time.

"I have some additional information on Renew Earth. It seems that they're actually discontinuing their business."

"Really," Gracie responded in surprise. "What's the reason?"

He referred to the steno pad in his hand, flipping over a couple of pages.

"Officially, Mr. Richter states that, and I quote, 'Deer Creek residents have created a hostile environment for those who wish to preserve the rural ecosystem. Furthermore, this hostility has forced Renew Earth to seek another location to further its campaign to save the pristine surroundings in pastoral areas of the United States.'" He paused and looked up from his scribbled notes.

Gracie rolled her eyes in disgust. "He's really full of it, isn't he? Did he say where he was going, by any chance?"

"No. I gather that they have things to take care of here before relocating." Roscoe flipped the pad shut, and he tucked it under his arm.

"What did he say about the activity on Jemison Road?"

"Mr. Richter wasn't prepared today to talk about that, but he did promise to call me for an exclusive interview," he added with some satisfaction.

"Really," Gracie said doubtfully. "He wasn't upset by your article then?"

"He barely acknowledged it actually. He mentioned the freedom of the press and something about contacting my editor, if he had questions."

She raised her eyebrows questioningly. "Are you sure he wasn't just tiny bit upset?"

"Not in the least. I let him know I would file the story with the editor in the morning." He glanced at his watch and pushed his glasses back into place. "I do apologize, but I must go. I have an appointment I must keep."

Gracie shrugged. "Sure. No problem. I'm going to check out some distances tonight between Greerson's Meadow and my cousin's house."

"Please be sure to note all of your calculations," he called back over his shoulder as he hurried back to the waiting car.

*****

The trip odometer on the RAV4 was at zero as she sat parked in the driveway of Jackson Farms. Gracie had decided to check out every possible combination to Greerson's Meadow. Dean, who was just leaving the office at the back of the big house, came over to talk to her. Carla waved to her as she unloaded drapery rods from the back of her car, which was next to Dean's pickup. She waved back, watching the woman finally corral the slippery black rods and start for the office.

"Is Carla working on something for Kim?"

"No. She's redoing the farm office right now. I think it's time for a fresh start in there."

Dean took off his Jackson Farms cap and then replaced it onto his thinning, short brown hair.

"That'll probably make it easier for you." Gracie replied. "You know, it'll be your office and not D. B.'s."

"It's a place to get the work done," he answered flatly. His dark eyes flashed with irritation. He looked at her notebook that rested on the dash, his eyes curious. "If you don't mind my asking, what are you doing?"

"Well, I'm clocking the distance to Greerson's Meadow from a bunch of different places."

"Is that right?" He was silent for a second. "Any particular reason?"

"Just trying to help Kim out with her alibi. D. B.'s phone records showed that he called the house, but Nolan thinks that she's on shaky ground because of the short distance. I guess the police must have asked you for yours too."

Dean's eyes hardened, his lips pressed together in a firm line.

"Sure. I had that conversation with the investigator."

The unwillingness in his manner to elaborate only encouraged Gracie.

"You were probably in the barn that night. I didn't see you at the protest," she said lightly.

"No," he said slowly, as if choosing his words carefully. "I was home with Carla that night. I had a touch of some nasty stomach flu. One of those 24-hour things."

"That's good then. At least you have an alibi. Kim is still trying to establish one."

"I'm sure it'll all work out for her in good time." He looked at his watch. "I'm due down at the barn. I'd be careful if I were you, Gracie. It doesn't pay to get too involved."

She was surprised at his harshness. But she chalked it up to the messiness of the farm transfer. As she pulled around the driveway, she saw Dean talking to his wife before he climbed into the pickup.

Haley sat panting in the back seat, always happy to be along for the ride. Gracie's first trip yielded a distance of 9.3 miles. She grumbled to herself. Nolan was right. Kim could have talked to D. B. at 8:30 on the house phone and then driven to the Meadow to shoot him well before 9:00. Logging her data in a notebook, she then turned the SUV around, reset the trip odometer, and drove toward Deer Creek. It was only 3.5 miles to Isabelle's. Much closer than she'd thought. She sat in front of her cousin's house, pondering the possibility and probability of D. B. getting into an argument with Mitch Allen, Ben Richter, or Cynthia Harkness. It wouldn't have taken long for any of them to shoot D. B. Or maybe Richter and Harkness were in it together and met back at the Renew Earth office. It wasn't out of the realm of possibility. Haley draped a front leg over the seat to push her way up front.

"Hey, get back there," Gracie scolded.

Reluctantly, the leg was withdrawn with a huff of disappointment.

"Let's see how far it is to good ol' Renew Earth from here," she told the dog. Haley whined in agreement.

The Renew Earth office was situated just off Main Street on Washington Avenue. The organization was housed in a converted colonial. Renew Earth occupied offices on the first floor on the left side. The right-hand space was vacant at the moment, although rumor had it that someone was thinking about opening a tea shop. Even though it was just after seven, there was plenty of daylight left. It was Mother Nature's reward for surviving long dark winters. After writing the short distance of 1.7 miles in the notebook, Gracie decided she'd better double-check her calculations and drove back toward Greerson's Meadow. Even with the bumpy road conditions, it took only seven minutes to pull up in front of the field.

Someone had finally cut the alfalfa, but a large rectangle of overgrown hay remained. Tattered remnants of yellow police tape still flapped sadly in the slight evening breeze. Gracie pushed the button to lower her window, leaned her head against the headrest, and sucked in the sweet smell. The even rows of drying hay gave the field order and symmetry. Haley pressed her face through the narrow opening behind the driver's seat to enjoy some of the fresh air. Curiosity overcame Gracie as she watched the yellow tape at the edge of the field. It would have been a cinch to sit hidden in the thick woods that flanked the edge. The murderer could have remained out of sight until D. B. was alone. Kim had said there was no hole in the tire. The police determined someone had let the air out. That meant the murderer had to have been watching for the right moment to sneak to the truck.

"Okay, girl. Let's go check things out."

Haley jumped effortlessly from the back seat. Gracie watched the dog run ahead. The blocky, black Lab kept her nose to the ground, her tail wagging furiously as she happily snuffled and sniffed.

A momentary nauseous feeling came over Gracie as she got closer to the bit of fluttering yellow police tape. Her steps slowed. What was she here for anyway? Mere curiosity? She wasn't sure. But maybe the police had missed something. Just thinking about someone actually lying in wait for D. B. made her look quickly to the woods, searching for movement. She whistled for Haley, who happily loped toward her. Standing in the wide rectangle of green, she couldn't see any impression of D. B.'s bulk in the matted down grasses. A wave of déjà vu washed over her. She'd been standing in a field almost three years ago, trying to save her own husband without success. Mentally shaking herself, Gracie forced herself to focus on the task at hand.

D. B.'s big truck had been parked behind the makeshift stage that night, and it had been close to the trees. She wandered further up the edge of the meadow, trying to remember the exact spot the truck had been in. Examining the ground in the high, uncut grass, she finally made out some faint tire tracks. She swung her foot from side to side to brush the grass out of the way to see if anything of interest appeared.

Haley, who'd been exploring nearby, suddenly raised her head and growled. Gracie saw a fat, brown mass ripple across the mown field in front of them. The dog made a beeline for the scurrying woodchuck, which undoubtedly was hoping to find the safety of its burrow. It disappeared into a large patch of burdock that looked to be flourishing from the benefits of fertilizer. Before she could call the dog, which was pretty pointless, Haley disappeared into the broad, dark green leaves. A yelp and a series of sharp barks brought Gracie running to see what sort of tangle the Lab had gotten into this time. Dirt flew up from the largest burdock plant.

"Haley, just leave it alone and get over here!" she yelled.

The dog yelped again, and Gracie plunged into the mass of new burs and ones from the year before, which were brown and ready to stick to anything that passed by. Grabbing Haley's wide collar, she hauled the dog from the large burrow. As she stepped back, pulling the over-excited dog with her, she felt something hard slide from under her foot.

CHAPTER 36

The barrel was dirty, as was the stock, but there was no mistaking that a shotgun lay half-hidden in the weeds. Gracie stood, heart pounding, a sour taste in her mouth as she stared at the gun. She clutched Haley's collar, her arm aching from dragging the dog away from the unusually feisty woodchuck. Bending down for a closer look, she pulled back the large burdock leaves. She sucked in a breath. Releasing Haley with a sharp sit-and-stay command, Gracie managed to get her cell phone from the narrow pocket of her Bermuda shorts. She hit "3" on her speed dial.

"What's up, Chief," Jim asked breezily.

She could hear music in the background. Either he had a date or was enjoying a couple with the guys.

"Well, I'm up in the Meadow, and Haley took off after a woodchuck, and ..."

"You're calling me about a woodchuck?"

"No. I'm not. I'm calling you about the shotgun I just found by the woodchuck's hole."

"What are you doing up there? You found a shotgun? Did you call the police? Did you touch it?"

She wasn't sure which question to answer first.

"I stepped on it, and I called you first."

"Gracie, call the sheriff's department. Now!" His take-charge tone broke through her daze.

"All right. I will. I ... I ..." she stammered.

"I'm on my way. Don't touch anything, and for heaven's sake, stay where you are."

She heard the call end. She stood looking at her phone as if willing it to dial itself. Grimacing, she punched in 9-1-1.

Jim's pickup bounced and jerked up Jemison Road. He parked behind the small red SUV on the shoulder and looked up the rolling green hill toward the pond. She waved to catch his attention. The faint sounds of sirens set Haley to howling mournfully. Jim lengthened his stride, hurrying to join Gracie, whose face was pale under her freckles.

"Where is it?" he demanded.

She pointed to the ground ahead of her. Haley licked Jim's hand and then began howling again. The sirens were closer.

"Dang! You'd have thought they'd have checked this area out. How could they have missed it?" Jim demanded.

"I don't know, but it's here," Gracie said glumly.

She shaded her eyes and looked down toward the road where three sheriff's department vehicles pulled up. They'd thankfully cut the sirens.

Gracie grabbed Haley's collar. The dog was anxious to inspect the group headed their way. Investigator Hotchkiss tromped ahead, looking exceptionally aggravated, dressed in a cap, jeans, and a black T-shirt.

The crime scene team went to work securing the area, while the investigator tossed out questions. Gracie answered each quickly, the old feeling of being a suspect returning. This was not earning any points with the policewoman. Why couldn't some passerby have found the gun? A cold sweat broke out on the back of her neck. The policewoman was not happy that a dog and human had contaminated the area. But who could have anticipated walking over a gun and possibly the murder weapon to boot? The low conversation of the deputies and guys in black T-shirts indicated they thought they had the real deal. The shotgun hadn't been there long either, according to the technicians. Gracie watched as they combed the area for any other evidence. Cameras clicked, but nothing else seemed to interest them. The investigator surveyed the newly mown field.

"Do you know who was here cutting the hay?" she asked, looking toward Gracie and including Jim in her gaze.

"Haven't any idea," Jim replied. "Jackson Farms was supposed to get the hay off the field, but you'd have to ask Tobias."

"Any idea where he might be?"

"Not really, but he's probably at home," Jim answered, scanning the edge of the woods where the trail led into the Meadow. "I think I hear a chainsaw. He could be down in the woods a ways. I'll go up and see."

"I'll tag along, Mr. Taylor," Investigator Hotchkiss affirmed, her eyebrows knit in concentration. "I hear that chainsaw too."

The gravelly buzz seemed louder. Now that it was beginning to get dark, Gracie wondered why Tobias would still be cutting wood.

The investigator closed a small black leather covered notebook and stuck it in her back pocket. She motioned for a deputy to join them. Gracie stepped back and watched them take off smartly toward the woods. She wasn't sure if she was off the hook with the investigator, so in the spirit of cooperation, she trailed behind the trio, with Haley heeling rather well for once. The trees draped a dark canopy against the setting sun, and it took a second for her eyes to adjust to the gloom.

Jim led the way toward the sound of the chainsaw. He waved his arms to get Tobias' attention, who was just finishing cutting up a small branch. The woodpile had grown since the last time she was up here. It was stacked at least four feet high now and maybe ten feet in length. Tobias had made good progress on cutting up the large elm. The saw rumbled to a stop.

Tobias was dressed in a dirty white T-shirt that stuck to his skin, soaked with sweat. He pulled a red bandanna from his back pocket and wiped his face. Jim called his name, and the wiry man looked up in surprise. His face registered shock and fear when he saw the deputy and investigator. Dropping the chainsaw, he turned and ran.

CHAPTER 37

Gracie put on a pot of coffee, while Jim washed his dirt-caked arms and face. Haley lapped half a bowl of water and then flopped into her bed by the fireplace with a groan.

"I'm telling you, none of this makes sense," Jim grumbled, drying off with a towel that was really meant for dishes only.

"Not much," she agreed. "I thought Toby's alibi was airtight with Roscoe. Do you really believe he found the shotgun in the woodpile?"

"Maybe." He threw the towel on the counter. "Judas Priest! I wish he'd quit climbing trees to get away," he griped, examining his scratched-up arms and rubbing his left elbow. He eased onto a stool and gratefully took the mug of steaming coffee from Gracie.

"At least he didn't slug any police officers tonight or threaten them with anything."

"A small favor. However, he's locked up again. I'm hoping Roscoe wasn't mistaken about the timeframe he was with Toby." Jim sighed heavily and took a quick sip of coffee. "His lawyer sure has his hands full."

"So, do you think," she began tentatively.

"No, I still don't think he killed D. B. He's stupid for tossing the gun in the field to get it out of his woodpile. If he'd only called the sheriff's department when he found it. What an idiot! Sorry, Chief, but I've gotta go home. See you in the morning." He took another gulp and slammed the mug on the counter.

Gracie had never seen Jim quite that angry, so silence and a weak smile were her response.

*****

The green Geo trembled and lurched into the kennel's parking lot, bright and early on Friday. It was a little too early for Gracie, who'd just left the house to walk down the long driveway to open up. It had been a very short night, and a migraine loomed as a distinct possibility.

Roscoe, who looked a little more disheveled than usual, called out a half-hearted, "Good morning."

She mutely nodded and snapped her fingers to keep Haley's attention on heeling, rather than sniffing Roscoe. He trotted to catch up with her, while Haley managed to lag behind to check out his shoes. He sleepily related his late-night interview with the sheriff's department. Tobias still sat in the county jail, his bail revoked. His fingerprints had been found on the shotgun, much to the District Attorney's delight. Roscoe rubbed a hand through his hair, his dark eyes worried.

"I know my notes are correct. I am always exact on details. Without fail," he confirmed.

"I'm sure the police will realize it and release Tobias. Jim would bet the farm that he didn't kill anybody."

She unlocked the reception area door and punched in the code to disarm the alarm. A chorus of barking greeted them as they walked through to the office.

"Jim is accurate in his assessment of Mr. McQuinn. He was not fond of Mr. Jackson. However, there are others who rather loathed him."

Gracie looked at him, a bit shocked that the mild-mannered, would-be reporter spoke so strongly.

"Anyone in particular?" she asked.

"After I complete my investigation today, all of the facts will be presented to Investigator Hotchkiss."

"Are you talking about Ben Richter? He's kind of an unknown quantity, you know." Gracie was getting irritated with his vagueness.

"I am quite aware of who Mr. Richter is. Once the information I've requested is received, he will be more than a suspect."

His voice was strangely confident. She looked at him in surprise. This must be the new-and-improved Roscoe.

She arched an eyebrow, trying to come up with the right thing to say. "Be careful," was all she could manage.

*****

Jim finished feeding the last of the canine guests, while Gracie put the day's receipts in the small safe under her desk. They'd sent everyone home a bit early, since all the pick-ups and drop-offs were completed way before closing. Haley came trotting through the door with Jim close behind.

"I guess I'm headed to Warsaw to talk with Toby's attorney," he said wearily, thumbs resting on his belt. "He won't talk to my parents, just lucky me," he sighed.

"Nice. Maybe Roscoe has come up with something this afternoon."

"Maybe, but I'm not holding my breath. I tried calling him a few minutes ago, but he didn't answer. Have fun at Isabelle's party. Must be quite the bash tonight."

"You've lucked out, my friend. I was going to ask you to accompany me. I'm actually hoping to scope out some information on Cynthia Harkness. She hasn't explained exactly what she was doing the night of the murder, from what Isabelle told me."

"Why would she talk to you about that?"

"No reason. But maybe the conversation will work its way around to it somehow."

"Then good luck to you. Watch your step though. She *is* a sniper."

Gracie shrugged with feigned unconcern. "I can take her."

He groaned and rolled his eyes. "Chief! Don't do anything stupid, please. Let the police handle this."

"But, of course."

Her phone buzzed loudly on a stack of papers piled on the desk. "My reminder alarm. Time to dress for cocktails at 6:30, Mr. Taylor." She raised a drooping hand as if waiting for a prince to kiss it. "Cinderella is off to the ball."

"All right. I'll lock up. Go get beautiful." He grinned.

"Thank you, kind sir. Come on, Haley. We're outta here."

In the excitement of the last couple of days, Gracie hadn't given much thought to what she was actually wearing to Isabelle's party. It meant something elegant and sophisticated, which wasn't her wardrobe's forte. She went through her closet twice without success. Sitting on the bed wrapped in a bath towel, she racked her brain in desperation. Her mother's voice chiding her about poor planning echoed in her head. Of course. She had a dress from two years ago that was as close to a cocktail dress as she had. It was hanging with the winter coats in the guest bedroom. Haley followed her down the hallway and into an untidy bedroom, where boxes of memorabilia sat in limbo. She slid the coats back until the navy blue chiffon dress was revealed, still in a drycleaner's bag. Breathing a sigh of relief, she hurried back to her room to finish getting ready.

The finished product wasn't bad, she decided, looking at herself from every angle in the full-length mirror on the back of the bedroom door. The sleeveless dress fitted her well with its sweetheart neckline and empire waist. A navy beaded diamond shape in the middle of the bodice gave it some pizzazz. She found the matching low-heeled sandals stuffed in the back of her closet. A quick wipe-down made them presentable. She'd swept her hair into a casual up-do with ready-made curls trailing gracefully down the back. The phone, which was on the bathroom counter, buzzed again, warning her that it was time to leave.

CHAPTER 38

The string quartet finished what Gracie thought was something by Handel. The three men were in tuxes, and the violinist wore a gauzy, cream-colored dress cut generously for her plus-size figure. Isabelle had carefully staged them inside the cedar-shingled gazebo.

A few guests were sipping wine, comfortably seated on the gazebo's deep cushions, enjoying the music up close and personal. The music resumed. The perfect June evening was balmy, and the air was sweet with roses, peonies, and honeysuckle.

Gracie looked around at the crowd that spilled out onto the manicured lawns. There must have been at least 40 or 50 people milling around. A few familiar faces drifted by, but it was obvious that the guest list was mostly from out of town. How she'd gotten invited to this shindig was beyond her comprehension. Isabelle was probably trying to upgrade her social status for her.

Obtaining information on Ms. Harkness was most likely going to be difficult. The sea of people planned to write big checks and consume a lot of food and alcohol. But the alcohol part might be useful, if Mrs. Allen had made the guest list again.

Gracie had managed to pick up a club soda and lemon from the bar, set up under a huge umbrella in the center of the yard. The dark-haired, Antonio Banderas-looking bartender was very charming. Several mature women, stuffed into sequin-plastered dresses, their necks and ears adorned with jewelry, seemed quite content to sip martinis near the big umbrella. Gracie suddenly felt severely underdressed. She'd even forgotten to put on a pair of earrings. Everyone else must have hauled out the family jewels for the occasion.

A hand on her elbow almost made her spill her drink. It was Ann Marie Allen. She had a martini glass in her hand and looked like she'd had more than one already.

"Oh, hi, Ann Marie."

"Hi, yourself, Jane." The woman smiled broadly and took a sip. She was dressed attractively in a scoop-necked, delicate green print dress. Strands of pearls dripped over her cleavage.

"Gracie. It's Gracie," she corrected, smiling.

"Sorry. That's right. Your cousin sure knows how to give a party."

"Yes, she does. Looks like you're having a good time," she answered. "Is Cynthia Harkness here by any chance?"

Ann Marie snorted and looked back over her shoulder. "She's over there with the congressman." She swung her glass around, sloshing the contents over the rim.

Cynthia was wearing a short red, strapless dress, which showed off her legs and other assets to perfection. The congressman didn't appear impressed as they continued an intense conversation. Ms. Harkness definitely wasn't happy, but then Gracie hadn't seen a real smile on her face—ever.

Before Gracie could maneuver her way toward them, Isabelle snagged her from behind. Fortunately, she mostly passed muster with her cousin, who steered her toward the food. The table on the patio was loaded with a stunning display of hors d'oeuvres. Crab puffs, shrimp, cheeses, tiny quiches, and fruit on skewers—she couldn't take it all in. She kept an eye on Cynthia, who was working her way through the crowd, shaking hands and looking generally pleasant. She was mentally rehearsing her opening line to see if Ms. Harkness would give her any idea what her true relationship had been with D. B. She took a crostini from a silver platter and drifted back toward the big umbrella.

*****

The Friday night crowd at Midge's was noisy. Harried waitresses hauled plates of fish as fast as Midge and her assistant cook could get them out of the fryers. Roscoe sat at a back table in the corner near the bathrooms with Allie, who had somehow managed to get the night off.

"Are you sure you should meet this guy by yourself?" she fretted. "I thought you said he has a bad temper and might have murdered his wife."

"Shhh. Not so loud, Allie. He wants to explain the development on Jemison Road. What better place than at the site? I'll have opportunity to take some photos before sunset. Because of the sensitive nature of the work, he's asked that I come alone. He's already explained that he doesn't want any other papers knowing about it before *The Sentinel*. I do have the exclusive." He beamed.

"Exclusive?" she exclaimed and then clamped a hand over her mouth. "I think it sounds fishy to me," the little brunette argued with barely subdued volume.

"Ah, fishy. Quite amusing," Roscoe smiled and dug into the crispy fried haddock.

Allie looked blankly at him and frowned. "You'd better call the police if anything suspicious happens. I really don't like this at all. Maybe I should go with you."

"There's no need. I have it under control. I'll pick you up at nine o'clock for our date at the drive-in," Roscoe said.

*****

The string quartet took a break while Congressman Streeker rambled on about his new economic plans for his rural constituency. More help for dairy farmers was on the way, and schools would receive more funding. The speeches never changed from term to term, Gracie thought, shifting her feet. They hurt already, and she was ready to find something more exciting than club soda if the politician kept droning on.

Surveying the crowd, she noticed Cynthia Harkness drifting toward the patio. It was time for another crab puff, she decided.

She found the long-legged aide sitting in a chair, her eyes closed and rubbing a piece of ice on her forehead.

"Are you all right? Can I get you anything?" Gracie asked, surprised at the woman's sudden vulnerability.

Cynthia opened her eyes and looked blearily at Gracie.

"I've got a blistering headache," she answered huskily.

"Let me get you some aspirin or something," Gracie offered, setting her glass down on a small wicker side table. She hurried to the downstairs bathroom and snatched a bottle of ibuprofen from the medicine cabinet, making a dash back to the patio.

"Here, take a couple of these," she said, popping the top from the bottle.

Cynthia opened her eyes and dumped four pills into her hand. She swallowed them with a generous amount of liquor from her martini glass.

"Thanks. It's been a hellish night. You're Isabelle's cousin, right?"

"Afraid so," she smiled bleakly. "I imagine your schedule is pretty demanding. It takes a toll," she sympathized.

"It was. But not after tonight," the woman answered. She finished the martini and put the glass on the table.

"Oh." Gracie was at a loss. "Finished with fundraising events, then."

"You might say that," was the crisp reply. "Now if you don't mind, I need a couple of minutes," she said dismissively, leaning back against the chair, eyes closed again.

"Oh, sure. I understand."

Gracie felt like a reprimanded first grader as she returned the bottle to the cabinet, desperately trying to come up with another conversation starter.

The sound of a male voice caught her attention as she walked across the living room toward the patio. She stopped short of the doorway when Cynthia's voice crackled with anger.

"He fired me. Everything is over. He knows about D. B. too."

"I thought that was handled. What are we going to ..." the man's voice stopped. The conversation discreetly ended while a group came in to load their plates.

Streeker's speech was over. Kevin made a smooth appeal for checkbooks to appear. The faithful dutifully got out their pens. Most headed to the tables for more food. A young woman in a blue-and-pink caftan rushed into the living room, looking for a bathroom. Gracie pointed her in the right direction, then decided to go out through the kitchen and formulate another plan to extract the information she needed.

*****

Roscoe eased the complaining Geo up the newly graded road toward the crest of the first hill. The car spewed dark fumes behind as it struggled up the grade. He needed to hurry to have enough light for the pictures he planned to take. If everything went as planned, he'd have the story filed with the editor before midnight. The western sky was streaked with streams of gold, pink, and rose. He was losing light fast. He'd tried talking Richter into meeting earlier, but he'd had another appointment to keep. Finally, he reached the top of the first hill and pulled over into the area where several pieces of heavy equipment were parked. It was a hike from here. The road ended. The car was definitely not built for off-road use. Richter had told him he'd be on an ATV at the top, inspecting the day's work.

Slipping the camera strap around his neck, he followed the stakes with orange strips of plastic flapping in the breeze. No doubt the rest of the road would soon be complete. The clearing at the top of the hill was empty except for a grader and a couple of heavy-duty trucks. He looked around for an ATV or any sign that someone was here. It was so still that he shivered involuntarily. A large pile of dirt was off to his left, and a mound of gravel sat next to it. Roscoe shoved black-framed glasses back up his glistening nose to investigate. He pulled out his phone from his pants pocket to check the time. He noticed there was no signal. As he rounded the dirt pile, he stopped short. A large, deep trench was immediately in front of him. The sound of an engine made him look up. It was the last thing he remembered.

******

The party wound down, and Gracie was anxious to go home. Her parents would be finishing up the mowing and weeding for the week. They'd be waiting for her on the patio with Haley. Except for the snippet of conversation she'd overheard between Cynthia and possibly Mitch Allen, there'd been nothing. Her whole investigative effort had been a bust. A constant dribble of guests said their good-byes to the hostess. Isabelle had pulled off another successful event. Everyone had admired her home and gardens *ad nauseam*. Gracie sighed. It was true. It had all gone very well.

She caught sight of Ann Marie walking slowly on the brick path from the gazebo to the patio. Congressman Streeker and a couple of staffers had left for another engagement at least an hour before, but Cynthia had remained. Her extended presence under the big umbrella was an indication of the amount of quality time she'd spent with the bartender and a steady supply of drinks. Mitch had spent a lot of time under the umbrella with her. Gracie was ready to call it quits, when Carla hurried up to her.

"I'm so glad I caught you, Gracie. I've got your bedroom plans in the car. I've been meaning to get them to you all week, but it's been so busy."

Carla was dressed in a baby blue, watered silk spaghetti strap dress. Her hair was in a carefully pinned-up do, embellished with an antique feather hatpin. Her necklace was a simple square-cut, deep blue sapphire pendant fastened to a gold chain. Gracie hoped she wasn't staring—Carla looked so well put together. Carla didn't have a curvy figure; it was straight, and her hands were large and manly. Fashion had never been Carla's strong suit, but tonight she looked every inch an up-and-coming businesswoman. Isabelle had probably coached her.

"I was just getting ready to leave. That was good timing, I guess."

"We just barely made it, no thanks to Dean. He's so busy getting ready for the transfer of the farm that I can hardly get him out of the barn or the farm office. We *both* have so much to do."

The smile on Carla's face was almost beatific. It was obvious she could hardly wait to have Dean in full control.

"Right. The transfer. How's the redecorating of the office going?" she asked, intentionally changing the subject.

"It's going great. Of course, it's difficult for Kim to see the changes, but I completely understand."

"I think things would be easier for Kim if she had a solid alibi. She has a lot hanging over her head right now."

"Absolutely. I'm so glad Dean and I were home together that night. The woman investigator was quite thorough. She really knows what she's doing."

The implication was clear that Carla was sure the investigation leading to Kim's door was on the right path.

Gracie took a sip of club soda to keep from saying something she'd regret. Clutching the glass, she swished the last bits of ice around, trying to devise a civil reply. Turning toward the big umbrella, Gracie observed Cynthia stepping away from the bartender, who had apparently shut her off. Mitch trailed after her like a lost puppy. She turned back to Carla.

"Looks like those two aren't very happy tonight."

Carla shook her head, her face dark with emotion. "D. B. was working them both over, but the whole lot of them is greedy. That woman had designs on D. B., you know," she half-whispered, her eyes narrowing. "Disgusting."

"Really?" Gracie scrambled through her mental list. Kim had mentioned the same thing. "Did you ever see them together, you know, as in ..."

"Well, I did happen to, one time." She hesitated.

"When was that?" Gracie prodded.

"It was ... well ... I'd rather not say, but the way she sidled up to him. It was obvious," she answered, making a face.

"Any reason she might want to do away with D. B.?"

Carla's face became conspiratorial. "Possibly."

Isabelle appeared from nowhere, Chanel No. 5 announcing her presence.

"I'm so glad you got that dress. It's absolutely perfect. And that necklace, Carla. Beautiful. They're *you*."

"I would never have chosen this dress without your help. Your fashion sense is perfect. Thank you, Isabelle."

Isabelle radiated with the pride of a benevolent fashion despot. She'd been right. It was all Isabelle's doing.

"I didn't even remember to put on a pair of earrings," Gracie muttered. "I'm not a big jewelry person, but the necklace is beautiful."

Carla's hand flew to the necklace. "It was an unexpected gift," she said, flashing a wide smile.

"Dean has good taste," Isabelle commented, her eyes never leaving the jewelry.

"Yes, he does." Carla's eyes searched across the patio to where Dean stood talking with Kevin.

"Ladies, let's get dessert," Isabelle said, herding them like a border collie toward the fire pit.

The string quartet was packing up. Dusk filtered over the lawn, pushing the rest of the stragglers toward the house. Carla excused herself, while Gracie followed Isabelle.

Ann Marie reached the blazing fire, holding her hands out toward the warmth. Fire was unnecessary on the warm evening, but it added just the right ambiance to the twilight seeping over the wide flagstone patio. Isabelle appeared with a tray of steaming coffee mugs. She set it down on a low, mosaic tile table near the fire.

The caterer, whom Gracie recognized as Kate, brought another tray out behind her. A huge bread bowl holding some sort of dip was carefully arranged in the middle of chunks of bread and fresh vegetables. Gracie planned on checking out the dip and then saying her goodbyes. A tray of small squares of cheesecake and brownies was on another table. The goodbyes might be put off a little longer, she decided, when she saw the tiny confections. Ann Marie teetered a little, and Kevin grabbed her elbow, steadying the woman, while directing her to a chair.

"Thanks, Kevin. Someone has to stand in for my husband," she said petulantly, eyeing Cynthia and Mitch as they reached the fire.

Gracie decided on a square of cheesecake topped with a perfect raspberry and a brownie drizzled with hot fudge. Cynthia took a mug of coffee and handed another to Mitch. Gracie noticed that Mitch's fingers lingered on hers. Apparently, Ann Marie noticed too. She rose out of the chair like a summer thunderstorm and knocked the mug from Mitch's hand. It shattered on the flagstone.

"Get away from my husband, you Washington whore. I know what you've been doing behind my back, and now you're stupid enough to do it in *front* of me."

Horrified, Mitch backed away from the two women, stammering, "Aaaah ... Ann ... Ann Marie. Stop it."

"Stop it? *You* stop it. You've gone through my money, and now you're screwing her to get more."

Ann Marie's face was bordering on apoplectic. Cynthia shot back daggers of hate at Ann Marie.

"You stupid drunk. I've gone to every green energy promotion and political function to keep your husband's business afloat. You can't even stay sober long enough to make it through a dinner. How dare you accuse me of even looking twice at *him!*"

The "him" was said with such contempt that Gracie could hardly breathe. The color drained from Mitch's face. It was as if time had suddenly stopped. No one moved. Isabelle coolly stepped in.

"Ladies, please. I'm sure we can ..."

Before Isabelle could finish, Ann Marie had taken a handful of dip from the large bread bowl and thrown it at Cynthia, who neatly sidestepped it. The plop of sour cream and spinach hit Isabelle squarely in the well-pushed up cleavage she'd showcased for the evening. It immediately spread down the front of her dress, and Gracie was sure, it was oozing down inside too. Isabelle screamed, looking down at the damage, too shocked to move. Cynthia picked up the dessert tray and whipped it at Ann Marie, who batted it away, cheesecake and brownies flying everywhere. Gracie felt one fall into her hair. She backed further away from the fray, picking brownie pieces from her hair. Isabelle regained her wits, and with a look that would turn a pack of hungry wolves away, grabbed the bread bowl and promptly dumped the contents on Ann Marie. The woman shrieked a string of profanities and stumbled toward the driveway, calling for her husband. Mitch, reminiscent of a frog about to be swallowed by a snake, ran after his wife. Cynthia smiled enigmatically at the stunned audience and stalked off behind them.

CHAPTER 39

Bob and Theresa Clark, comfortably seated on the small wicker sofa on the patio, enjoyed the retelling of Gracie's party adventure.

"Unbelievable! Isabelle must be mortified. I can't wait to hear her version of this fiasco tomorrow." Theresa laughed. "I won't be able to stop myself from dropping by to ask her how the party went."

"I think you should pass on some of the other information to that investigator," Gracie's father admonished. "If you heard these people correctly, it might mean one of them killed D. B."

Gracie nodded unenthusiastically. "I know. I'm just not absolutely sure what they were talking about."

"Just tell the police and let them handle it. I keep telling you this, but you don't listen, her mother advised. She stood and turned to her husband. "Come on, dear. Let's go home."

Gracie watched the taillights of her parents' car disappear down the road. A text notification from her iPhone chimed. She grabbed it from the round side table on her patio. It was from Jim: *r gone ... called cops ... looking 4 him*

She called him and got voicemail the first time. She hit his speed dial number again. He answered, but it was obvious he was running. He told her he'd call her back. The house phone rang. Gracie grumbled about getting up to answer it to a snoring Haley. Jim must have dialed it by mistake. Without looking at the caller ID, she answered, "You called the house phone."

"Hello? Is this Gracie?" The male voice was familiar, but she'd expected Jim, and she was at a loss.

"Oh, yes. I'm sorry. I was... Who's calling, please?"

"This is Dean. Uh, Carla asked me to call you about the plans."

"The plans. Right. I forgot to take them when the food fight broke out."

"Yeah. That was quite the scene. I guess I would've shown up sooner if I'd known the entertainment was so good." He chuckled. "Anyway, she wants to drop them off tomorrow."

"Sure. I'll be home all day. Not a problem. Say, you've got good taste in jewelry. That's a nice necklace you got for Carla."

"Huh? Oh, yeah. Well, I've got to check on some things at the barn. Goodnight then."

Her cell phone buzzed. She grabbed it from the breakfast bar.

Jim's voice was strained as he brought her up to date. Both the state troopers and sheriff's department were combing Greerson's Meadow and Richter's property above it. They'd found the Geo in the Meadow—doors open, key in the ignition, but no sign of Roscoe. His laptop was smashed and his camera gone. Gracie raised her eyebrows when Jim told her that Allie had called the police and him when Roscoe hadn't shown up to take her to the drive-in.

"I had no idea," she said incredulously. "Allie, huh?"

"That's right. Allie. Sorta out of his league, but, hey ... Good for him. She said he had a meeting with Richter up here, but she wasn't sure where. Anyway, Toby and I are going up with the cops. Who knows what he might've gotten himself into? They're trying to find Richter right now too. He seems to have taken off."

"I just hope Roscoe's all right. And they'd better find that rat, Richter."

"Agreed. I'll let you know."

She sat down on a stool, stomach churning. She'd consumed way too much rich food. She felt a tad nauseous. Roscoe was missing again, and it seemed as if all her suspects were on the loose tonight. It was like the kids' game "Fruit Basket Upset." Quite similar to how her stomach felt. She groaned and stretched her legs out, rubbing sore calves. Wearing heels always did her in.

She looked at the kitchen clock. It was 9:30. If everyone was out hunting for Roscoe and Richter, Investigator Hotchkiss wouldn't be interested in hearing from her until tomorrow. She decided to make a list of her suspects, which might clear things up. She sat down at the breakfast bar, grabbed a pencil from the container by the phone, and dug through her bag to find the notebook.

Richter was the prime suspect as far as she was concerned. If he'd hurt Roscoe or worse.... She blocked the possibilities from her mind. He and D. B. had certainly produced enough ill will between the two of them. Maybe D. B. had pushed Richter a little too far, which wasn't a stretch. But the erstwhile environmentalist had his beady eyes on the Meadow property. He'd also threatened just about everyone. And it looked like the group was skipping town. His alibi didn't add up either. He couldn't prove he was at dinner anywhere, but Cheryl had seen his vehicle along with Cynthia Harkness at the Renew Earth office. He would have had time to shoot D. B. and meet up with the sniper.

And that led her on to Ms. Harkness. She was supposed to be at a meeting with Kevin and D. B., but instead she'd been at the Renew Earth office. The timeframe still worked for her to shoot D. B., and she was an expert shot. Of course, you didn't need to be an expert to use a shotgun. And if D. B. was having an affair with the woman, it could have been a crime of passion. Ms. Harkness had to be up to something else that wasn't apparent yet. She'd lost her job with the congressman tonight. What was that all about? Had D. B. known something about her that was dangerous?

Gracie jotted down three question marks after "Harkness" and nibbled at the end of the pencil eraser. All roads still led to the Meadow property. Cynthia wanted it for the wind farm. But would she kill for it? Why did she want it so badly? How could she be sure that killing D. B. would get her the property? It could have been a lover's quarrel. Mitch Allen had designs on Cynthia. That was completely obvious tonight. Maybe he and D. B. got into a fight over Ms. Harkness. But Mr. Allen seemed like a weak man to her. On second thought, that characteristic might make him more dangerous. His alibi was pretty solid though. He'd been at Isabelle's right on time for the meeting. She scratched his name out.

Shifting to a more comfortable position on the stool, she scribbled "Dean" next on the list. He had entered her mind in the last couple of days. He was in an all-fired hurry to get the farm into his name and kick Kim out the door. It was out of character, but maybe he was over the edge. He'd have to be if he'd killed D. B. His alibi was nice and tidy though, just like Mitch Allen's. Then again, a spouse vouching for a spouse might not be the best either. That warranted some further research. There was something else she couldn't put her finger on that nagged at her about Dean. She'd come up with some questions for Carla tomorrow. The ringing house phone jarred her from her detective reverie.

CHAPTER 40

Kim had an alibi—finally. Gracie was almost dancing around the kitchen listening to the unbelievable news.

"I don't know why I didn't think of it before, but at least I've figured it out now," Kim bubbled.

"Wow! What a relief! Have you called Nolan yet?"

"Not yet. I wanted to call you before I called him. It was so simple all the time."

"Thank the good Lord for online shopping," Gracie laughed.

The upshot was that Kim had been logged into a home decorating site, ordering new accessories for the living room re-do. She'd been logged in and active for 45 minutes total, from 8:11 p.m. to 8:56 p.m. The true beauty of it was the auto logout feature, which activated if the user wasn't active on the site for 10 consecutive minutes. It had been a continuously active session. The reason it had all come back to Kim was the delivery of the backordered pillows, candlesticks, and a shelving system today. The order date on the packing slip had jogged the crucial memory.

"I may be able to get some sleep now that they can focus on D. B.'s real murderer. I'm so grateful you believed me from the beginning. Everyone has looked sideways at me since the police started questioning me. What a relief!"

"I'll say. Make sure you call Nolan tonight."

"I will. Just as soon as I have ... Hello?"

Gracie looked at the phone receiver and answered, "I'm still here, Kim."

The phone went dead.

CHAPTER 41

Gracie turned into the long driveway. The porch light wasn't on, and she couldn't tell if there were any lights on inside. The curtains must all be closed. She could only hope she was overreacting. The phone line had been constantly busy when she'd tried calling Kim back. Maybe she was on the phone with Nolan, but that wasn't her first guess. Kim's car was parked outside of the garage. She jammed the SUV to a stop behind it. There were no other vehicles around, except for an ATV on the lawn.

Running to the door, she pressed the doorbell twice. No lights switched on.

She began pounding on the leaded glass sidelight. "Kim! It's me, Gracie. Kim, please open up!"

Unable to budge the locked door, she ran to the back of the house, crossing her fingers that she could get into the farm office.

Fortunately, the door was unlocked. A banker's lamp burned steadily on D. B.'s desk. Drapery rods leaned against the filing cabinet. The top desk drawer was open. Papers were scattered across the floor. The door from the farm office to the main house was unlocked. Gracie breathed a sigh of relief when she found herself in the dark kitchen.

Moonlight glowed through the windows and gave enough light to find the way into the dining room and foyer. She waited for a moment by the coat rack next to the front door to formulate a plan. She had none. She wasn't even sure what faced her or where to look. A flash of recollection brought a very bad feeling, and a wave of nausea surged in her stomach. Steeling herself, she started for the stairway. A thin glimmer of light caught her eye at the top of the stairs. It was the small lamp on the console table on the landing.

Before she went any further, she should probably call for backup. She crept into the darkened living room to make the call. Yanking the phone from her shorts, she punched in 9-1-1. The crash of glass from upstairs stopped her hurried explanation to the dispatcher.

"Please send help to the Jackson Farm," she hissed and pressed the "End" button before the 9-1-1 operator could ask any questions.

She couldn't wait for the deputies to show up. She'd have to do this on her own. She looked around for any sort of weapon. Nothing. She'd have to hope for the best.

Turning the corner to face the grand staircase, she tentatively called out, "Kim? Are you here?"

Her ears strained to hear the slightest sound, but silence prevailed. She tiptoed up the winding stairs, still calling for her friend. As she reached the landing, a muffled cry broke the stillness; a dull thump sounded. Gracie saw light filtering from Kim's doorway at the end of the hall. She called again, frozen in place. The door sprang wide open, and a disheveled Kim stood, wrapped in a white cotton robe, trembling in the doorway.

"Gracie! What are you doing here?"

Kim's tear-streaked face was caricature-like in the odd shadows that played off the walls. She gripped the doorknob with one hand. The other clutched the robe around her throat.

"I ... I couldn't get you on the phone. I was worried."

"You shouldn't be here. Go home, please ... please go home." Her voice caught in a wrenching sob, her eyes full of terror.

"You're *not* fine, and I'm not going anywhere. Who's with you?" Gracie demanded, suddenly feeling brave.

She was halfway down the hallway when the muzzle of a Glock 9mm loomed larger than life behind Kim's head.

"Don't come any closer," Carla snarled, stepping out from behind the door. Her face was flushed, her eyes glinting with rage. "Stay where you are."

Gracie's heart pounded like a bass drum in her ears. She felt as if she were drowning.

"Carla, what are you doing? Tell me what's going on here. I want to help."

She backed toward the railing on the landing, grasping it with both hands behind her back.

Carla pushed Kim forward with the pistol. Kim stumbled, then ran toward Gracie. Carla scrambled forward, screaming at her to stop. The gun blast made Gracie's knees give way. Kim cried out, sprawling face first in front of Gracie, the right sleeve of her robe soaked with a widening stain of crimson. Carla pitched forward like a football tackle, the black handgun raised to strike. Kim rolled to her left, struggling to stand, effectively knocking Carla off balance. Gracie rose from her knees, and threw herself toward Carla to ram the teetering madwoman down the stairs. The pistol flew from Carla's hand, hit the railing, and clattered to the hardwood floor below. She screeched, blood trickling from her nose, struggling desperately to regain her balance. The gangly woman missed the railing by inches and then tumbled down the winding stairs, while Gracie tried unsuccessfully not to be sick on the carpet.

CHAPTER 42

Ambulance lights pulsed in the darkness, and Kim was whisked away. It didn't look good, from what the EMTs had murmured to one another as they'd tried to stabilize the unconscious woman. Carla sat handcuffed in a cruiser, staring zombie-like into space. She seemed none the worse for wear after the fall. She'd refused treatment, even though her left wrist was swollen with a lump the size of a baseball. The thick carpet had probably saved her from any major injuries. Lights pulsed in the darkness from the bevy of law enforcement vehicles parked at odd angles all over the lawn. Crime scene people were hard at work in the house.

Jim stood by Gracie, who had just finished her statement to a furious Investigator Hotchkiss. She was now explaining it all over again to Jim, who was of the same mind as the policewoman.

She sat shivering in the warm night air on the edge of a cruiser's backseat, while Jim towered over her, arms folded across his chest.

"I know it was stupid not to call anyone sooner, but everyone was looking for Roscoe, and I wasn't really sure anyway. It all happened so fast. I didn't expect it to go quite that way, you know."

Tears streamed down her face, streaking the remains of her party makeup into puddles on her cheeks.

"Chief, you were almost killed tonight, and Kim is in really bad shape."

His exasperation was more than evident, and the worry lines on his face made her feel somewhat comforted. He squatted down and took her hands in his. He squeezed them tightly, released them, and stood abruptly.

Jim turned to look at the activity around the house. A crime scene team member ran from the house to Investigator Hotchkiss, who squinted as she studied what looked like a small bottle. A deputy shone his flashlight on it, and the woman barked orders to him.

Jim returned his gaze to Gracie, who snuffled and wiped her smeary face with the back of her hand.

"I'll take you home," he said simply and pulled her to her feet.

Her parents met them at the house. Haley was eager to see her mistress, but Gracie could hardly function as she willed her sluggish legs to carry her across the floor. The dog, immediately subdued, followed Gracie and Theresa into the bedroom. Her mother helped her undress and was uncharacteristically mute throughout the process. Gracie felt herself slip into nothingness under the cool, smooth sheets.

******

Sunlight flooded the bedroom. Gracie groaned and forced her eyes open. They felt gravelly and swollen. She looked at the alarm clock on her nightstand. It was 9:36. Panic surged through her, and she swung her legs out of bed to hurry to the shower. Bob and Theresa were in the kitchen when she appeared, wrapped in her robe and a towel around her wet hair. Their faces were grim, and she knew the news wasn't good.

Kim was in a coma. The bullet had torn through an artery and she'd lost a lot of blood. The quantity of sleeping pills that were in her stomach had complicated the situation. Carla had forced Kim to swallow almost an entire bottle with D. B.'s Glock pressed to her head. She'd gotten a call from Kim about the accessory order that had helped her establish an alibi. Unhinged that Kim would no longer be a suspect, Carla decided that Kim should commit suicide out of guilt before her alibi became public knowledge. Until Gracie had shown up, it had almost worked. Gracie sat at the breakfast bar, the reality of death staring her in the face.

"What about Roscoe? Have they found him? Is he all right?"

She desperately needed some good news. She tore the towel from her head, dropping it on the stool next to her. Jim appeared at the kitchen screen door as if on cue. He had a crooked smile on his face and a box of sweet rolls in his hand.

"They found Roscoe last night on Richter's property. He's got a pretty good knock on the head and he's banged up, but he's going to be all right. They pushed him into a trench and tried to bury him. The man's tougher than we thought."

She heaved a sigh of relief. "Thank you, God, for something good," she breathed.

"Get some caffeine in your system and tell us what happened last night," her mother instructed while she handed a mug to her daughter.

Gracie nodded miserably and began the complete report.

"I was thinking the murderer was Dean because he was acting pretty hostile toward Kim. It wasn't like him to be so forceful. When I started up to the farm, I remembered he'd told me that he was going to the barn. It's an easy walk to the house from there. There was something about that necklace Carla was wearing that nagged at me, though. Then I remembered when I got into the office. The sapphire was exactly like the ring Kim wore. That couldn't have been a coincidence. I had mentioned it to Dean, and he acted like he knew nothing about it. I guess he didn't."

Jim, who was finishing a hunk of caramel brown gooeyness, held up a hand as he finished chewing. Swallowing the last of the roll down with a slurp of coffee, he said, "You were right about the necklace. She took it from D. B.'s truck the night of the murder. It was a gift for Kim that D. B. had picked up that day. Carla considered it payment for pain and suffering, I guess. Poor Dean!"

Gracie frowned and shook her head. "What was she thinking? If Kim had seen the necklace, she'd have known right away. The way Carla talked, it sounded like she and Dean had a good marriage."

"What you don't know was that Carla had been pushing Dean to force D. B. to sell out to them for over a year. D. B. had messed around with Dean and the partnership for a long time, and Dean was content to bide his time. He was sure that D. B. would retire in the next year. Carla apparently didn't believe the retirement plan would happen and decided to move things along. Dean told me last night that he'd suspected something was going on between D. B. and Carla. They weren't having an affair, but Carla kept making hints to D. B. that it was time to speed up his retirement plans. She started redecorating the house to suit her own tastes, and with Kim's blessing. Once D. B. figured out what she was up to, he finally told her to back off. His retirement would be on his own timetable."

"Kim thought D. B. was having an affair with Cynthia Harkness," Gracie broached. "She spent a lot of time with him the last few weeks he was alive."

"There's an ongoing investigation into Ms. Harkness' dealings with New Energy and federal grants," Bob Clark chimed in, holding up the newspaper and rattling the pages. "Looks like a big scandal for Streeker, who says he's the one who got the FBI involved. Paper says she's disappeared though."

Jim huffed in disgust. "She's probably on some island, counting the loot."

"Probably," Gracie agreed. "Streeker fired her at Isabelle's party. Maybe she's run away with Mitch Allen," she said, half-joking.

"Oh, no," said her father, holding up the newspaper again. "He's been arrested and is facing an indictment for fraud and a list of other charges from the government."

"What about Dean's alibi? Carla vouched for him," Gracie asked, rubbing her temples to ease a headache.

"Dean was really sick. So sick he was flat on his back when he wasn't in the bathroom. He said that Carla could have come and gone 50 times that night and he wouldn't have noticed," Jim said. "The kicker was that she'd told him she had an evening appointment earlier in the day. When the police started questioning him, she swore she'd been at home all night because Dean was sick. She acted like the loyal wife, and Dean was grateful for a solid alibi."

"This whole thing makes my head spin," Theresa complained. "It's a wonder you weren't all hurt or worse."

"It *is* a wonder," Gracie agreed.

Chapter 43

The strawberry social was well underway. Shortcake, whipped cream, and bowls of ruby-colored strawberries swam in their sweet juices, waiting to be ladled into bowls of biscuits and huge squares of white cake. Long tables stretched across the church lawn, filled with just about everybody in town. Marlene and Theresa were in the middle of the serving crew, making sure there was plenty of everything available for the crowd. Gracie sat with Kim, Amanda, Sara, and Duane. Kim was still recovering, but her much thinner, pale face had a look of determination and peace.

"I'll be leaving for Philadelphia next Saturday with Amanda," she said, putting her spoon on the white paper tablecloth. "It's time to get out of Dodge and stay out. When the farm sale is finalized, I'm going to Virginia to live near my sister."

"I can understand that," Gracie replied. "What is everyone else doing?" She waved a hand toward the three adult children.

Duane spoke first. "I'm transferring to the University of Virginia. I agree with Mom. I need to get out of here too."

"And he'll bring his laundry home on weekends to check on me." Kim smiled at her son.

"What about you two?" Gracie looked at Sara and Amanda.

"John and I will hang around here. We just bought a house last year," Sara answered. "We're thinking about starting a family," she added, glancing at her mother.

"And I'm staying in Philly. I love my job at the publishing house, and Philly's a great place to live. A little more metropolitan than Deer Creek," Amanda said, smiling.

"Is Dean going to stick around?" Gracie asked, wondering how in the world he would ever pick up the pieces staying in Wyoming County.

"Only for Carla's trial, which we will come back for," Kim said bitterly. "He's working out a deal to sell the farm to the Strykersville manager. With his share of the sale, I'm sure he'll be able to make a new start."

She nodded solemnly. Carla's dream of living in the big house would most certainly come true in a whole new way. Gracie was grateful to be alive and doubly grateful that her friends were getting the chance to move on.

"I'll never be able to thank you enough for saving my life, Gracie. The whole thing is still unbelievable." Kim gingerly extricated herself from the table. Her slow and deliberate movements made it clear she was still healing physically. The emotional healing—she wasn't sure if that ever ended. The two women hugged. Gracie watched the Jackson family stroll to the parking lot.

Roscoe and Allie were quick to take the Jacksons' place across from her. Tom and Kelly followed right behind the couple, huge bowls of strawberries and shortcake in their hands. Roscoe actually had some color in his cheeks. Allie had a little glow about her, too. Gracie suppressed a grin and began eating the hunk of shortcake drowned in juicy strawberries.

Roscoe was eager to fill her in on the loose ends in the search for the Richters. They'd reappeared in Vermont. His first wife's family had slapped Ben with a wrongful death action. Some new evidence had recently come to light about her "accident." There were a few other legal woes pending, most notable of which was Mr. Richter's disbarment. The Wyoming County DA was also working on indicting the Richters and the De Francos for their attempted murder of Roscoe.

"It couldn't happen to nicer people," Gracie said between mouthfuls.

"And Roscoe found out that the Richters wanted the property because of gas." Allie beamed, her large brown eyes batting at the embarrassed man.

"Gas?" Gracie put her spoon back in the bowl, looking puzzled and amused at Roscoe.

Tom chuckled. Kelly suppressed a giggle.

"Let me correct that—*natural* gas," Roscoe amended, his cheeks stained with red. "A rather large deposit actually. Ms. Harkness found out and was trying work out an agreement with the Richters the night of Mr. Jackson's demise. She said if they agreed to submit grant paperwork for a wind farm, she would ensure they received money to finance their land acquisitions, which would take care of their cash flow problem. No one ever intended for the wind farm to be built there. They were looking for quick cash from the grants, which would finance the fracking operation. Ms. Harkness would have received a generous cut of the profits for her assistance. It was an uneasy partnership at best, and fortunately, it's been disbanded."

"Chalk up one for the good guys," Gracie snickered. "At least my tax dollars were saved on that deal."

Roscoe sat up straighter on the bench, his chest puffed out importantly. "The other news is that *The Sentinel* has offered me a position as a reporter."

"That's great! Congratulations! You deserve it after all you went through to get the skinny on those slime balls."

"Thank you, Grace. I've turned them down actually. There's an opening for an investigative reporter on a lesser known publication where I'll be able to pursue my study of extraterrestrial visitations."

Jim joined the table, as did Dan and Darlene Evans, owners of the hardware, just as Roscoe made the announcement. Another round of congratulations ensued with some raised eyebrows, and Roscoe looked like he was going to pop all his shirt buttons. Allie clutched his arm, her eyes shining with adoration.

"Did you ever find out about the lights in the sky after D. B.'s murder?" Jim asked while he pressed the juicy strawberries into his biscuits.

"Not really. Mr. Richter denies using the equipment that Mr. Jackson's son had hidden on the property. He did, however, call the police the night of our nocturnal investigation. Someone had let it slip that the perpetrators of the hoax were picking up the equipment. It's amazing the information to be collected at Midge's." He looked meaningfully at Gracie, who blushed. He continued, "The Air Force had no aircraft in the area, and the Weather Service didn't have any weather balloons. That unfortunately remains a mystery, one that will require further research," Roscoe finished officiously.

"It'll give an ace reporter something to investigate," Tom joked.

"I plan to continue my UFO research, but I do have other priorities at the moment." Roscoe's face was serious, his eyes bright with puppy love as he gazed at Allie. Leaving their strawberries behind, the unlikely couple made their way across the church lawn, hand in hand.

"Who would have thought?" Jim said.

"That is a definite mystery," Gracie replied. "Why have you guys been absent from all the festivities of late?" she quizzed her brother.

"Well, we've been busy with a few things," Tom answered, his voice quavering nervously.

"What things?" Gracie demanded.

Kelly slid her left hand across the table. A sparkling pear cut diamond adorned her ring finger.

"Really? You're really ..." Gracie stopped, her eyes filling with tears, rising to hug her best friend and veterinarian. An excellent combination, in her book.

"Yup. It's official. We just let Dad and Mom know. I had some things to work out with Jan and the custody arrangement with Emma. Jan's decided to go back to Texas. She has a good job there and friends to help her through another divorce. Emma will live with me and visit her mother over the summer," Tom answered. He stood and put an arm around Kelly, who hadn't stopped smiling.

"Well, congrats, Tom. You're a lucky man," Jim said, standing to shake Tom's hand.

"So when's the big day?" Gracie asked.

"We're not sure yet," Kelly said. "I've been dealing with some issues at the clinic, and I'm thinking about opening up my own practice. It's been pretty stressful. I've been off the grid to figure things out. Once we know for sure what I'm doing, we'll set the date. It won't be too long, right, Tom?"

"Yes, dear," he responded with an exaggerated sigh. "I don't want Kelly to lose interest, and Emma is demanding a quick wedding date."

Gracie laughed. Her niece was a chip off the old block. No patience and a woman of action.

*****

Gracie stood in the warm June night, inhaling the scented dewy air. The sky was brilliant with stars. The Big Dipper seemed to sparkle with unusual brilliance tonight. For the first time in a long while, everything seemed in balance. It was a good feeling. She'd had a surprise phone call from Marc. They'd talked for over an hour, catching up on life. Then he'd asked her if she'd come visit him in Arizona. A rush of emotion had made her answer "yes" without hesitation. It felt right, especially after Tom's and Kelly's announcement.

Haley rustled through the lilac bushes, critter hunting. The peepers and crickets sang with gusto in the humid darkness. The Lab abruptly stopped her search, growling and looking up at the sky. Startled, Gracie followed the dog's nose toward the horizon and the woods behind the kennel property. Blue and white lights pulsed steadily over the trees. She watched them advance slowly over the field, ascending higher. A flash of white light stung the darkness and the lights vanished.

Thank you for reading Fly by Night. I hope you enjoyed the third mystery in the Gracie Andersen mystery series. If you have a moment, please post a quick review of *Fly by Night* online and help other mystery fans discover Gracie too!

–Laurinda Wallace

ABOUT THE AUTHOR

Laurinda Wallace lives in the beautiful high desert of southeast Arizona where the mountains and fabulous night skies inspire risk taking. A native of Western New York, she loves writing about her hometown region including Letchworth State Park. A lifelong bookworm and writer, she made her foray into the publishing world in 2005. She's contributed to a variety of print and online magazines, and along the way created the Gracie Andersen mysteries, and more.

Visit **www.laurindawallace.com** for more information and be sure to sign up for the Mystery Mavens Society. Subscribers receive free short stories and insider book news. Your email is never shared or sold.
Books by Laurinda Wallace

The Gracie Andersen Mysteries

Family Matters

By the Book

Fly By Night

Washed Up

Pins & Needles

The Mistletoe Murders

True-Crime Memoir

Too Close to Home: The Samantha Zaldivar Case

Inspirational

The Time Under Heaven

Gardens of the Heart

Historical Fiction Short Story

The Murder of Alfred Silverheels

Historical Mystery

The Disappearance of Sara Colter

www.ingramcontent.com/pod-product-compliance
Lightning Source LLC
Chambersburg PA
CBHW071142260626
47162CB00003B/879